TRESPASS

TRESPASS

ANTHONY J. QUINN

PEGASUS BOOKS
NEW YORK LONDON

TRESPASS

Pegasus Books, Ltd.
148 West 37th Street, 13th Floor
New York, NY 10018

Copyright © 2017 by Anthony J. Quinn

First Pegasus Books hardcover edition November 2017

ISBN: 978-1-68177-550-0

10 9 8 7 6 5 4 3 2 1

Printed in the United States of America
Distributed by W. W. Norton & Company, Inc.

To Eileen, Rhoda, Nuala, James, Paul and Charlotte

PROLOGUE

Midwinter darkness. Another bad night: he no longer knew why. Sleep came and went, his mind haunted by an image of his younger brother that was comical yet deeply disturbing. He dreamed they were in a large windowless room with a low ceiling and a parquet floor creaking beneath their feet. It was very dark and late and, for some reason, they were alone and clasping each other, his brother whispering 'Quick, quick' and 'Now, now' as they followed the moves of a dance, a blinking spotlight tracking them across the floor. Somehow it seemed normal that they should be holding each other in this intimate way, even though it was not his brother as he now knew him, but a much younger version, dressed in a soldier's uniform with a strange, watchful expression on his glistening face.

They were keeping perfect time together, which surprised him, because neither of them had ever been light on his feet. The rhythm of the music, the unhindered stretch of floor, and the shimmering light seemed to suit them. For a while, it felt as though the dance were sweeping away the long shadows of the past, all the years of ambition and bitterness that had soured their relationship.

Through the gloom, a figure moved towards them. He tried to pull away gently, embarrassed by the show of brotherly affection and the growing awareness that someone was following them around the floor, but his brother's grip tightened. The mood between them changed, the warmth draining away and the music speeding up. He turned around, scanning the darkness for the presence hovering there, but his dance partner was now vaulting across the hall, and his feet struggled to keep up with him.

It struck him that there was something very odd about this ageless, athletic version of his brother, the uniform he was wearing, his solicitude, and the glinting light in his eyes. His brother was sweating heavily, not humming but making animal noises, a series of pig-like grunts as he grabbed him closer. It no longer felt like a dance, but something more dangerous, a test or an experiment conducted under a tracking searchlight, which they were both trying to evade, the shadows pouncing all around them.

Then he saw her properly, the figure of a young woman, silhouetted as the light swung behind her, a black hood covering her head. He closed his eyes and concentrated on the music, and the gliding movements of his brother, using his momentum as a guide as he missed several steps. Although it had been decades since he had last seen the girl, the memories of that night had never quite left him, the sound of her stressed breathing gulping at the hood, and the frail

2

thump of her fists battering the car window as they drove her away. He kept catching glimpses of her on the dance floor, her oddly upright stance, her head drooping forward, indescribably sad in her dark hood. Was she sleeping or about to faint? He looked up at his brother, who seemed unconcerned, immersed in the music, his mouth set in a grin, his gaze watching him closely. He tried to prise himself away, but failed. He grew frightened, trapped in an embrace that had more to do with the sinister hold of the past than keeping up with the music.

'You're tensing up,' said his brother. His pupils were large, his eyes completely black. 'You've danced all these years, following your steps well, why get stage fright now?'

However, the fear had been with him for decades, rising up silently, coiling around his chest, probing between his ribs, thrusting towards his heart with a piercing pain.

'I have to stop.'

'Oh Jesus, Sammy, it's too late for that.'

'I'm an old man,' he complained. 'I'm exhausted.' He glanced down at his brother's pointed shoes, flying in and out of the ring of light, not so much dancing as skipping across the floor. By comparison, he felt like a beginner, a fool out of his depth and lost on the dance floor. If it weren't for his brother's grip, he would have fallen to pieces long ago.

'I can't keep up any more.'

'You're doing all right.' His brother wore a forced look of cheerfulness, his eyes dark and glittering. 'Hold me tighter, and remember, you're not meant to think about anything else.'

'What do you mean?'

'Just follow the spotlight, and stop looking so serious.'

'I'd rather stay in the dark.'

'Why?'

'It's easier to forget things there.'

'Don't be such a bloody coward.'

His legs grew heavy and his feet clumsy, the darkness creeping all around him. After the girl had disappeared all those years ago, his brother had warned him not to talk about her, not even to mention her name. He tried to drag himself out of the light, but his brother swung him back in, planting his feet firmly in the dance moves, weaving him round the room again.

'One more dance, that's all I can manage.'

'Haven't you worked it out, Sammy?' His brother's lips leaned into his ear. 'This is a conspiracy, not a dance. You can't quit until the music's over.'

The beat quickened, and the empty hall stretched interminably ahead. Beside them, the figure of the missing girl sank to her knees and became a shadow, slipping into a darkness that was full of crashing music all night long.

CHAPTER ONE

Samuel Reid woke, trembling, from the strange dream that had been haunting him for weeks. His first impulse was to look through the curtains and check the forlorn darkness of his farmyard for signs of strangers. Afterwards, he lay back in his bed, waiting for the dawn light to come, trying to comprehend fully the message of his brother's sinister embrace. All winter, he had been constantly on the alert, glancing over his shoulder, straining his ears, starting at any sudden noise, hiding even from the wind that blew through the keyholes and the cracks around the doors and windows of his farmhouse. Although he lived alone, he could not escape the sensation that people were watching him from within the house's warren of cramped rooms, the notion that if he suddenly turned round he would meet a row of eyes staring at him. Each day he felt their rays of suspicion falling upon him, wearing his defences thin as he navigated from his bedroom to the kitchen and then back to his bed at night.

There he rolled in an old blanket and waited helplessly for his brother to return in his dreams, full of youthful bravado and poise, eyes watching him without a trace of pity, ready to lunge him masterfully across the floor for one more dance.

He could not see his watchers but he felt their eyes touching him with their glare, gripping him in a state of guilty apprehension. The past was drawing near. He felt it in his nerves and in the hairs of his neck. He saw it repeatedly in his dreams, and in the landscape beyond his window, which resonated with clues: the spindly trees standing stiffly to attention, the quivering nettles, the warning calls of crows and blackbirds, the blackthorn tips that tapped the window like the suppressed subconscious of his farm, and the wind that rose louder and louder, carrying the shouts of murder and revenge along the overgrown hedges.

Each day he puttered about the house and farm, feeding his pigs and mending broken fencing, keeping his dog and his brother's old army rifle close, trying not to be noticed, feeling watched and inspected even in the bathroom, not even looking at his reflection in the mirror, still less at his eyes, which were the eyes of a man who had been blinkered from the truth about the missing girl for too long, a truth that was deeper than any nightmare.

January drew to a close, the winter passing slowly in a long-drawn-out wait. He gave up tending to his farm and just sat in the kitchen or bedroom, trying to steel himself against his fear, feeling his nerves tightening by the day. His hours of consciousness had now become a grim survival against an unseen enemy.

And then, on 15 February, something happened that he

could at last connect to the dreams and his sense of growing unease. A group of strangers arrived at his farm. They turned up without warning a few hours after noon and set up camp at the edge of his land. Alerted by the commotion of their vehicles churning in the mud, he clambered into his jeep and drove down the lane.

A young woman wearing a dress too short for the raw February afternoon emerged from an opening in the field by the river. There was something inviting and frightening about the look she gave him as he passed her, her eyes flashing a sly signal, the fleeting brightness of her red dress against the dark hedge stirring his memories of another girl, one who belonged to the distant past. He drove on, afraid that her eyes and his memories would encircle him and drag him back down a forgotten road. When he got to the gap in the hedge, he could not resist looking over, and when he saw the three caravans camped there, the open fire surrounded by children and dogs, the rusted white vans, the piebald horses tethered by ragged ropes, darkness settled around his heart.

He spent the rest of the afternoon scraping ice from the farmyard, but the white glare of the caravans in the murk of the winter landscape kept distracting him. His fingers and mind went numb in the cold. The temperature dropped further, and the air grew empty and calm. It began snowing, a skin of whiteness settling over the fields and hills. Numbly he watched as more caravans arrived, slowly negotiating the freezing lanes, settling in before nightfall like an army preparing for a dawn attack.

At first, any hostility was purely Reid's and not something inherent in the travellers' proximity or their behaviour, but as the days passed, their campsite began to exude an air of squalor and menace. He was surprised by the speed at which they took over the fields and wood by the river, turning them into a fully functioning halting site, four-by-fours and caravans wallowing in the icy mud. He became obsessed, watching them from the hedges that bordered his fields. Some days, several of the families would take off in their caravans, circle the roads around his farm and pitch up on the grass verge overnight. These strangers had no sense of belonging, he thought; their restlessness made them more troubling than ghosts.

He grew convinced that the gypsies were involved in criminal activities, principally smuggling. He watched young men unloading consignments of what looked to be cigarettes and tobacco, stashing them in sofas, which then went out in furniture lorries. When it grew dark, he could hear the rumble and whine of the loaded vehicles straining along the narrow roads, the snarls and barking of the travellers' dogs, drunken bellows and bottles breaking. One night he counted about a dozen vans arriving and leaving the site.

Driven into a state of indignation, he contacted the police and the council authorities, only to discover that the travellers had bought the fields they were camping on, and applied for planning permission. To his dismay, the council informed him that until the planning appeals process had been exhausted, the travellers could not be evicted.

Some nights later, during a storm, his dog sprang up from its rug by the fire and began barking frantically. The suddenness of the animal's arousal made him drop the ragged bible he had been reading. He grabbed the dog and bade him to be quiet. He listened intently. He switched off the light and leaned into the cold east-facing window of the farmhouse. The only sound was the icy rain drumming upon the roof and sluicing down the drains. He parted the curtain and caught a brief flurry of movement. He could not fully discern what was out there in the heaviness of the downpour, but what he thought he saw was the figure of a solitary man bent over and hurrying towards his door.

Afterwards he wished he had ignored the bell. He ought never to have answered the call. He ought to have held his dog and sat by the fire waiting for the visitor to pass by. There were forces set in motion by strangers in the night that should be shunned and feared by old men. However, he felt drawn to the door, which in its squeaking and creaking in the wind radiated a sense of looming threat. He wanted to show whoever it was that he was alert, on guard, and that he was prepared to defend himself and his home, if necessary. He stared at the door handle, feeling a feverish sense of anticipation. His dog snuffled and whined at the threshold. He shivered and listened to the wind roaring against the roof tiles and threshing through the trees. In his imagination, it sounded as though the storm were trying to batter and pound a vengeful mob to death.

CHAPTER TWO

For most of that winter, Inspector Celcius Daly had not been in his right mind. The detective's elderly neighbour Nora Cassidy had seen it every morning in his erratic movements around his cottage, the way he criss-crossed his unkempt garden and fields in his work suit and coat, the way he huddled in the thorn thickets, rubbing his forehead as though afflicted by a persistent headache. She ought to have been alarmed by his baleful figure wandering the edges of his deceased father's farm, his silhouette fluttering in the windy dawn light like a slow-burning fuse, but from her hidden vantage point at the kitchen window, her principal emotion was sadness. Daly was forty-four years old, divorced and childless, and her nearest neighbour. She had known him since he was a little boy, but since the beginning of winter it was as though a gulf had opened up between them.

Glancing through the window one morning as she washed the breakfast dishes, she followed Daly on one of his strange lumbering half-runs across the fields. She was captivated rather than frightened by the seemingly haphazard direction of his flight. What was he searching for amid the meaningless tangle of the overgrown hedges? What undisclosed secret was driving him to these early-morning stunts of madness?

She worried that if she did not hurry up the lane and say something to him she would spend the rest of the day distracted, troubled by the fear that he was about to crack under some unimaginable psychological strain. She had been planning to approach him for weeks now and offer him some words of consolation, but what could you say to a police officer who had recently discovered a terrible family secret, one that implicated his former colleagues in murder and cover-up?

Over the autumn, details of Daly's investigation into the murder triangle of the 1970s and his mother's death had leaked out and become the talk of the lough-shore parishes. The case had ended with an unexpected twist: the suicide of Daly's former commander Donaldson amid rumours that he had facilitated the Loyalist gang's assassination of its victims. There had been press calls for a public inquiry into the killing spree, until journalists discovered that the main perpetrators were either dead or too senile to be interrogated and the media circus had eventually moved on. But not before a reporter from the *Irish Times* had travelled through border country looking for Celcius Daly and his cottage. Amid all the tawdry details of murder and betrayal, the journalist had seemed most fascinated by Daly's reclusive existence, and the black hen he kept for company. She had asked the detective's neighbours questions about his domestic routine, as though the hidden story of the murder gang lacked any real interest for her readers in the Republic. She had hung around for the weekend, bothering everyone in the parish, while Daly, who had a terror of publicity, conjured up a disappearing trick and wasn't seen for days.

The journalist had confided in Nora that she found Daly's farm set-up so very mysterious and romantic. What a perfect escape from a day job detecting serious crimes and investigating the legacy of the Troubles, she told her. The old woman laughed. The journalist had it wrong. The men that Nora knew intimately, her husband and her sons, got in touch with their solitary souls by taking up fishing or duck hunting. Sometimes they would disappear all day, but eventually they returned to comfortable homes and their families, dinner in the kitchen and TV by the fire. A sliver of nature was all they needed to help balance their lives, to prevent the demands of home and work from stifling them. Daly's problem was that he had no home life whatsoever. All he had was his wild farm and the ghosts of the past haunting him.

Not much happened along the lough shore during winter, and the detective's behaviour and his dispiriting domestic life had kept preying on Nora's mind. Somehow, the urgency of his gait and the emptiness of the landscape made his restlessness loom larger in her imagination. What was he trying to do every morning? It was perplexing and the last thing she expected of a professional police detective in the circumstances. Even on mornings when the wind blew in gales and the rain lashed the trees, the detective's figure appeared on the brow of the hill, waiting under the thorn trees, before taking off on his clumsy pilgrimage of his fields.

Watching him that morning, as he took shelter from the wind, she decided that she would have to speak to him. It was time she confronted him about his erratic behaviour. She tightened her shawl about her head and struck off from her front door. She thought she had worked out why Daly was so unsettled, why he wandered the fields every dawn with the air of a man looking for something he did not know how to find. She was determined that she would give him the benefit of her opinion, which was that there was only one way for a person to settle gently into middle age, and it did not involve living on your own surrounded by the shadows of the past.

It wasn't right to interfere, but it made her sad that Daly lived such a lonely life, and that there were no children for miles around, just old farmers and their wives floating along in their solitary routines like weeds trailing in a stagnant pond. She could not help thinking about Daly as a boy, and the other lough-shore children. She wanted to see their bright faces again, hear their laughter, and tell them stories about the past and the great characters that once sailed and fished the lough. Perhaps she was projecting her own acute longing for the children who would never exist, but whose voices she kept hearing in her imagination. In her view, Daly was of just the right age to start a family. He should free himself from the downward pull of the past, the weight of his father's tragedy, his sadness and silence, and the guilt over his mother's death, the murder he could never avenge. What was the point in being a detective if you could not tie up the loose ends of a decades-old crime and get on with your life?

It was an invigorating, bad-tempered morning, the roar of the lough sinking deep into the thorny hollows and dips in the lane. Nora was almost out of breath when she came alongside the trees beneath which the detective had been sheltering. She was caught off guard when she saw him standing only a few feet away, immobile and tense, his mouth open, his eyes luminous in the glimmering dawn, eyes that just blinked and blinked without registering her presence. A buffet of apprehension hit her. Perhaps she was getting old and fretting too much over this reclusive man who still had many good years ahead to decide what to do with his life. She should mind her own business and not bother him with her opinions.

Nevertheless, she tried to catch his attention by shouting a harmless remark about the weather. The detective did not appear to hear her over the roar of the wind. His hands were clenched by his sides, his tendons contracting, his eyes squinting as leaves and broken twigs blew around him. He seemed to be listening intently to the trees, which shifted in the wind with a rising chorus of injured, squeaking noises. What had so fixated his attention that he seemed oblivious to the weather and human company? She watched as his fists tightened and untightened, and his eyes swivelled back and forth, as if searching for some stimulus to release the tension in his body. For a few moments, she shared his lonely refuge, this space of cold air beneath the churning trees. Part of her wanted to reach out and console him, even though it violated the rules of respect for a neighbour's grief. It seemed to her that the man beside her was not a detective, but a troubled only child who had yet to lead the life that had been promised him.

However, she was afraid of provoking him into an outburst. There was something dangerous and vulnerable about the look in his eyes, like that of a starving carnivore hunching over its fresh kill. She waited for the right moment to say something. The morning sun peeked out from behind the rain clouds and the sky became a tumult of orange and red. Slowly he became aware of her presence. His eyes turned to take her in, flashing a look of dreadful surprise, and then, to her dismay, he bowed his shoulders and took off at a run back to the house.

She hurried after him, shouting, 'You can't go on like this, Celcius Daly. You need a normal home, with someone to love. It's time you took a chance in your life.' However, the wind was too strong for her voice to carry. She tried to keep up with him, but he turned along the line of a high hedge and disappeared between the trees. She lingered for a while, saddened to find no further sign of him. The wind grew wilder, and the lough-shore waves filled the horizon with their queasy greyness.

CHAPTER THREE

When Samuel Reid opened the door that stormy night, he was surprised to find not a gypsy, but a tall, well-dressed man in his late thirties. The rain was whipping relentlessly at his face and raincoat, seeping its way along his shirt-neck and tie, and into his cuffs, which looked relatively dry, although his trouser bottoms were sodden and heavy. It seemed to Reid that he had not walked too far. The man's coat filled with a blast of wind, and he gave Reid a look of desperation.

'Sorry for calling at this time of the night,' he explained in a southern English accent. 'My car's broken down and I can't get a signal on the phone.'

He pointed back at the swirl of darkness, the toiling trees, and the puddle-strewn lane disappearing into the mesh of border roads. His face winced in the cold and rain. He looked lost. He clutched a mobile phone with a younger man's reliance on expensive gadgets. However, there was something in his eyes that unnerved Reid. A lingering grievance, as though

Reid were to blame for his motoring misfortune. What was a strange Englishman doing travelling such remote roads at this time of night?

'I only need to make a phone call. It'll take less than a minute. My car's at the bottom of the road.'

The rain intensified, the puddles boiling under the weather's fury.

'You'd better come in.'

Reid led him to the phone, a reassuring relic from the past, with its circular dial and metallic black receiver. Then he slipped into the front room and watched the stranger through a tiny secret window in the wall. He hesitated, transfixed by the sight of the visitor slowly replacing the receiver and opening the drawers of the telephone desk. He watched him root through the contents, examining old letters and notebooks.

He stepped back into the hall. 'What do you think you're doing?' he asked.

The stranger stood upright, caught in the act.

'You haven't come here looking for help,' Reid said aggressively. 'What are you up to?'

The Englishman raised his hands in the air, in an attempt to reassure his host. 'You're right,' he said. 'My car didn't break down, but I do need your help. I'm a journalist researching a story. I'm trying to trace a woman who went missing from these parts many years ago. She was a traveller.'

An old instinct kicked in. 'I don't know who you're talking about. You should leave now. Before I call the police.'

The journalist's hands dropped. 'Her name was Mary O'Sullivan. I need to find out what happened to her.'

Reid cleared his throat. 'What makes you think I can help?'

'I'm finding it hard to locate anyone who can remember her at all. I heard she worked for a while on the farms around here. Does the name ring a bell?'

For a bad moment, Reid felt the chill of his dream travel along his spine. The journalist now looked oddly familiar, as though his face was something presented not out of the rainy night but from the darkness of his subconscious. 'Nobody along this part of the border is interested in a gypsy story from the past.'

'Trust me, a lot of people soon will be.'

Reid raised the back of his hand to cover his mouth, which was thick with spittle and dread. It was an involuntary movement, and he tried to conceal it from the journalist. He extended his hand to steady himself against the doorframe. 'Have you any identification?'

The journalist fished out his wallet and handed Reid a press card. He studied it carefully. Why had this Englishman come after all these years, intruding upon his company at this time of the night, annoying him with the dark deeds of the past? 'Don't you have more up-to-date stories to write?'

'I've spent months tracing the geography of this woman's short life. Her story deserves to be told.'

'But this country is full of missing people. Every twist in the road, every thorn tree has its secrets. Who cares about a forgotten gypsy from all those years ago? Maybe she got into trouble and had to emigrate. The past is the past, and shouldn't be interfered with.'

'I heard she was suspected of being an IRA informer. A gang of men raped and murdered her before hiding her body.'

'Where did you dig that rubbish up? None of that was in any of the newspapers. What sort of journalist are you?'

'A journalist with some influential contacts.' His eyes glinted with satisfaction. 'They told me that her last job was at this very farm. Your brother was a friend of the police officers who investigated her disappearance.'

'She worked here for a few months, and then she left.' Reid focused on a spot somewhere behind the journalist's head in an attempt to remain composed. 'That's the way with gypsies. They come and they go; no one knows their business.'

Outside, the sound of the storm grew wilder. The light in the hall flickered, and in the shadows, it looked as though the journalist was grinning, but from the grave tone of his voice, he was not. 'If you know something about what happened to her then the law demands you should bring it to the police.'

'Whose law are we talking about? The law that allows gypsies to pitch up next to my land and run amok? You want a story then go down to that camp at the bottom of the lane and watch what happens at night. I've seen shocking things with my own eyes. Smuggling alcohol and god knows what else across the border.'

'I want the names of the men who abducted her.'

'I can't help you any more. It's time you left.'

'Before you kick me out there's something I want you to look at.' The journalist removed a folder from his jacket. Reid noted that his fingernails were dirty. What grubby secrets of the past had the Englishman been digging up? He stood his ground, but accepted the folder. He had lost the momentum of his anger. For a moment, the hall was quiet, and the two of them stood motionless, neither of them speaking.

'This was so long ago,' said Reid, looking up from the documents.

The journalist leaned closer. 'You seem bothered. Perhaps you should look at them sitting down?'

Reid grunted with irritation. He did not need to sit down. He did not want to be detained by the past. He glanced at the journalist and saw it again, a dangerous light glittering in his eyes. Why were people of his profession always meddling, always asking dangerous questions? They did not seem to anticipate or care about what might come to light, or imagine the events that might be set in motion when a question was answered truthfully. They were like mischievous children, pinpricking the dark deeds of the past, as though they were harmless balloons to play with.

'A lot of things happened along the border that are none of your bloody English business,' said Reid. Nevertheless, he opened the folder and went through its contents.

The first photograph he saw was of a group of men in uniform, including his brother Alistair. They were wearing the same soldier's uniform that hung in his wardrobe. He stared at the faces of the brave young men, cousins and brothers, who had bonded together to protect their border farms from IRA gunmen, to keep their country from slipping into chaos, only to find themselves betrayed at the last when the Ministry of Defence disbanded the regiment and refused to give part-time soldiers a proper pension or redundancy payment. All those nights they had spent lying in cold ditches, operating checkpoints on lonely roads, reading passages from the bible and singing psalms to keep up their courage. All those days cleaning their guns in the back yards of their farms and tending to their livestock in between mounting dangerous foot patrols under the gaze of IRA snipers and praying at the funerals of their colleagues.

Another photograph slipped from the folder. He recognized the young traveller woman immediately. Perhaps he really did need to sit down. The trusting expression on her face looked so familiar to him, as did her dark eyes and the centre parting of her lank hair. She was wearing lipstick, which struck him as odd. He did not remember her wearing make-up. He wondered who had taken the photograph. Somehow, the lipstick made her look more vulnerable, more open to danger. He stared at her eyes. What were they communicating to the photographer? A shared secret? Some moment to remember? Then he noticed the full roundness of her belly. In another photo, she was beside the sea, this time with a young baby in her arms. There was a date below the photograph: 4 April 1976. This would have been about a month before her disappearance.

There were old newspaper reports in the folder, much less pleasing to the eye. They were grubby and accusing, cut-outs from the *Irish News* dating back to the late 1970s. His eyes strained in the gloom to read the newsprint. They described the search for the missing traveller Mary O'Sullivan on both sides of the border, the futile police investigation, and then, later, protests by travellers claiming that not enough was being done by the authorities to find her.

Reid trembled inside. The photographs changed everything about what he thought he knew. A birth and a disappearance. The young woman and her baby. A journey over and another just beginning. This journalist with his quest for the truth was well informed. There was no doubt about that. He felt a surge into the maw of the past, the secrets that lay beneath what he remembered, the details of the young woman's pregnancy, her disappearance and the mystery of her baby. He was confronted by a truth that his own family had protected him from during his secluded life on this lonely farm.

'You're not looking at the pictures,' said the journalist. 'You're thinking of something else.'

Why are you searching for her? Reid wanted to ask the journalist. Is it to find out the facts or seek some form of atonement, a confession, or perhaps something darker – retribution or revenge? The questions hung in the air, demanding answers.

The journalist watched him more closely. 'Don't you want to know what happened to the baby?'

'I don't want to know anything.'

'Why? If it were me, I'd be desperate to know.'

'I don't like thinking about the past. For one thing, it reminds me of how old I am. For another I'd rather sleep tonight in peace.'

He opened the door in a gesture that signalled it was time for the journalist to leave.

'What do you mean, sleep in peace?' asked the journalist. 'If there was a secret I didn't know I would want to discover it. Not knowing would keep me awake at night. Especially if it were a secret that others had kept hidden.'

Reid pushed the folder back into his hands, but the journalist refused to take it. 'Is that all you have to show me?'

The journalist stared at him silently.

'Have you anything else to say?' asked Reid. 'What else do you want from me?'

'Did you rape her?'

Reid's heart began to pound. 'I never touched her.'

'Then help me solve the cover-up of her murder.' His eyes were unmoving, black and glittering.

'Help you? What sort of cover-up are you talking about?'

'Don't look at me with that stupid expression on your face.' The journalist's tone was no longer polite. 'I want to know: will you help me find her killers?'

'What if I can't help you at this stage of my life?' Reid's voice rang out in the narrow hallway. 'Would that be so terrible? Think about it. She disappeared a long time ago, and memories grow weaker by the day. What difference would it make to her if no one remembered? Give us a few more years and everyone who knew her will be dead.'

'It would make a difference to me.' The journalist's face was full of darkness.

'Then go to the police,' said Reid. 'If you've new evidence show it to them and ask them to open the case again.'

'I've wasted enough time talking to them. They tell me there's neither the funding nor the political will to open up these old cases.'

Reid was quiet. His visitor was less a reporter, more a ghost that had floated up from the underworld to haunt him with bad news. He did not need these questions. A surge of defiance welled within him.

'I'm no telltale. I won't go blabbing about the past.'

He flicked on the outside security light and angrily ushered the journalist out of the door. The rain had stopped and the yard was empty. However, close to the farm gate, he spied a dirty-white traveller van, its headlights flicking on.

The reporter turned back briefly before walking towards the van. His eyes were filled with the dregs of contempt. 'Now that we've found you, Mr Reid, be prepared to suffer.'

CHAPTER FOUR

The most uninhibited man in Armagh courthouse was the judge, from whom Inspector Celcius Daly detected a faint whiff of alcohol as he marched past him from his side chamber. One of his shirt collars protruded at an odd angle and his cheeks glowed red, his puffy eyes barely acknowledging the assembled ranks of solicitors as he perched himself at his leather seat, like a jockey getting ready for the starting gun. His state of inebriation appeared to have little detrimental effect on his performance, however, and he was soon making improbable headway though the list of uninsured motorists, drink drivers, and petty drug dealers, having memorized many of the details of that morning's cases. The row of clerks and prosecuting solicitors worked at a feverish pace beneath him, prodding each other with files and pecking away at keyboards, struggling to keep up with his delivery as the stacks of papers beside them grew into towers.

Exasperated by a time-consuming domestic abuse case, the judge broke into a rant at the court, castigating the solicitors for their habit of adjourning hearings at any excuse, and the police for the lengthy delays in their investigations. Daly had heard it countless times before, and that morning's slightly drunken diatribe was no different, at least outwardly, from any other. Consequently, he was not overly concerned when he took the witness stand. He had barely taken the oath when the judge indicated with a vexed wave of fingers that he should sit down.

'Are you the investigating officer?' asked the prosecuting counsel.

'No, I am not,' replied Daly, eyeing the judge.

'Are you aware of the details of the investigation?'

'Yes, I am.'

'Can you connect the accused with the charges before the court?'

'Yes, your worship.'

The prosecutor rattled through the details of the case, and then a silence fell upon the room. For the last six months, Daly had taken refuge in his role as the stand-in prosecuting detective, covering for officers who were on holiday, off sick or too busy to attend court; a role that not only provided distance from the scrutiny of his colleagues and commanders, but also served to mask his sense of professional unease. He could no longer be held to account, nor did he have to defend himself and his actions, since it was the detective work of others, rather than his own, that was under scrutiny. It was a relief to watch the jostling of other egos, the careers being made or broken, but what comforted Daly most were the silences, and the repetitive quality of the court exchanges, the defending solicitors and the prosecutors eyeing each other closely, listening to what each other said. The way they nodded gravely and waited with caution for the judge to speak, standing in the same positions every morning and speaking at the same volume, as if everything was subordinated to invisible but strict stage directions.

There were even times when Daly thought he might be able to forget the events of the previous winter, and the sense of betrayal he felt from his former colleagues, that the deaths of the rogue officers and Commander Donaldson had been a form of punishment in itself. There were glimmerings of hope sometimes in the witness stand, when he was able to relegate the details of his mother's murder, but then the feelings of guilt would re-emerge, the self-doubts, the worry that he had not done anything, or at least not enough against the system of cover-ups and silence that had kept victims like him in the dark for so many decades.

He scrutinized the behaviour of the defendants and their solicitors, as though it might be possible to find in their simple crimes, in the intervals of silence between their scripted monotone excuses, a trace of the crime that had tarnished his childhood. As if he expected his mother's murderers to appear in the dock, shuffling in their turn, like ghosts in the dank light under that vaulted ceiling.

Daly's principal problem was that back at headquarters, he usually felt bereft, but he was unwilling or unable to reveal his grief to his colleagues, who also seemed at a loss whenever they strayed into small talk with him, unsure of the lines they were expected to recite. He had no doubt that

Special Branch Detective Derek Irwin and his boss Inspector Ian Fealty found his company prickly and exasperating. After the journalist Jacqueline Pryce had published her reports on the murder triangle of the seventies, they had launched an internal investigation into his role in helping her and into the disappearance of Daniel Hegarty, a former IRA spy. They'd asked questions of Daly's professional reliability at a time when the police force of Northern Ireland was under unprecedented scrutiny by the media and politicians. They'd even accused him of instigating political instability during a difficult period in the peace process.

'What did you think you were doing, making contact with a dangerous spy?' the new police chief, Commander Alan Sinclair, had asked him at an informal disciplinary hearing.

'My job,' was Daly's simple reply.

'Well, you can forget about leading any major investigations until this inquiry is over.'

'How long will that take?'

'These things can run for months.' The sight of Daly's pained reaction prompted a hint of sympathy from the commander. 'Listen, Daly, it might do you good to get a break from the front line. It's what we all need from time to time.'

'True,' Daly had replied, knowing that in his case it definitely wasn't.

Nevertheless, he had accepted his reassignment to court duties with equanimity. He tried to convince himself that the courtroom was not a prison, and that he was not being punished. I am a senior detective, he reminded himself as he stooped before the judge, serving up cases that were the work of other detectives, while all the time nagged by the worry that forces in Special Branch were conspiring to dismantle his career and reputation.

His subordinated role meant that the details of the cases, even the most shocking and violent, were fixed at a remove, like half-submerged buoys in a fog-bound sea. He had no explicit connection with the investigations, or the anonymous figures of the defendants as they passed through the dock. Weeks had slipped by, and virtually nothing of note happened on the surface of his life. Deep down, however, he was lurching towards a painful transformation. During those mute, constricted hours waiting for his call to the witness stand, he came to realize that as a divorced forty-four-year-old the chances of him salvaging any sense of fulfilment in his career or troubled personal life were rapidly dwindling.

The cases had blurred into each other that morning, Daly sitting half-numb to what was going on, time totally lost to him. On a submerged level, he felt they were all doomed, the lawyers, their clerks and the police officers, even the omniscient but tipsy judge sitting at his elevated perch, defending the indefensible, a justice system that was too weak and underfunded to deal with the countless ills of a society emerging from forty years of conflict and murder.

The silence in the court had grown uncomfortably long, and when Daly glanced at the judge, he was surprised to meet his eyes, no longer puffy but shrewd and aggressive-looking, staring back at him. The judge addressed Daly slowly and deliberately, as if every word was a trap laid for his prey.

'Have you heard what I just said, Inspector?' His cheeks had turned a livid warning colour. 'If you are doing this deliberately to frustrate the proceedings, then I will charge you with contempt of court.'

The silence in the courtroom deepened as Daly straightened up and tried to recall which case the judge was dealing with. The piercing gaze directed towards him obviously constituted a professional threat, but he racked his brains, trying to think of how he might have drawn his ire.

'I want us to understand each other so you must explain to me why you refuse to answer my questions,' said the judge with an unpleasant smile.

The prosecuting counsel leaned forward to whisper something at Daly, but the judge irritably gestured for her to be quiet. Daly was still under oath, but his mind was a blank and he had no idea what to say. To make matters worse, the defendant in the dock was a complete stranger to him. He glanced about the room, catching glances from the solicitors and their defendants. The judge kept his eyes fixed upon Daly, and though the words sounded professional and calm, Daly could sense the fury behind them.

'You are not the detective in charge of this case, but you have sworn in this court that you are aware of the details.' The judge let his words hang in the air.

'Yes, your worship.' Daly hunched his shoulders, feeling as though a protective hood had been wrenched from his head, robbing him of his invisibility. He glanced towards the exit. At the door stood a young female solicitor, gazing at him with sympathy, her shoes a bright red in the dull light of the courtroom.

'What is your name, Inspector?' snapped the judge.

'Inspector Daly.'

'I would like to have your full name, Inspector Daly.'

'Inspector Celcius Daly.'

'I want you to explain to this court, Inspector Celcius Daly, why it has taken your colleagues more than six months to pass on a medical report of the victim's injuries to the prosecution service.'

Daly tried to keep a dignified bearing, while the judge's cheeks glowed ever more dangerously. A solemn hush fell over the courtroom. The truth was that the investigation teams dealing with minor assault charges were often overwhelmed. It was a chaos inherited from the Troubles, when resources had been routinely directed towards foiling terrorist plots and solving sectarian murders. Even now, so much of police time was spent monitoring and obstructing the terrorist activity of dissident paramilitaries. However, Daly suspected that the judge was in no mood this morning to hear excuses.

'There is no explanation, your worship.'

The judge's eyes darkened. 'Meanwhile, the defendant remains in limbo while the investigating officers drag their heels.'

Daly leaned forward, his mouth dry. The judge's comments chimed with his own unfulfilled longings. He thought of all the victims of the Troubles who were also in limbo, waiting for the justice system to prosecute the murderers of their loved ones.

The prosecutor began to outline possible dates for an adjournment but the judge interrupted her in a low but thunderous voice. 'I don't think counsel understands fully what is at stake here, so she should kindly let me finish.'

The prosecutor sat down, blinking in distress, and the judge turned back to Daly.

'Tell me, Inspector Daly, exactly what progress has been made since the last adjournment in December?'

The unease in the room increased, the solicitors sensing Daly's humiliation.

'No progress at all, your worship,' replied Daly.

'Then either your colleagues are incompetent or they are wilfully obstructing this investigation in the hope that the defendant will remain in custody for as long as possible.'

Daly watched the lines on the judge's brow deepen, his anger looming towards him like a gathering storm.

'What irritates me the most is that you, sir, came to court knowing in advance the dire state of this investigation, and were content to simply sit here, prepared to go through the motions without asking any meaningful questions of your colleagues.'

Daly said nothing. He was reluctant to reply because to speak now would be akin to confessing, and he was afraid that any confession would worsen his situation and be used as evidence against him. The judge had singled him out as though his apathy were to blame for the paralysis of the entire legal system. He could feel the savagery in the judge's stare, like that of a caged bird of prey outraged by the endless monotony of its imprisonment. The hushed courtroom no longer felt like a bunker for Daly, safe from hunting eyes. There was no dark place for him to retreat into; he could not move from the witness stand. He was frozen to the spot, transfixed by the judge's glare. He was aware of the rows of solicitors dipping their heads in embarrassment, and the faces in the public gallery, rapt at the unfolding drama. The only one who returned his glance was the young solicitor by the door, watching him closely. He felt hollow inside. He told himself he would have a few extra glasses of whiskey that evening, perhaps even some cigarettes. He was sure there was a mouldy pack somewhere in the drawers of his furniture.

'What do you think, Inspector?' The judge was leaning far out of his seat now, clearly enraged by Daly's lack of reply. 'You think you can dodge my questions by your silence. Let me remind you that this is my court and you will follow my instructions. You will act professionally from now on. You will work within the code of conduct that this court sets and according to the duties that it assigns to you. We cannot afford the luxury of a character like you wandering around, holding your silence, coming and going as you please, avoiding doing anything of any real worth.'

Daly stared fixedly ahead of him. The judge turned away from the detective and heaved a great sigh. 'We must ask ourselves the question: What sort of justice are we delivering, ruining a man's life, leaving him in limbo, wasting taxpayers' money and court time, waiting month after month for vital evidence to substantiate the charges?' The anger in his face gradually dissolved. The silent detective had been a tonic for his frustration. 'Inform your colleagues, Inspector Celcius Daly, that if the report is not forthcoming in two weeks, I will strike off the charges and order the defendant to be released.'

Daly nodded and left the witness stand. Any damage to his self-esteem was only temporary. Nothing serious. However, he felt tired to the core of his being, tired of the grinding slowness of the justice system, of the deadening weight of unsolved crimes, and of his own mindless role within that system. What sort of justice did people expect while the shadow of the Troubles still loomed so largely, while former paramilitaries enjoyed the highest positions in government, while the political set-up decreed that stability was more important than uncovering the truth? How could anyone believe in law and order when the authorities pretended that some victims never existed and that their ghosts did not haunt their loved ones?

A dark cloud, outlined in edges of golden light, passed over the high windows, adding a leaden weight to the court. The solicitors began their whispering again, shuffling papers, pacing relentlessly back and forth between their clients and the prosecutors, casting half an eye up at the judge, wondering fearfully if he might pounce on them. Slowly the wheels of justice began to grind again with their rhythmic monotony.

There was still light left in the sky when Daly left the courthouse that evening. He drove to his cottage on the southern shore of Lough Neagh, his foot pressed hard against the accelerator, as if he wanted to bore the bonnet of his car into the landscape unfolding before him. The lough was invisible until he crossed a low hill and a ridge of trees, and hit a brief rain shower. When it lifted, he had entered a different landscape altogether. Ahead of him, a swathe of triangular fields and marshland sloped down to the lough shore where waves were washing up and breaking in their winter fullness. For a few moments, his over-preoccupied mind made him feel like a stranger, as though he had been away on a long journey.

The car dipped and bounced over the uneven road, twisting through straggling gorse hedges and birch trees. He could navigate his way blindly along the roads of his childhood, orientating himself by the feel of the road alone, or the sight of the snow-dusted Sperrin Mountains in the west, and the evening stars twinkling in the sky. His body always returned home first, his thoughts and moods later, and the sight of the waves rising and falling gradually drained away the traces of his frustration and humiliation. His driving slowed and became more measured, his mind lifting, even if his suit and jacket still reeked with the odour of defeat. As he pulled up on to his little lane, he found himself looking forward to one of his few remaining consolations: the sight of his black hen roosting in the porch of his cottage.

The creature had not laid an egg for years, and was economically worthless, but, as the sole survivor of his father's brood, Daly was determined to keep her alive from each winter to the next. After his father's death, he had taken indifferent care of the flock until one brutal moonless night when the foxes slunk out of the hedges and attacked the brood. To his shame, he had forgotten to close and bolt the coop door before going to bed. Ever since, the black hen had kept close to Daly's heels, always trying to follow him indoors, flapping in his footsteps and roosting every evening in the porch, waiting for him to carry her back to the coop, which he always made sure to bolt securely. In many ways, he was glad that her old-maidenly presence had entered his life.

She clucked at his arrival, but instead of allowing him to

pick her up, she lifted her glossy wings and flew off, landing a little bit away, her beady eyes watching him. As soon as he approached, she flew off again, skimming across the dead nettles and thistles in the garden, before alighting on an abandoned wheelbarrow.

She glanced back at Daly, waiting for him to draw near, and then she made off again. Lunging at her, he managed to grab one of her wings, but she let out a squawk, flapping furiously, her broken feathers falling at his feet. She was quick and nimble, and struggled out of his grasp. He kicked at the weeds in frustration. It was an evening to retire to the fire and seek comfort in a bottle of whiskey, rather than chase a flustered old hen around his ruined garden. He went to the kitchen, gathered some breadcrumbs and paced after the bird, scattering the crumbs in an attempt to lure her closer.

For half an hour, the hen kept evading his clutches, as though in the space of a day he had become a dangerous enemy. With the tactical sense of a wild creature, she beat off along barely visible tracks through weeds and blackthorns. The farm was riddled with such paths, worn out by his restless feet and the tread of wild animals, wandering as no human way should, switching back and forth across the hillside, veering through thickets that over the winter had become his favourite refuge from ill feelings. He ducked and scrambled through the thorny cover until his feet were caked in mud and his hands scratched.

He took stock of his predicament. His father would be cross, tut-tutting at his terrible fowl keeping. Here he was, a detective confined to the smallest possible professional stage, unable to concentrate on the important details of his job, and failing to tend to his father's legacy, this unkempt farm and its only remaining charge, a wayward hen. In future, he should tie string to the creature's feet and allow her only the smallest possible range of flight. Why should he permit her to roam freely, when he had no freedom at all, and no choice but to sit mindlessly at court each day as he had been instructed by his commander, trapped as much by his own clumsiness as by the political forces within Special Branch?

Taking a breath and looking up, he gazed at a view of Lough Neagh that eased his heart. Low clouds were shifting over the expanse of water, the waves swelling against the shore, their flanks dark and foaming. The hen's wings flared over the top of a bush, the wind dragging her ungainly form to the far side of the thicket. He felt transported by the sight of her. If his troubled spirit could take form, it would be in the shape of this bird, broken-feathered and unbiddable, reverting to wildness within the blackthorn trees.

CHAPTER FIVE

Next morning, Daly returned to his usual berth alongside the prosecutors in Armagh courthouse. He had only one case to cover, but not knowing when the judge would call it, was unable to escape until lunchtime. Raindrops pecked against the high skylights, and then began falling in earnest, drumming against the glass, adding to the weight of the mood within the room. Daly wondered if his hen had found a comfortable roost at the bottom of some hedge. Perhaps she had dragged herself back to the safety of the porch, and was sheltering there right now, safe from the attention of foxes. Either way, he was not looking forward to another evening stumbling through shrubbery in the near darkness, trailing in her wake.

The atmosphere in the courtroom grew stifling, the hands of the clock above the exit barely seeming to move, the judge squinting at him from time to time with barely concealed scorn, as if waiting for him to make another wrong move.

He was glad, therefore, when a note, passed along the bench and addressed to him in hastily scrawled handwriting, offered him an excuse to leave.

'Please, Celcius, I need your help, urgently', it read, followed by a signature, 'Rebecca Hewson'. It was the young solicitor in bright red shoes, who had flashed him a sympathetic look the previous day. The familiar tone of the note surprised him. Within the confines of the court, solicitors tended to refer to police inspectors by their surnames, fellow lawyers by their first names, and the defendants by their first and last names, usually reversed. Such were the hierarchies of the justice system. He had never spoken to the solicitor, and here she was sending him a pleading note hinting at dark legal undercurrents. He grew cautious. He read the note again, and slipped it into his pocket. He looked up from the shadow of the witness box and saw her standing next to the public gallery.

She concentrated her gaze upon him, and he frowned in response. He was at a loss to fix a context for her request. It might have been something to do with a case he was covering, which made him dubious about her motives. He glanced at her again, feeling drawn to her pretty face, her glittering eyes. He detected something speculative and defiant in her stare and the way she eventually moved towards the doors, confident she had reeled him in.

He waited for the judge to stop speaking, her mute appeal intensifying in the air like a suffocating gas. When he rose and awkwardly excused himself before the judge, she flashed him a triumphant little smile and slipped into the public waiting room. He barely raised his eyes as he followed her out, feeling slightly embarrassed at the impropriety of a middle-aged detective running after this attractive-looking young solicitor. He thought he was dashing to her assistance, but in reality, it was his own no man's land he was fleeing. The note and her eyes had formed the basis for his rescue. They were the first signals of the deliverance he had been longing for since uncovering the truth about his mother's murder.

Rebecca Hewson leaped forward as soon as Daly entered the waiting room, dragging him to a corner where her client, a distraught young woman, was trying to comfort a crying baby. She began talking quickly about her client's predicament – a single mother, brought to court on charges of shoplifting, who had been unable to find a minder for the infant. Daly followed the story bit by bit, focusing on Hewson's pretty face in order to better tolerate the impact of the baby's crying on his eardrums. To sum up, the woman had appeared before the judge with the baby in her arms. In a fit of irritability, the judge had immediately adjourned when the baby started wailing, warning the mother that bringing a child to court was not a get-out-of-jail card. Unless she found a babysitter, the judge threatened to cut short the hearing and punish her with an immediate custodial sentence.

Daly stopped the solicitor, without looking directly at the mother or her child. 'What do you want from me?' he asked.

'We need someone to hold the baby while I defend my client. It will only take a minute.'

Daly reddened slightly, his expectation and curiosity changing rapidly to discomfort. He hadn't expected such a request. He looked at the mother. Her face was young but her hands holding the infant were lined and chapped. Her stricken eyes disturbed him. 'Why are you asking me?'

'Because this woman needs help. She's at risk of going to jail rather than getting a community service order, the usual punishment for a first shoplifting charge.'

Daly shook his head. It had been a week of strange humiliations.

'Can't you see how distraught she is?'

'Is there no one else?' He was not used to dealing with children, and the fact that he had responded so heedlessly to her request for help made him feel foolish. He glanced at the forlorn crowd in the waiting room, the grey-faced defendants and their relatives, hardly the pool of people from whom you'd recruit a reliable babysitter. 'What about the father of the child?'

'I'm sorry we don't have time to go through all the options. The judge has just recalled the case.'

A security guard opened the court doors and called the mother's name in a stern voice. She turned to Daly with imploring eyes.

'Don't worry, Inspector,' said Hewson. 'The mother is much more likely to go into hysterics than the child.'

Seeing how defenceless the young woman looked, how she lacked the confidence or strength to persuade him, he reluctantly agreed and took the baby into his arms. Ignoring her plight would have been churlish of him. Better to risk his own discomfort than appear rude, he reasoned, even if it meant looking ridiculous in front of his colleagues. The mother thanked Daly, while Hewson leaned against the doors, pushing them open for her client and ushering her through.

Daly glanced at the solicitor's bouncing dark hair and the neat curves of her dress. She flashed him a smile, her eyes shining, and disappeared into the courtroom.

Not knowing what else to do, Daly held the infant against his shoulder and patted its tiny back. Almost immediately, the wailing increased in intensity. Daly clenched his jaw, praying that the judge would give the case a quick hearing. He was a complete stranger to the child and there was nothing personal in its reaction to his clumsy attempts at soothing it, its rigid limbs and its hideously loud crying. He walked in small, anxious circles, feeling concerned for the baby's welfare but impotent to help it in any meaningful way. He glanced around the waiting room, catching sympathetic but futile looks from the security guards.

He groaned in exasperation. The solicitor's request had jarred him, thrown him back upon himself with nothing to hold on to, nothing to assert his role as a senior detective, a professional with more than twenty years' experience in the police force. He had never before considered what happened to the babies of shoplifting mothers. It was unexplored terrain. The only skills he had were measured in terms of the cases he had solved, and the bitter mistakes made along the way. If he had a talent, it was in his stubborn and diligent approach to detective work, but was this any qualification for the task at hand? He put his head to one side and tried to communicate with the child's angry face. His stubbled chin brushed its cheek, setting off another protracted wail, which echoed through the waiting room and along the corridors of the courthouse.

Trying to coax some sound other than crying, he asked

the baby questions, but its tongue jutted out of its mouth, its distorted forehead bulging like that of a gargoyle. Out of blind reflex, its fingers clung on to Daly's jacket, fastening on to him with a surprisingly ferocious grip.

Daly caught a glimpse of his reflection in a glass door, a suited detective holding a distressed baby with a solemn, regretful air, as though he had just broken terrible news to it. He retreated to a less conspicuous part of the court, walking along the public information shelves, trying to distract the baby with the colourful leaflets.

Miraculously, the baby began to settle in his arms, its wet face nestling into his neck. He rocked the infant back and forth, and little by little, it edged towards sleep.

The minutes ticked by, and the warmth of the baby's body and its soft damp cheeks released a tangle of feelings that lay knotted in Daly's chest. He thought of his deceased mother. Not the remote, almost fairytale figure from the time immediately before her murder, but a physical memory, thrusting up from his earliest days, the smell of her freckled skin, the closeness of her breath, her mouth humming with happiness as she swung him in the air.

An image of his father's last days also sprang to mind: the old man's arms folded across his narrow chest as he rocked himself into emptiness, the sunspots on his yellowed flesh, and the frozen grey of his eyes, a final barricade against human interaction. Daly had loved them both, but they had been taken from him. He realized that since his father's death he had not loved or cared for another human being. If he could have lived his life differently, he would have had children with his wife Anna, but it was too late now to have such thoughts. It would take a miracle for them to resume their relationship and start a family and he did not believe in miracles. Just as he did not believe in fate or destiny. Nevertheless, he shivered at the thought that he might be destined to roam his father's farm for the rest of his days, burning with loneliness and guilt. What age was he? He was broaching his middle forties, so didn't he still have lots of life to live, more opportunities to fill the cramped rooms of his cottage with the sounds of family life?

He should renovate the place completely, he thought, put on a new roof and insulate the walls, drive out the primeval damp that seeped up from the floorboards and the ghosts of the past that followed him through the tangle of tiny rooms. The cottage needed bigger windows that he could open fully to the lough-shore air, and noisy children clattering in and out of the doors. Such were the thoughts that ran through his mind as he watched the baby settle into a deeper sleep. He gazed at its still face, entranced. So focused was he on tiny events – the flutter of the infant's eyelids and the rasp of its slow breathing – that at first he was not aware of the shadow looming beside him.

Hearing a chuckle, he looked up and gazed blankly at the face of Special Branch Detective Derek Irwin.

'What's up, Celcius? Interrogating your prime suspect? Or have you been keeping something secret from us?'

Daly felt as though he had been woken from a reverie. He bowed his head, and considered the baby lying defence-less in his arms, its mouth slightly agape.

'It's a professional matter,' he said gruffly. His voice sounded pompous and tense.

The Special Branch officer watched for several moments, marvelling at the sight of the solitary and childless detective holding a baby with such solicitude. Some colleagues swanned past. With a jerk of his head, Irwin drew their attention to Daly's arms, and they clocked the baby with bemused grins.

'How old is it?' asked Irwin.

Daly said nothing.

'No, seriously. I'm interested. How old?'

Irwin was grinning. It was clear to Daly that he was not serious at all.

'Come on, at least tell me its name. Is it a boy or a girl?'

Daly knew none of the answers. He grew tense staring at Irwin's mocking features.

'Strange to have known you all these years,' said Irwin, 'and not realized you were keeping such a cuddly version of yourself secret.'

'What is it that you want to talk about?'

Irwin stepped forward and adopted a more confiding tone. 'You're hiding here, aren't you?'

'Hiding?'

'Yes. That's why you're down here every day. Pulling stunts like this. For Chrissakes, you're a fucking detective, you should be solving cases and catching criminals.'

'What makes you think I'm hiding?'

'Don't pretend you're not.' Irwin was enjoying his discomfort, his grin widening.

Daly could not deny the truth in what the younger detective was saying. The courthouse had become a refuge, while police headquarters felt more like a front line, a place where colleagues and enemies, the past and the present converged dangerously. Neither of the two men spoke. The only sound was the rasping of the baby's breathing.

Still Irwin lingered. Whatever the reason, he was not staying to be companionable.

'You can't hide here for ever,' he warned, staring intently at Daly. This time the words felt more like a threat than a jest.

Daly stared back with a steely gaze. He has come with his sardonic grin to test me, he thought. He's here to gauge my innermost thoughts and feelings. He must think that because I look ridiculous with this baby, I have become vulnerable. And now he is threatening me; he wants to see me flustered and uneasy so that he can exert professional pressure and gain an advantage over me.

Irwin leaned closer. 'Here's a word to the wise, Daly. We're following up every lead on Hegarty. We're sniffing round everyone who had contact with him before he disappeared. We're very efficient in that regard.'

'Does that include his former handlers in British Intelligence? I could help you out with some names.'

'No need for that. There's been enough scandal dredged up by that old bastard already. Look at the mess he entangled you in.'

Finally, Irwin's words snagged and caught something in Daly. His irritation rose to the surface. 'Are we talking about policing or are we talking about politics? Call me hopelessly idealistic but I thought our job was to protect the public, rather than the reputations of former commanders and security chiefs.'

'You're not idealistic, Daly. Far from it. Just dangerously stupid. Regardless of the meddling of traitors like Hegarty, this country is going to have to find some accommodation with its past. It's the only way to avoid a return to violence.'

'Wrong. All you want is what's best for the top floor in the security services.'

However, Irwin was already backing away. The fun had gone out of the exchange. 'Some day, Daly, you'll realize we're on the same side. We should be working for the future of that baby in your arms rather than creeping about in the shadows of the past.'

Daly watched Irwin disappear into the foyer, feeling something very dangerous surge from deep within his chest. Irwin had given his loneliness a terrible new edge. Suddenly he did not want to be in the courthouse holding this stranger's baby. He shut his eyes, craving darkness or some sort of refuge, a secret hiding place in his father's fields. The baby started crying again, and he stared at it with unblinking eyes. He wanted to be kind and patient to it, but his kindness and patience were nothing but a veneer hiding his raging frustration. The baby cried louder, its face burning with anger. The vulnerable lightness of its body set against the heaviness of Daly's chest made him feel dizzy. He shut his eyes again, his mind full of darkly swaying blackthorn hedges. This is insufferable, he thought, I can't do this. I can't handle this baby's anger and mine combined. We are heading towards disaster.

A woman appeared and gently prised the baby from Daly's arms. He looked up, breathing hard. It was the mother returned from court. She gazed at Daly with grateful eyes, while the solicitor surveyed the handover with a victorious smile. Judging from their happy demeanour the case had gone in the shoplifter's favour. Daly nodded curtly at them, unwilling to share in their relief. He resisted the attempt to make an admonishing remark to the young woman and did not look again at the baby. He walked away and felt a surge of release tinged with melancholy.

He slipped back into the courtroom, grateful to return to its long silences and his scripted role in the witness stand. Later, he realized that it was no accident that the solicitor had sought him out with her imploring eyes that morning. Not that it was fate or destiny either. It was something darker and more profound, a rite of initiation for the disturbing drama that was about to unfold between them.

The next morning the winter darkness lifted along the shore of Lough Neagh. Daly's nearest neighbour, Nora Cassidy, woke to the sight of the hedges filled with shining white blossoms. The first tentative signs of spring had arrived and the hard-cornered fields seemed to swell and shimmer into softer, more mystical dimensions. She walked around the cottage enjoying the changed patterns of light, the new rhythms of life. Still curious about her lonely neighbour, she stepped out and walked up the lane to Daly's cottage.

It had been a long, dark winter, with barely a glimmer of the sun, and the arrival of the blossom in such profusion felt like a miraculous intervention. A white wave of flowers surged along the lane, rising as though to drown the thorn thickets, leaving the detective's cottage stranded like an island surrounded by a sea of blossoms. She saw his figure standing at one of his usual spots, dressed in his black coat, half-camouflaged by the drifts of light and darkness. She drew level with him and saw that he was staring at the horizon, his eyes full of glittering light. However, on this occasion, he was smiling. There was no urgency or restlessness about him this morning. He looked refreshed, without a worry, as though the arrival of the blossoms had insulated him from all harm and death. Perhaps there was no need for him to find a girlfriend or a wife, after all, she thought. During a lough-shore spring, men like Celcius Daly could live as though they were just floating, so weightless that not even the terrible crimes of the past could hold them down.

CHAPTER SIX

After his visit from the journalist, Reid had tried to put the folder of photographs and news clippings out of his mind. He had hidden them in a bottom drawer in the kitchen, but they were like a stash of whiskey to an alcoholic, impossible to leave alone. In an attempt to gain some form of mental equilibrium, he had returned to the drawer in the early hours of that morning.

He lifted out the photographs and news clippings, and arranged them on the table, as if he could organize his fears and put them in their correct place. For a while, he switched the documents around, teasing apart the connections between the news clippings and his memories, rearranging the sequence of events, trying to work out the facts that had been hidden from him for decades, before returning them to their original order. His thoughts were so muddled he could no longer summon the energy to think logically.

He stared at the picture of Mary O'Sullivan and her baby

with a sense of dread. What did it change? Everything. No one had told him about the infant, or what had happened to it after the traveller girl had disappeared. He had been infatuated with Mary, the obsession of a shy young man that had come to nothing. Or so he had believed. She had been a capable and resourceful worker on the family farm, but his parents immediately sacked her on the day they discovered she was pregnant. Fearing a scandal involving one or other of his sons, his father had given her cash to travel to England and procure an abortion. She had left with a large sum of money in her pocket. It was months before he saw her again, turning up at the farmhouse door, asking for her old job back. When his parents refused, she took to hanging around the periphery of their lives, bothering the other workers on the farm, until his brother and his friends in the regiment had taken her away one night for questioning, claiming she was an informer for local paramilitaries.

His memory of what had happened to her and the evidence of the photographs and the clippings contradicted each other. They were like two halves of a magnet, refusing to join, no matter how much he fumbled with the details in his mind. He was prey to all sorts of suspicions. His brother had told him O'Sullivan had eloped with a traveller cousin, and that not even her parents knew exactly where she had gone. Somewhere in the south, he had heard. O'Sullivan belonged to a world he knew very little about, and it had been easy to convince himself that she had disappeared in the back of a caravan into no man's land, that web of secret roads zigzagging the border. It was a completely different explanation for her disappearance than that suggested by the news clippings detailing the travellers' campaign to have her body found. Why the divergence? And why the secrecy around the baby when there should be no reason for secrecy?

In the midst of his suspicion, the sounds of winter drew very close. They were unlike the noises of other months, edgier and more hollow: branches groaning in the wind, the fidgeting of hungry birds on the roof, the weather vane rattling in the wind, doors creaking in the draughts, and the clang of church bells carried over a mile of frozen bog and gorse. He had little sleep that night.

When he struck off across the fields the next morning he was almost delirious with tiredness. The whole world felt lighter, the trees seeming to lift towards him, his fields uneven in the low sun, tilting beneath his feet, as though they might upend and sweep him away into the darkness of the valley and the gypsy camp. He hunkered low over the humps of weeds and made his way to the edge of his farm. There he stood still for a long time, staring through the thorns.

A small bunch of gypsy children lined the far side of the hedge. Their pale unreadable faces seemed to float amid the black twigs. Strictly speaking, they were doing nothing wrong, but their presence bothered him. They stood there, staring back at him through the holes in the hedge, without making any sound. He rubbed his watery eyes. He thought he spied another face amongst theirs, the face of the missing girl, rising up like doomed ballast from the depths of the past.

Farther along the hedge, he spied a couple of older boys removing a sheet of corrugated tin that he had used to fill a large gap. He roared like a bull and chased them, but they were quick, darting creatures, and wriggled beyond his grasp.

He shouted at the remaining children and waved his arms in the air. They remained where they stood, their stubborn gazes haunting him like the eyes of the missing woman in the picture. He did not want to think of the past. The thought that it had returned and might be as close as the other side of the hedge terrified him. As long as the secret of Mary O'Sullivan's disappearance was kept hidden, it endangered no one, he reassured himself. Panting hard, he strode back to his outhouses and equipped himself with a hook and pitchfork.

For the rest of the morning, he set to work on his hedges, hacking with his hook and ramming with the pitchfork. He filled in all the horrible holes with cuttings of branches, driving them in tight, blocking out the sight of the children. In his toil, he slashed his hands but he barely noticed the pain. Step by step, the hedge grew into a swaying fortification of thorns, the boughs creaking with the burden of dead branches. He stood back and stared at the impassable barrier with a grimace of satisfaction. Then he moved on to the next field and worked on the gaps there.

If only he had confided his concerns about the woman to someone else, he grumbled, then it would no longer have been his secret to carry. He had told no one and concealed the truth because that had been the easier course to take. His conscience had been yielding and passive, giving in to the demands of his brother. As the months and years went by, his silence and passivity had shaped the secret, adding gravity to it. He had allowed it to sink to the back of his mind, almost forgetting it, unaware of the grave danger it would one day bring him.

No matter how busy he kept himself on the farm during the rest of the day, tending to his pigs, repairing the outhouses, digging and cleaning the vegetable patch, he was unable to alleviate the sense of looming disaster. He felt sick with dread at the disarray the gypsies seemed to threaten, the nonchalant way they wandered the fields around his farm, the insolence of their stares as he strode by them. That evening he could barely settle inside the house. The transformation in his behaviour and mood was so complete it fascinated him. It was as though a stranger had supplanted him. Since the travellers had arrived he had become someone else. He tried to remember the sense of peace and contentment that had dominated his life before, but all that he could recall was a sense of aimless anticipation, an aura of mystery hanging over his hilltop farm, which had never dissipated, a set of questions he had never dared to ask.

The next morning Reid awoke with a start from a whiskey-induced sleep to the sound of whooping and cantering hooves in his yard. He pulled on his boots, feeling braver, ready to tackle what the day might throw at him.

Outside, a group of teenage travellers were riding their ponies around his outhouses. They circled him, showing off their horsemanship, marshalling their beasts with reins made from rope and straw. There was a sneaking admiration in his gaze at first, but as they raced by him, they began pulling faces and shouting obscene threats. He ran into the middle of them and spat out a stream of equally coarse insults to which they responded with delight.

The travellers rode into the nearby field and returned to the yard with sticks and branches, whirling them close by Reid's cowering frame. The mood changed, became more threatening. He backed into a pig shed, his legs shaking. He steadied himself. Surely, they meant only to intimidate and not harm him. All he had to do was endure their little game and wait for the ponies to tire. To calm himself, he gave his full attention to his pigs. Disturbed by the commotion and squealing noisily, they shoved against his legs, treading on his boots with their hooves. He grasped their snouts and squeezed them back against the railings. For what seemed like an age, he was trapped with his livestock, listening to the gypsies circling the sheds in waves of shrieking and laughter, their ponies whinnying and snorting for breath.

The smell of smoke wafting through the air signalled a dark turn to the game. Through the slats of the shed, he saw the boys riding with balls of orange and red held aloft, circling the outhouses in silent glee. He caught another whiff, the sweet smell of an accelerant, most likely petrol. They were wielding burning sticks, he realized. It was no longer a joke, or a nasty exercise in intimidation. They were intent on harming him.

He hunkered in alarm as one of the sticks soared through the air in a low arc, marking its target in a pile of bales at the back of the shed. More of the flaming missiles landed in, whizzing past Reid. Some burning embers touched his hair and he crawled about on all fours, shaking his head vigorously. Smoke filled the shed as the flames took hold, leaping from bale to bale.

Reid released the gate of the pig enclosure with his

fumbling hands, and urged the frightened animals to stream past, but in their panic, they butted his body to the ground. When he staggered to his feet, the fire had already advanced up the stack of hay and was licking the timbers of the roof. Burning bales fell apart, unfolding into eruptions of yellow flames that climbed into thick columns of overpowering smoke. The loose hay around him ignited, worms of flame taking hold and eating their way along the floor. He felt as though a dirty rag had been stuffed into his mouth, the acrid smoke coiling its way into his lungs.

Gasping for air, he lay down on the barn floor. There were flames everywhere, immense flames catching hold of every-thing his eyes fixed upon, arching overhead with the sound of a ferocious wind, shaking the air with igniting sparks.

He was about to give up and close his eyes for good, when he noticed a tall figure quivering beyond the curtain of fire. With all his strength, Reid concentrated his gaze on the figure, watching it draw closer and wrinkle in the heat. He shouted hoarsely for help and through the blaze, a voice answered back. Miraculously, the figure loomed above him and, lifting him to his feet, dragged him out of the inferno.

'They're trying to kill me,' croaked Reid, clutching at his rescuer.

'Relax,' said the figure.

Reid's smarting eyes cleared, and he saw the face of the English journalist.

'I was driving by and saw the smoke,' he explained.

'Where are the gypsies?' Reid's throat hurt with every word.

'Don't worry, I've chased them off.'

Reid smelled petrol on the reporter's clothes. He stared wildly at the Englishman's face, his emotionless eyes glazed by the flames of the fire, and the gloves on his hands.

'What sort of game are you playing at?' He choked out the words. 'You rescued me too easily.' He struggled to his feet as the reporter kept his silence. 'It was you who gave the gypsies their starting orders and then called them off.' He backed away. 'Get out of my yard.'

'I want to keep you alive.' The reporter sounded exasperated, following him. 'What's so bad about that?'

'Why do you care whether I live or die?'

'Because no one has spoken the truth about what happened to Mary O'Sullivan.'

Reid tried to count the pigs in the yard to make sure they were safe. They were zigzagging across the cobbles, out of control. He turned back to the reporter, whose blank face was like raw fuel for his anger. 'I told you to leave.'

'I am your friend, old man. It's time you started listening to me.'

'You're my interrogator, not my friend.'

'You're not fit to protect yourself, and I won't be able to keep rescuing you from harm. You need to start talking to me, or leave this place for good. More travellers are arriving this weekend. They're coming from a wedding up the country. Soon they'll have you completely surrounded.'

Reid considered the possibility that the arson was just the beginning, a preliminary tactic, before the travellers got down to the serious business of interrogation and torture. The reporter's eyes glinted, seeing that Reid had understood the message.

'I'll pay for the damage to the barn,' he offered. The sun peeked out through the dark smoke, lighting up flecks of soot as they fell on his curly hair. 'I can tell you want to find out the truth about her as well.'

Reid felt a vague sense of trouble welling from inside his chest. It was a religious unease, his conscience yearning to reveal everything that he knew. Deep down, he still hoped for some form of redemption, to be rescued from the cursed island of his farm.

'Where did you get the photographs of the girl and her baby?' he asked. 'I've been thinking about that. Who gave them to you?'

'This has no bearing on what happened to Mary O'Sullivan.'

'But before I talk you have to tell me what happened to her baby,' said Reid.

'I've been waiting for you to ask me that question.'

'The baby survived, didn't it? It was raised by its grand-parents.'

The reporter shook his head.

Reid was troubled. 'It must have gone somewhere?'

'The baby belonged to nowhere and to nobody.' The reporter shrugged. 'We've more important things to talk about first. It's time you told me what you know about its mother's abduction.'

Reid turned back to the blaze, closing his eyes to the all-consuming flames. 'There are secrets I must keep.' He seemed to be addressing the fire rather than the reporter. To his surprise, the flames answered back with the sound of wood splintering and timbers crashing to the floor.

Part of the roof collapsed, releasing the trapped roar of the fire. They crouched together as a heavy blanket of heat rolled over them.

'Were you one of the men who raped her?' asked the journalist.

'I never harmed her. I warned her to be careful and that the others were planning to get her. I heard them say terrible things about her.'

'Then now is the time to talk,' shouted the reporter. 'Who are you protecting with your silence?'

'There's no point twisting a story from me,' complained Reid, the heat hurling his voice to the back of his throat. 'I can't say for sure who took her away or how many men there were. Maybe half a dozen, maybe less. I only knew their nicknames, and they changed them all the time. They came to see my brother, not me.'

'Where did they come from?'

'They belonged to my brother's army regiment.' He was stupefied by the fire, worn down by the interrogating force of its flames. 'They moved from base to base along the border. They were dangerous men. Why should I risk my life by betraying them?' A sudden whiff of heat blasted over him. He felt his legs weaken under the force of the encroaching blaze.

'All I need are some lines of inquiry. Names and addresses. Did the police ever investigate this gang?'

'I don't think so.' Reid's voice was reduced to a bare croak. 'All I remember is the name. They called themselves the Strong Ulster Foundation.'

The reporter hauled him back to the shadow of the

farmhouse. He left and returned with a glass of water from the kitchen. He helped Reid sip it. There was a look of wolf-ish cunning in his eyes.

'This is good,' he said. 'We're making progress.'

'What is it you want? Justice or revenge?'

'I'm not the police. It's not my job to collar criminals and drag them before the courts. I have a private vendetta to settle.'

They watched as the flames died back, the shed reduced to a skeleton of blackened rafters.

'Give me a few days,' said Reid. 'I need to ask some ques-tions myself. I'll find out what I can and report back to you. And then you'll tell me what happened to the baby.'

'Don't worry about the baby. It belonged to the next generation. It did not have to suffer as much as its mother.'

It took a considerable effort for Samuel to pick up the phone that evening and ring his younger brother, Alistair. Over the years, his brother had become more and more unreachable to him. Alistair Reid had not hidden himself away on a lonely farm to escape the past. He did not need to. He operated in a completely different environment, the arena of politics, but one that was just as steeped in secrets and shadows. Alistair had climbed through the ranks of local government, and was now a successful minister in the Northern Ireland Assembly. Surrounded by his political colleagues, the apparatus of power, and a cadre of excellent lawyers and advisers, he was impervious to criticism about the past. No one dared dispute the persona he had created or the stories he told about the dark days of the Troubles. He was too big a fish and too accustomed to the highest levels of government power to be harassed by a bunch of itinerants and a reporter with a knack for barbed questions.

'I need to speak to you,' Samuel told him. 'It's urgent.'

Almost immediately, his brother's familiar voice irked him. 'Things are difficult for me right now, Sammy. What's it about?'

'The missing traveller girl. Mary O'Sullivan.'

His brother was silent for several long moments. He seemed to condense a lifetime of thinking in the pause, trying to straighten out the entanglements conjured up by that name.

'I'll tell you everything when we meet,' said Samuel.

'Where?'

'Home, tonight. But be careful, the place is being watched.'

His brother turned up that night with a driver in a black BMW. He slipped into the house quickly, barely giving Samuel a glance, and sat down by the fire without taking off his coat. He acted like a man connected to important facts, the running of a country, the solving of sectarian feuds, the balancing of difficult financial budgets, the sort of things that were far beyond his older brother's understanding. His shadow flickered in front of the fire, agile, sinister, as if getting ready to haunt Samuel in his sleep.

'Who have you been speaking to?' Alistair's voice was tired. His eyes swept the room but avoided looking at Samuel.

'There's a reporter on the prowl. Asking questions about O'Sullivan. You remember her, don't you?'

'What sort of question is that?' His brother sounded

injured. 'What are you trying to do to me?' He began rubbing the dog's head, firmly and rhythmically. For the first time their eyes met. 'What are you trying to do to me, Sammy, dragging me back here to talk about the dead?'

Samuel dropped the folder of photographs and newspaper clippings on the seat beside him. 'The reporter gave me these.'

The politician did not move. The dog put its head to one side and began rubbing the back of its head against his hand, cajoling him to keep petting.

'What paper did he say he worked for?'

'He didn't.'

'What leads does he have?'

'He knows about the Strong Ulster Foundation.'

His brother sighed heavily. He glanced at his brother up and down as though he were an object he was contemplating for the first time in years.

'Perhaps now is the time for you to come forward and tell the authorities what you know', said Samuel. 'You've friends in the right places; they'll look after you.'

'I can never do that.'

His brother leaned back in his chair and began to explain why his past had to remain a secret. To Samuel's ears, it sounded like a story rehearsed for the benefit of reporters. He already knew most of the facts, but Alistair recounted them anyway. The Strong Ulster Foundation had been a maverick unit of soldiers, operating without official sanction, who'd resolved to take on the IRA at their own game. Sometimes they strayed over the line in terms of their reaction to IRA atrocities. Alistair had only ever been a junior member of the gang, barely involved in their operations. He didn't want to describe their misdemeanours, or the laws they might have broken. His involvement ceased, when, during the early eighties, a local political party invited him to stand as an MP. After a successful election campaign, he retired from the army. The unit dissolved soon afterwards and its members swore to keep silent about their past. Ever since, he had been at pains to avoid bumping into them.

'Where are they now?'

'Some of the members were already alcoholics, a few found God and took up preaching on street corners. Most of them managed to keep their heads together and lead normal lives. They're married now with grown-up children. They do as their wives tell them. Their days of roaming the border with guns are over.' He looked closely at his brother. 'I thought those times were dead and buried. Long forgotten. What does this journalist want to know?'

'Everything that happened to Mary O'Sullivan.'

'Military Intelligence believed she was informing for the IRA. She worked on border farms and set up young men for their deaths. She had connections with the wrong sort of people. When she turned up at our house, I contacted my friends and they took her away for questioning, and that was the last I saw of her. Is that enough for you?'

'It is for me. But not for this reporter. Perhaps you should talk to him.'

'What you are suggesting is too dangerous. Someone must be in contact with the reporter, drip-feeding him information. Have you considered that he might want to blackmail me over these secrets or discredit me? If word gets out about my connection with the foundation my career will be ruined.'

In the sharp aftermath of silence that followed, Samuel imagined that his brother was making a series of haunted, moaning noises, but then he realized that it was the sound of the wind wailing down the chimney, and that his brother was mute.

'You should have told me what happened to O'Sullivan from the start. Perhaps I would have understood.'

'Promise me not to speak about her to anyone. Or mention my name in connection with the events of the past. None of us is at fault over what happened to her. The problems of that time are at fault. All this is buried in the past and we must learn to forget.'

'I've kept quiet all these years.'

'And because of that I am indebted to you.' Alistair spoke through a clenched jaw and mouth, his face taut and soldierly-looking, like a drill sergeant at dawn. 'Do I have your word?'

Samuel reached forward and crammed some turf into the fire. 'Yes. You have my word.'

'Then we will speak no more about it.' Alistair relaxed visibly. The two men said nothing for a while, witnesses to the deal that had been struck.

'What about the reporter?'

'Make it clear to him that you know nothing. Eventually, he'll stop annoying you.'

'You're wrong. His search for the truth has just begun. He and the travellers will be back. They won't stop tormenting me. They've already burnt down one of my sheds. The next time, it'll be me.'

'Are you afraid of them, Sammy?'

'The only one I fear is God.'

Alistair sighed. 'Give me the reporter's details and I'll make sure he won't bother you again.'

'What do you mean by that?'

Alistair started stroking the dog again, but he did not reply. Reid looked up at the mirror over the fireplace so he could get a clearer view of his brother. He saw that the politician was perfectly composed now, his face detached and serene in the flickering light of the fire. The dog shivered and snuggled closer to him. Reid knew that the other questions he was burning to ask would never be answered. In particular, the ones about the woman's baby. By contrast, when he looked at his own reflection, he saw a face full of darkness, the eyes obscured, as though someone had placed a blindfold over them.

Perhaps lies and deception are inevitable, he thought, part of living, and the past a terrain full of ambiguities and shadows. Only a child would expect always to hear the truth. How many evenings had they spent talking about other people, nephews, cousins, strangers, but never about themselves? And now when the evidence lay between them, he still could not find the conviction to ask the question: What dark deeds have you done, brother?

Alistair leaned back in his chair, and allowed his body to go slack, but his eyes were alert. The two of them stared at the fire, which flickered with reminiscences, none of them pleasant. Turf smoke hung in the air, carrying burnt hints of gruesome bogs and petrified oak. Samuel sat down in an armchair and drifted off to sleep. When he awoke, the embers had sunk to ashes, and his brother had gone.

Before going to bed, he went into his brother's old room

and lifted his soldier's uniform from the musty wardrobe. He stared at it for a long while. He imagined that the sins of the past might be as evident as the brass buttons on its collar. He touched the beret, the epaulettes, the loyal things that had once ruled his brother's life, searching for some form of reassurance transmittable through the cloth, a tactile escape from the guilty silence left in his brother's wake.

CHAPTER SEVEN

Shortly before the noon recess at Armagh courthouse, there came, into the stupefied hush of the waiting room, a noise that sounded like a woman wailing. Daly, who had been taking a break from the court proceedings, got up and stared over the railing into the lobby below. The cry of distress had not come from a defendant or a stricken relative, but from one of the smartly dressed female solicitors. A commotion grew as the woman, who seemed to be in a desperate hurry, pushed through the wall of defendants and their relatives. When Daly hurried down the stairs to investigate, he was surprised to see that the solicitor was Rebecca Hewson.

Somehow, she had lost her professional grip; her face and hair were in disarray, and one of her high heels had broken. She let out another wail that had an explosive effect on the crowd, making everyone turn and stare in her direction. Daly watched her anguished face as she steered through the bodies. She was breathing with difficulty, bumping into people, hobbling mechanically, her eyes scanning the faces she met. She drew close to Daly and when her eyes locked on to his, a look of relief passed across her features. She called out his name and swerved towards him. He stood still, trying not to flinch, a sharp and secret dread welling within him. The fact that she had singled him out from the crowd made him feel exposed and somehow implicated in her distress. Now that she was almost upon him, he could see that tears were bursting from her eyes, and her hair was soaking wet. He felt his temples throb. He had stored up a great lake of professional solitude, and now that reservoir was about to be broken. His deliverance was just beginning.

'What's wrong?' he asked her.

'My son is missing.'

He glanced at the court security staff, the uniformed officers in the building and thought: *Why me, again?* Was he the only one capable of helping a mother in distress?

'Please, you have to do something.'

'When did you last see him?'

She moved closer to him. The habits of silence and loneliness he had acquired since his divorce made the proximity of her stricken face and the intensity of her eyes overwhelming. He was struck by the look of terror that dwelt there. Compared to the shoplifting mother from the day before hers was a wretched and primitive display of vulnerability.

'About an hour ago,' she said. Her voice snagged and then started again. 'I left him in the car.' She pointed at the glare of light from the lobby. 'I just popped in to give a file to a colleague and for a quick chat. When I went back to the car park he was gone.'

In spite of her agitation, she had the confidence to keep staring at him, demanding a promise that he might not be able to keep.

'Please, you must find him. He's ten years old.'

He began asking questions. He brought his entire attention to her answers. It was the first time in weeks he had listened so carefully to another person. Behind the half-choked words, he detected a sinewy note of control in her voice. It was clear that her usual self-command had been overwhelmed by a rising tide of panic. He groped for some words of reassurance, but was unable to think of anything that might resolve her anxiety.

It was time for action, he decided. He arranged for announcements to be made in all the courtrooms. He organized the security staff to search the building from top to bottom. All the toilets were checked and the public galleries, too. Then the court proceedings were halted. However, no one had seen a ten-year-old boy matching Rebecca's description.

As he led her out to the car park, he marshalled the police officers in the lobby of the court. 'Check for eyewitnesses in the court grounds and nearby houses. Someone must have seen the boy.'

So distracted was the solicitor that it took her a while to locate her vehicle, and when she found it, she could not move. She stood with the key in her hand, flicking the door locks on and off, a lost look in her eyes. She seemed unable to accept that the empty car was hers. The car's sidelights flashed. She looked at the car and then at the key in her hand. There was a mental gap she could not overcome, a rift in her field of vision. She pointed the key at the car and walked around it, as though it were someone else's vehicle, someone else's fate to have a child disappear in broad daylight.

'Where was he sitting?' asked Daly sharply.

'In the back.'

Daly moved her aside, noticing that there were no signs of forced entry to the vehicle. He opened all the doors and then the boot. He shut the doors and circled the car, once, twice, and then again. There was no trace of the child or evidence that he had been abducted. However, he still did not have sufficient grounds for launching a full-scale police search for the boy. The greatest likelihood was that he would soon turn up, safe and well. Nevertheless, he stepped back, thinking of the possible evidence he might have contaminated. He tried to determine a space around the car that he might use without destroying more clues.

'He must have followed you into court. How long were you gone?'

'Barely five minutes,' she replied, but Daly suspected it might have been considerably longer. 'The security staff at the door said they haven't seen him. I've already run up and down the road. I thought he might have got bored waiting for me, and wandered off.'

'Has he ever taken off without telling you before?'

'No. Something has definitely happened to him.' She stared into Daly's eyes. She was finding it difficult now to maintain the intensity of her gaze. 'I want you to call in help. Block off all the roads. Just do something.'

Daly nodded. 'But first there are things we must try here.' He asked her if anything had been taken from her car. When she checked and said no, he got her to go through the sequence of events in case he had missed something. 'Was there any sign of anything out of the ordinary in the car park?'

'Not really.'

The only things he had to work on were the boy's absence and his mother's fear. But didn't mothers fear for their children most of the time?

Catching the questioning expression in his eyes, she said she knew how it looked. She had been negligent leaving her son alone in the car, but she had only slipped away for a few minutes. She had been sure he would be safe and that nothing bad would happen to him in broad daylight. Daly reassured her that the boy had simply wandered off. He began planning a course of action based on this assumption.

'Where would he most likely go, into the court grounds or along the road to the shops?'

Without hesitation, she pointed to a thick laurel hedge and shuddered. 'He's always playing in the trees.'

Leaves gently stirred in the wind, revealing a deeper darkness within. Daly organized the search party so that no one would overlap, and took the lead himself, exploring the margins of the court grounds. Soon he was trampling through the hedge, following the sound of rustling leaves. Within a few minutes, he could hear a child shouting and the sound of brisk footsteps.

Through a sudden hole in the leaves, he saw flickering movement, the sight of what looked to be a child's legs running for dear life. He raised an arm to fend off the bushes and pushed on, twigs and branches snapping and buckling under the force of his intrusion, but the shapes remained indistinct, dissolving into the green gloom of the hedge. A heavy branch pinned him back, and he had to squeeze beneath it. More sounds trickled through the air, a child shouting and crying. Was the boy trapped somewhere? he wondered. He listened carefully, but the cries grew garbled and faint, broken up by the wind and the groaning branches. He plunged deeper into the cover. For a while, all he could hear was the sound of his shoes squelching in the mud, and then the wind gusted and a noise rose into the air that sounded oddly like laughter. He heard other children's voices, much closer now. In spite of the dense undergrowth, he pushed and charged in a straight line towards the source of the sounds. The voices came again, this time farther to his left. The wind picked up, the shifting branches moaning together, and the voices were blown back. He crawled through a tunnel of trembling leaves, and eventually broke free, blinking into a cold draught of sunlight.

The light sharpened around the outlines of a young woman and a dark-skinned boy. Their eyes opened wide as Daly dragged himself completely free of the hedge. He froze, breathing hard. He saw the flash of more colours, like bunting in the wind, a carefree crowd of children rushing with curiosity to see what the commotion was about. The clawing branches had released him, breathless and sweating, into a school playground. The children circled him, laughing and screaming, making him the centre of their game. Then a bell sounded, summoning the children back to their classes, leaving behind several worried-looking adults. Daly remembered that a primary school lay next to the courthouse, and began to feel he had made a mistake. He introduced himself to the adults.

'Have you seen a missing boy?' he asked. 'His name is Jack Hewson.' He gave a description but no one had seen the child. He *had* made a mistake, he realized. He stood there like a dejected dog, and then he vanished back into the hedge without a further word.

By the time he returned to the car park, the place had begun to resemble the scene of an abduction. A van had pulled up and police officers were clambering out with search dogs. Daly heard their cries of encouragement as they guided their dogs to Hewson's car and directed them to sniff the seat in the back. The handlers shouted more encouragement and the dogs began to whine around a nearby empty parking bay that bore an oil stain from the vehicle that had been sitting there. They refused to budge despite the efforts of their handlers. The trail had ended, it seemed.

The police and security staff ceased their searching in the court grounds. They approached Hewson, and then at a certain point halted. They waited and glanced at her with an impending sense of doom, while she stood, watching the whining dogs, rooted to the spot beside her car. Even her colleagues had stopped trying to reassure her. She had given up retracing her steps and ransacking her mind for the last memory of her son. She no longer had the heart for any form of conversation. Her face was immobile with fear, as if she was falling into a hollow car park that grew emptier and quieter by the minute.

Daly needed to see the car park exactly as it was the moment she had left the boy in the car, what vehicles were parked in the location that had attracted the sniffer dogs, and who was coming and going at the time. He checked with the security staff but, unfortunately, the court's CCTV cameras had been trained on the building itself and the entrance doors, and they had seen nothing suspicious throughout the morning.

In the car park, Rebecca's husband had appeared. He embraced her, almost in an aggressive manner, as if testing her to refuse his gesture. She submitted to his attention and they spoke together quietly. Then he broke away and began to pace restlessly about the place, not speaking to anyone. He was more composed than his wife, seemingly deep in thought. Daly watched him with interest. His dark hair was bushy, thrust upward, and his pale, freckled skin gave him a very Irish look, but he spoke with a pronounced southern English accent. Daly walked over and introduced himself. There was something tough and optimistic about the way Hewson shook Daly's hand and began firing questions at him, which contrasted sharply with his wife's frightened vulnerability. He told Daly that his name was Harry, and that he was a journalist. He knew that suspected child abductions usually turned out to have simple and innocent explanations. Nevertheless, he wanted Daly to employ the full resources at his disposal to find their son as quickly as possible.

Then Hewson turned his attention back to his wife. Daly listened to their conversation. Some old annoyance seemed to have resurfaced between them. Rebecca's pretty mouth was fixed in a frown, her eyes enlarged with something other than fear.

'I wanted to leave him with you,' she said. 'But you didn't answer your phone. You were meant to be working from home today, but I couldn't find you anywhere. No one in your office has seen you for weeks.'

He mumbled something in reply.

'I don't know where you've been for the last fortnight.' There was exasperation, even anger in her expression. 'What are you not telling me, Harry?'

'It's not important right now. Let's talk about it later.' He glanced at Daly with a look that said they were working something out between them.

Accustomed to seeing the effects of stress on the parents of missing children, Daly moved away. He spoke to Commander Sinclair, on the phone, apprising him of the situation.

'OK, Daly, set up the search party as you see fit,' said Sinclair. 'Tell me what help you need and I'll see you get it.'

'What about the Internal Affairs investigation?'

'I'll have to check with them, but in the meantime you're the lead detective on the search.'

Daly slipped the phone away and glanced over at the couple. A coldness had come over Rebecca, the coldness of loss. He looked at her husband. He had walked away, and was holding his phone to the side of his face, not speaking but smoking. Daly got the impression that he was using the phone as a mask. He began to feel genuinely uneasy. This was how family tragedies began, with strangeness and moments of standstill, parents waiting for the carefully maintained balance of their lives to tip into chaos.

It began to rain. Figures bustled along the fringes of the court grounds, searching for cover. Only the mother and father kept their ground, standing to attention, their coats flattened against their bodies by the wind and the rain.

Harry kept glancing around him, a reflex gesture. Was it to keep looking for the boy or to check who was watching them?

For a moment, Daly felt swamped by concern for Rebecca, thinking of her anxiety and how in her stricken state she had called upon him to play a part in this unfolding drama. He was no longer a stand-in or a spectator. He was the lead detective. He felt hot with a sudden rush of emotion. What's got into me? he thought. He wasn't the leading man in the tragedy, that role belonged to Harry Hewson, but part of him wanted Rebecca's eyes to seek him out again and hold his gaze, her trusting, desperate eyes.

He turned to walk away, but then Veronica O'Neill, one of the junior detectives at the court, rang through on his mobile phone. She had been going door to door along the road, interviewing householders, searching for possible eyewitnesses. Her voice spelled urgency. By a stroke of luck, she had got talking to some workmen who were doing a job at number 31. From the windows, they had a clear view of the car park.

'They were taking a tea break about an hour ago when they saw a group of young men escort a child into the back of a white Mercedes van,' she told Daly. 'The vehicle pulled on to the road so quickly it hit the pavement. Thankfully they thought it suspicious enough to take down the van's registration.'

Daly strode over to the Hewsons and kept talking. 'Did they give a description of the suspects?'

'Thin build. Medium height. Dark-haired. They're sure they were travellers.'

'Send out an alert and trace the owner's address.'

The couple were staring at the patch of empty tar where the dogs had been sniffing around, as if they still might find a trace of their child's presence there. Noticing Daly's confident walk, they looked at him with hope in their eyes.

'We now have a lead on the vehicle that took Jack,' Daly told them. 'There's a suspicion the occupants might have been travellers. Officers are checking for the owner's address. In the meantime it would be best for you to come down to the station where we can keep you informed of the search.'

He offered them a lift.

'It's OK, Inspector,' said Harry. 'I'll drive my wife there.'

'No. I want to take my own car.'

'Then I'll go with you.'

Again, Daly noticed the moments of blankness in the way they communicated with each other, anger flickering between them like a set of faulty light bulbs. The stress of their predicament or some deeper marital tension? he wondered.

'It's better that we drive separately,' she told him.

'Don't make me suffer any more, Rebecca.' His voice was resentful. He tried to get closer, took her hand.

However, she didn't reply. She brushed him off and pointed her keys at her vehicle and the lights flashed back. She planted her hands in her coat pockets and walked to her car. Daly saw Harry's face transform momentarily with a look that expressed inner torment or anger. He had lost his air of self-assurance. His frozen stance suggested defeat.

'We'd better go now, Mr Hewson,' said Daly. 'Time is of the essence.'

As Daly climbed into his car and placed a warning siren on its roof, he felt a sense of release. Was this what it felt like to be freed and rehabilitated, he wondered as he accelerated out of the courthouse car park, to be singled out by an intensely gazing woman for exoneration, to be relieved of an insufferable burden, to be given the chance to discharge the ills of his mind and the sins of the past?

CHAPTER EIGHT

Even though the traveller camp had been quiet throughout the night and his dog had not stirred once, Samuel Reid had felt compelled to rise several times and switch on the security lights, scanning the yard for intruders. He walked up and down the old plank landing, unable to sleep. He checked the locks on the front and back doors. He turned the kitchen light on and off and checked the yard again. He prowled from room to room, sniffing, on the alert for travellers. He switched on the radio, and slept for about an hour. His dreams were brief and sudden, bits of the past gusting up like scraps of paper, flashing their terrible messages at him, overwhelming him with their secrets. Afterwards, he lay on his narrow bed and waited, his eyes wide open.

He got up and switched off the radio. The dog was still fast asleep, a sign that all was well. He checked the doors and the view from the kitchen window. He now lived in a zone of heightened suspicion, one from which it was impossible to escape. He took out his brother's rifle and made sure it was in working order. His movements were his way of controlling his fears, giving him a sense of purpose and destiny. He placed the gun back in the cabinet and checked the view from the upstairs window.

In the fields beyond, the traveller camp lay in silence and complete darkness, with no sign of its swarming life. He sighed. Its nearness had placed an unbearable mental strain upon him. In his imagination, it represented all the nagging squalor and entanglement of the past. Yet, staring out at the shrouded encampment, he felt as though the gypsies had helped him understand something important about the past. Within that murk, a fabric of connections was beginning to emerge, a network of clues that led straight to his brother and the Strong Ulster Foundation.

As soon as it was light, he drove down to the site to see if he could locate the journalist. He was convinced that the only way to end his anxiety and the dragging nights was to tell Hewson everything he knew about Mary O'Sullivan. He stopped at the gates and shouted the journalist's name, but there was no sign of him, or any answer from the camp. The dishevelled caravans lay still and exposed in the morning air, their doors and windows wide open. It looked as though the place had been ransacked.

He got back in his car and headed home. Along the lane, he met a throng of traveller children with their dogs. As he drove past them, the front of his car connected with something and rose slightly into the air, the wheels bouncing as though he had hit a hidden pothole. He heard a cry of pain, half-human, half-animal, but drove on. What had he hit?

A dog or a young child? He dared not think that he might have harmed a human being. He glanced in the mirror and saw the children standing in the middle of the road, waving at him to stop. He felt the past eddying around him, and a sinking feeling inside. His mind went blank and he drove on, suppressing his memories. He no longer felt like hiding at his farmhouse. He drove in circles along the border roads, skulking between the high hedges, drawing close to his familiar fields and then speeding away. The roads were winding and dangerous but he no longer cared. He hit the accelerator pedal as though he had reached the end of his tether, swerving along introverted little lanes at the very edge of the country. His entire life, he'd been meandering along the border like this, he realized, with no proper goal or destination in sight, as though what he was looking for had always been moved somewhere else, the track leading up to his hill top farmhouse a dead end for his lost and restless spirit.

By the time he felt calm enough to return home, it was late afternoon. The fields lay empty and lined with shadows. In the distance, the sun rolled its bleak rim towards the horizon. He stood in the farmyard. A sound rose and fell with the wind, like the sound of an angry sea gathering in strength, darkening the air. It seemed to be coming from the traveller camp. He looked in its direction. Still absent were the smoke of the gypsies' fires and the sound of moving vehicles. He walked across the potato patch and listened. Loose noises drifted across the fields – the sound of someone singing or lamenting, but the wind kept pulling it apart. He clambered through the mud to the camp, and gradually the sound became unmistakable. It was the sound of someone wailing bitterly, a high-pitched keening sound that came and went in gusts of emotion.

Almost in a trance, he walked through the gates and past the empty caravans searching for the source of the moaning. He came across the figure of an old woman bent over a burnt-out fire, her creased face full of tears. She gave him a look that was inscrutable, neither friendly nor hostile.

'Why are you crying?' he asked.

From her voluminous skirts, she removed a photograph. It showed a young woman, her image already stamped indelibly in his memory. He felt relief that this was the source of her grief. Perhaps he had run over no one that morning. He could not resist taking a longer look at the picture: the corners of the girl's smiling lips; the darkness of her eyes. *Come closer*, her wronged ghost seemed to beckon him. *These photographs are the only evidence that I ever walked the earth, these and a handful of newspaper clippings.*

But what about your baby, he wanted to ask her ghost, was that not your continuance, your revenge? They never found your body but yet you live in the minds of those who have not forgotten, like this old woman, and in the fitful dreams of those who have tried to forget but failed. He turned to look at the old woman, noticing that her lips were blue and trembling.

'It's wet and cold. Shouldn't you go inside?'

'If it's wet and cold for me then it's worse for her. Think of her lying out there along the border with no one to comfort her.'

'Was she a relative?'

'She was my daughter.'

A cold chill ran up his spine.

'Why are you here?' she asked, scrutinizing him closely.

'I wanted to see the journalist. He believes I'm the only person left who can help solve the mystery of her disappearance.'

'You're the farmer Reid, aren't you?' she said, the look of recognition lighting up her dull eyes. She leaned forward and gripped him by the wrists as though she might fall to the ground. He recoiled slightly, afraid that her grief might travel like a current through her bony fingers. She looked to be barely breathing. Her eyes were shut and her mouth had folded in upon itself. She seemed about to collapse but, in reality, she was gathering strength for what was coming next. Taking a deep breath, she opened her mouth, revealing the black gutters of her toothless gums. A long undulating wail rose from the back of her throat. The intensity of her emotion shook Reid, and left him panting with anxiety. It was the most impressive display of sorrow he had ever witnessed. He grew afraid of her, and the vehemence of her grief, which veered between doleful and angry, tender and bitter, the tears streaming down her face, her cries rising into the air and echoing harshly against the dark hills. He wrenched himself free from her grip and ran homewards, feet splattering through the mud.

Along the lane, the shadows of trees swam all around him, leaving him dizzy and disorientated. He leaned over at the side and saw the girl's ghostly face pour itself along the watery bottom of the ditch. He looked again, but the ditch had thickened with darkness. By the time he got to the farmyard, he was shaking with exhaustion and fear.

He was in such a hurry to get indoors that he failed to

notice the signs that he had a visitor, the fresh tyre tracks in the mud and the marks of forced entry at the back door. Believing he was all alone, he sank beside the fire and began to cram turf into the grate. He lit the pile, and watched the flames take hold, warming his numb hands. He listened to the licking sounds of the fire and the wind shaking the loose doors of the outhouses.

He turned around suddenly and stared into the gloom, distracted by the sensation that someone was watching him. He did not trust the instinct at first, but eventually he could no longer ignore it. Making his way into the kitchen, he saw, at the periphery of his vision, a figure in a soldier's uniform in one of the barns outside. It was standing on top of a stack of hay bales, its head hidden from view. He could see that it was his brother's uniform that the figure had donned, the jacket hanging slightly askew, the buttons unfastened, and a pale hairless belly poking through. He thought some tramp must have crept into the house and stolen the uniform. He watched the figure for several long moments, as it remained motionless, hanging in the space above the hay bales.

His incredulity edged towards anger. How dare someone break into his house and steal his brother's precious uniform. He hurried upstairs and located his gun, and then he stepped outside and crossed the yard. The figure was hard to make out, unmoving and half-hidden under the rafters. There was something confrontational, almost mocking about its pose. He stood below and stared upwards. Was he seeing things? He strained to make out the face of the figure, but there was no face, at least not one that was recognizably human. Barbaric, he thought, the blood draining from his face.

He could now see that someone had dressed a dead pig in his brother's uniform and hoisted its carcass from the rafters. He pondered the dummy's design. Like a bizarre animal suicide. He could see the pig's face clearly now, the dirty snout and gaping mouth, the blood-black tongue, the flaps of cheek and neck slobbery and raw against the collar of the uniform. The feature that most fixated his attention, however, was the slitted eyes, through which something malevolent seemed to be peeking at him.

Whatever the motive for placing the pig there, it was the contempt that disturbed him the most, the disregard for the honour of the uniform. He felt aggrieved by the grotesque way in which it had been displayed for him. He wanted to demonstrate his defiance towards the hidden enemy that had desecrated the uniform of his brother's regiment and killed a dumb creature in the process. Leaving his gun behind, he clambered up the bales of hay and hauled himself level with the figure. He reached up to untie the ropes that were suspending the dead pig, but his movement caused the carcass to swing through the air and butt against him. He gritted his teeth and cursed, shooing it away with his arms as though it were a living thing with a mind of its own.

A sound like someone suppressing a snigger came from behind. The tower of bales swayed underfoot and Reid cursed, teetering for a second, and then regained his balance. The dead pig swung against him again, a block of lifeless flesh, its eyes rolling in its head. Reid turned and squinted at the darkness towards the back of the shed. He could make out the dim outline of the rafters, the straggles of old rope, the cobwebs and birds' nests, but something was different about the alignment of shadows. He peered closer, trying to make out the details in the gloom. The little piggy eyes loomed again, and the dead creature leaned against his shoulder. Reid bullied it away and craned his neck. There was another figure there, alive and watching him, but he could not make out who or what it was. He felt terror tug at his guts. What sort of trespasser lay there waiting for him, having lured him to this dangerous brink?

CHAPTER NINE

The lead on the van that had taken their son provided only a temporary suspension of the Hewsons' anxiety. Within minutes of arriving at the family suite in Dungannon police station, the tension had returned to breaking point. Daly watched them through a window in the door, sitting at a table as stiffly as a condemned couple. As a solicitor and journalist, they were used to taking notes when visiting local police stations. They had built their careers on what was transcribed in interview rooms like the one they found themselves in, but now, relieved of such duties, they clenched their hands tightly, wringing their fingers together, unsure of what to do with them.

Daly brought them in some tea and biscuits, and felt their fear and confusion fill the room like a heavy gas. Their eyes fastened greedily on to him. He groped for some fresh words of reassurance, but was unable to think of anything that might resolve their anxiety.

'I've two questions I need to ask you straight away,' he

told them. 'I want you to think carefully. Do you remember seeing a large white van in the car park?'

'Yes.'

'Was it there before you arrived?'

She paused. It was an effort to recall the world that existed before the boy's disappearance. 'I think so,' she said eventually.

'OK. How many people knew you were going to court this morning?'

'No one. Like I told you, I just popped into court to give a file to a colleague.'

'Now I want you to think back over these past few weeks. Has anyone visited your house and given Jack more attention than you felt they should have? Looked at him or talked to him in any way that made you feel uneasy or worried?'

She gave him a blank look.

'What about when you were at the local park or shopping centre. Did anyone approach him there?'

'Jack's a shy boy. He doesn't engage with anyone he doesn't know.'

'But think carefully. Did anyone look at him or seem interested in him that made you hesitate, even for a split second?'

Rebecca sat upright but said nothing. They were uncomfortable questions, asking a mother to rake over the happy hours of family life, searching for a sinister shadow in the background. He ran through in his head reasons – other than the one most feared – why the occupants of the van might have abducted the boy. The fact that the mother was a solicitor involved in criminal cases might be a motive. Perhaps she had made enemies among the travelling community.

'Have you had any trouble with travellers in the past?' asked Daly.

'What do you mean, Inspector?' said Harry.

'I mean have you been involved with them in any legal cases?'

'Who hasn't?' she replied with a helpless shrug.

'What about travellers behaving suspiciously around you or your home?'

She took a deep breath and glanced at her husband. The look of panic returned to her face.

'We and our neighbours have been having a little bit of bother recently,' intervened her husband. 'A small group of travellers camped illegally on land next to our housing estate.'

Something seemed to pinch Rebecca's throat as she struggled to say something.

'At the start no one was bothered by them,' continued Harry. 'But then they began gathering scrap and more caravans arrived. There were rumours they were involved in illegal activities, possibly cigarette smuggling. Eventually the police moved them on. Really, they didn't bother—'

This time it was Rebecca's turn to interrupt. 'I found them in my back garden one morning. They were talking to Jack.'

'Those were just children, Rebecca. They didn't mean any harm.'

'Can you describe them?' asked Daly.

'The oldest was about thirteen or so. He had a horrible look on his face. When I asked them to leave he shouted an obscenity.'

Harry shifted his chair slightly. 'Jack said they were just

looking for old bikes,' he told Daly. 'Look, Inspector, we're not sure they were from the camp. They might not even have been travellers.'

'But they knew my name. And they knew you were away,' said Rebecca, turning to her husband. 'They'd been watching our house. I was concerned they were going to come back and look for us.'

Her husband placed a steadying hand on her shoulder, but she shrugged it off.

'Tell me about the traveller camp,' said Daly. 'Which clan did they belong to? Do you know where they moved afterwards?'

'I think we need to stick to what's relevant, Inspector,' said Harry, a note of anger covering up his anxiety. 'My son is missing and my wife is clearly distraught. She's not capable of thinking straight at the moment.'

Something in his manner suggested to Daly that he'd had dealings with the police before, and not all of them had been amicable. He made a mental note to check the details of the traveller camp afterwards. The police and council agencies would have taken an interest in the movements of the clan. He hoped they would be able to give him something to work on.

'We're trying to work out what happened to your son, Mr Hewson,' said Daly. 'Unfortunately, we have no CCTV footage of the car park, which means I'm going to have to ask questions to find out what happened.'

At that point, Detective O'Neill popped her head round the door and beckoned him.

She spoke to Daly in the corridor outside. 'We've got the details of the van's owner, but I'll bet he's in hiding now.'

'What do you mean?'

She had conducted a computer check of the vehicle registration and traced it to a Thomas O'Sullivan, from 6 Dunmanagh Drive in Dungannon. Daly raised an eyebrow. The name and address were familiar to him. O'Sullivan was the head of a local traveller trading empire that imported cheap furniture from Eastern Europe. He had made his fortune during the Celtic Tiger years when the country was awash with cash, rich pickings for door-to-door sellers like O'Sullivan, whose astute investments in property had also helped fund the building of a lavish mansion in Dungannon and a brand-new fleet of Mercedes vans. However, like the majority of his clan, O'Sullivan was usually nowhere to be found. His Dunmanagh home might be his official address, but his true home was on the road. The mansion was merely a bolthole, a place to stay while he buried his dead, organized family reunions or celebrated Christmas and Easter.

'I've sent two patrol cars to check the address,' said O'Neill.

'Send out an alert to all mobile patrols and the ports and airports to be on the lookout for the van,' replied Daly. 'Let me tell the Hewsons what we're doing and then we'll pay a visit to O'Sullivan's house. Let's hope we find a trail there.'

CHAPTER TEN

The suspect's address took Daly and his colleagues to one of the strangest ghost estates he had ever seen, with its avenues of lavish-looking mansions in the sort of tree-lined setting dreamed up by a high-end architect yet not a single soul in sight. A granite plaque with silver lettering on a gatepost told Daly he had arrived at number 6. He pressed the buzzer next to the electric gates but nothing happened. He sounded the horn of his car as officers from the patrol cars lined the black railings. The place seemed unnaturally quiet, but unlike the many ghost estates dotting the countryside, this one had no for-sale signs or unfinished buildings. Daly stared at the three-storey mansion at the end of the drive. It was utterly still, deserted. In fact, the entire estate had the air of a place where all the inhabitants had fled some impending disaster.

For travellers there was death and then there was settling down, hence the gloomy, unused feel to the houses. O'Sullivan and his relatives had built these dwellings as temporary refuges in times of celebration or uncertainty, locking them down for the rest of the year while they took to the open road, travelling between Ireland and Britain, and into Europe, doing business, laying tarmacadam, ferrying cheap cigarettes, or selling furniture and electrical goods at knock-down prices. The extravagantly designed houses had statues on gate pillars, high-security fencing, stone cladding and garages with double electric doors, but they existed as grandiose fragments, without any connection to the town or ordinary settled life. They were trophy properties, as extravagant and empty as the monuments the travellers erected for their departed in graveyards.

Through the gates, Daly saw a manicured garden adorned with life-size marble statues of children playing, while next door's had a bronze boat with sailors holding up spyglasses. He felt as though he had been sidetracked, misdirected into a labyrinth of frozen figures and enchanted houses, while the real action was taking place elsewhere.

Impatient for some clue to O'Sullivan's whereabouts, he clambered on to the gates, wedging his shoe in a gap in the metal bars and pulling himself up to the spikes, which were more decorative than burglar-proof. He paused for breath and lowered himself to the other side, half expecting a dog to come barking at him, but the house and garden remained silent. The gate shook with the efforts of the other officers following his example.

A cold wind, a remnant of the winter just past, stirred the shrubbery in the garden. A flock of sparrows flitted over the high evergreen hedge, settled for a moment on the ghostly white garden statues and then scattered. Daly's feet crunched on the gravel as he approached the front door. He rang the bell and knocked on the door loudly, but there were no signs of life from the house. He stared through the large windows and rapped at the glass. Still no one appeared.

'O'Sullivan's hit the road. What does that say?' said O'Neill, joining him in the shadow of the house.

'Only the guilty run,' replied Daly. But then, travellers were always hitting the road. 'We'll have to get a warrant for his arrest and put a stop to him using his passport.'

They walked round to the back, O'Neill gesturing towards the garden statues, which, according to rumour, had been erected in honour of O'Sullivan's offspring. 'They say he has a few more rows hidden behind the rhododendrons for his illegitimate kids.'

On a whim, Daly tried the back door and was surprised to find it unlocked. He pushed it open and stepped inside.

'Wait. Don't we need a search warrant first?' said O'Neill.

Daly barely paused before answering. 'I heard someone shouting for help inside,' he lied.

She frowned, but followed him into the silence within. For half an hour, they searched for any signs of the boy or clues to his abduction. They found nothing at all. What they saw was a pristine interior far removed from the untidy jumble of the traditional traveller's caravan, but one that had been drained almost completely of any sign of habitation or personal touches. Daly made a mental inventory as he moved from room to room, the marble tiles reflecting the weak evening light, the solid oak doors closing soundlessly behind them, the kitchen looking as abstract as a laboratory with its smooth floor and empty worktops. A nauseating smell of bleach hung in the air. They walked into a number of sitting rooms that resembled large white cells, filled with spotless furniture and rugs. The most striking theme of the interior design was its blandness. Glittering ornaments and crystal decked the glass cabinets, but not the type Daly would ever wish to see on his own shelves. The walls of the rooms echoed as they searched for some sign of O'Sullivan or the boy's whereabouts. With every step he took, Daly felt the air grow colder and emptier. The sense of abandonment grew oppressive.

The only hints of a family life were the photographs in heavy silver frames, mostly of weddings and christenings, filled with pneumatic young women in puffed dresses and false tans. O'Neill pointed out O'Sullivan to Daly, a moustachioed figure in the centre of the photographs, usually in an open-necked white shirt, a big black-haired man, who looked as though he enjoyed eating and drinking as much as wheeling and dealing.

They went upstairs and checked the bedrooms, which again looked barely lived in.

'This place doesn't feel like a home,' said O'Neill. 'It's a show house. There's nothing secret here. Not even a locked door or safe.'

Daly nodded. 'The boy's not here. Perhaps he never was.'

They were about to leave when his phone buzzed into life. Daly listened as the voice of Commander Sinclair drifted in and out. The reception was weak and he had to walk to a corner of the kitchen to get a clear signal.

'I'm sorry, Daly,' Sinclair was saying. 'Turns out only the chair of the panel can authorize your return to normal duties.

If we're going to put you in charge of this case, we'll have to do this through the proper channels.'

Daly frowned at the phone. 'What are you saying?'

'I'm taking you off the search.'

He went quiet.

'It's not up to me. Internal Affairs have insisted only they can decide if you're fit to conduct this investigation.'

'But the inquiry has been dragging on for months.'

'They're close to making their decision.' Sinclair's voice seemed to be suppressing something. Daly wondered about the meetings that had taken place to discuss the future of his career. Meetings that Sinclair must have attended.

'Should I assume the worst?'

'Not necessarily.' There was a change in his tone. 'For one you have my support. Give me an hour or so to discuss this with the relevant people.' Daly heard paper rustling. Sinclair was searching through his notes.

'OK.'

'Don't do anything until I call you back. In the meantime it would be best to let O'Neill run things.'

Daly didn't reply. He felt the silence of the house tower behind him, room after room of mocking stillness.

'Anything you're not clear about?'

'No,' replied Daly. 'I'll await your call.'

O'Neill looked surprised when he told her she was in charge until further notice. The expression on his face must have betrayed his embarrassment and irritation.

'What should I do now?'

'Check all the usual traveller haunts. Someone must know where O'Sullivan has gone to ground.'

She promised to keep him informed and then she left. Daly stood in the house, watching the other officers follow O'Neill, unable to join them. He felt angry and restless, like a bear that had been dragged back to its cage. He prowled from room to room as though he might find some refuge in the stone-cold emptiness of the house from the indignity of deferring to a junior officer. He should really have returned to police headquarters and awaited Sinclair's response but he lingered in the mansion, feeling protected and isolated within its sterile silence. He wondered what it would be like to live in such a dwelling, a brand-new building with all the mod cons, spotlessly clean and bright, rather than his cramped dark little cottage, its geometry twisted out of shape by his family's tragedy, its windowsills mouldering in the damp lough-shore winds, and plaster crumbling in its walls.

He perused the rooms again, carefully opening and closing the doors. Was it his instinct as a detective that kept him there or something more flawed, a voyeuristic curiosity that he could not shake? It was an untouched house, in whose crypt-like rooms nothing changed, and through which visitors wandered like impostors or ghosts. He tried to understand O'Sullivan's relationship with the house. Had he abandoned it because inevitably every refuge begins to feel like a prison after a while?

The quality of light through the tall windows changed, grew heavy, soothing his mind. He stood in a kind of trance, suspended by the silence of the rooms. He still worried about the fate of Hewson's son, but it was mainly the behaviour of travellers like O'Sullivan that occupied his thoughts. Did they lead happier lives with the escape route of the open road always at hand? Without the grind of a fixed work routine, their world was bigger than his, more expanded in space and time, but did that make it more comprehensible or less? Daly knew so little about their lives. He remembered as a child his father referring to them as tinkers and lamenting their plight. They were a race left over from another time, uprooted during the years of the Great Famine and forever doomed to walk the roads, their status debased, their lives rendered mean and pointless by their lack of belonging and their broken attachment to the land. During the Troubles, both sides of the community had regarded them with deep suspicion so that they were often caught in the crossfire between warring factions. Daly had heard the reports of brutal attacks by the old police force, the B-Specials, as well as by paramilitaries and vigilante gangs, who were keen to expel travellers from their turf or exploit them for their own purposes. During the darkest days, Unionist politicians had openly called for them to be incinerated, while Republicans intimidated them into smuggling explosives and collecting intelligence information. Even after the ceasefire, traveller families were likely to be firebombed from their illegal campsites.

He kept searching the rooms for clues about the elusive O'Sullivan. Men like him were impossible to pin down, wandering the dangerous territory of exile and homelessness. They belonged nowhere. Was that why they were always viewed with such suspicion? Was that why they needed huge houses like these, places in which they might feel safe for a night or two, where they might take respite from the suspicions of society, the interrogating gaze of police officers, where they could prove they belonged to a place like everyone else, even though deep down they knew they would always be strangers?

What unsettled Daly was the realization that these were the same reasons he kept himself confined to his father's dishevelled cottage. His fear of uprootedness and not belonging; his inability to shake off the notion that deep down he was a stranger, too, in a society emerging from a long and bitter conflict into peace, and that he could never belong anywhere if he did not feel at home in his childhood berth. Such was his dread of displacement that he had not spent a single night away from the cottage in more than seven years. Other people changed homes, jobs, and loves with easy regularity, but he had tenaciously held on to the same four walls, the same piece of ground and dwindling set of opportunities, a prisoner who thought he had found refuge in the farm's bleak geography of thorn trees and hummocky fields, while a widening gulf slowly separated him from the rest of the world. Who would he become if he left the cottage and abandoned the farm? Would he be able to reinvent himself if he moved to the city? The questions tantalized him.

In a drawer in one of the bedrooms, he found a hardback history of the Irish travellers, consisting mostly of old photographs. Wrinkled men and women with suspicious frowns next to their high-wheeled caravans. And children. Many children. Grinning with their grown-up faces and heavy stares. He flicked through the images. Straggling families cast adrift on muddy lanes, camping at the edge of towns and villages. A lost tribe emerging from darkness, carrying and hauling their cumbersome burdens, moving slowly on an endless road to a destination they would never reach.

In one of the pictures, the hooves of the horses pulling the caravans were padded with straw and bound with strips of red flannel. Men with furtive faces posed alongside the animals, guiding the caravans along secret paths in forests. In the caption, Daly read of the long stealthy marches the travellers made across the border during times of heightened suspicion, when they had to muffle the sound of their horses' shoes to avoid the detection of the settled population. He wondered if that was what O'Sullivan would do now: creep away into the darkest reaches of the old border roads, making himself invisible between the jurisdictions of the two different police forces? Even if he had not abducted the boy, O'Sullivan would still run; it was the traveller instinct to avoid police attention at any cost.

But this was the past he was contemplating, not the modern-day world. Travellers were no longer invisible, transient visitors beyond the reach of the law. There were no secret roads left for fugitive souls in present-day Ireland. The law of both jurisdictions would not relax until they had found O'Sullivan and his van, pinned him down in whatever corner of the country he was hiding.

He put the book away and collected his thoughts. He was still angry but he felt resigned to whatever decision the inquiry panel made about his fitness to return to normal detective duties. Whatever the outcome, he shouldn't stay any longer in the house. There was nothing he could do here to advance the search for the missing boy. He was an intruder, acting without any official permission, pointlessly sniffing around the traces of a suspected child kidnapper, a flawed detective who had been content to continue with the sham of his career in Armagh courthouse, living off the scraps of his colleagues' work. He was in danger of no longer fitting in, of joining the ranks of people like O'Sullivan and his clan.

As this melancholy thought filled his mind, the sound of breaking glass made him start. He peeked outside in time to see three men climb through one of the ground-floor windows. He did not move, holding his breath and listening intently. He was reluctant to phone his police colleagues in case they asked awkward questions about why he was in the house in the first place.

'Spread out and do the ground floor first,' one of the men ordered. 'Then we'll do the bedrooms.' His voice wielded the dangerous authority of a criminal.

'What should we be looking for?' asked a younger voice.

'Any documents to do with Mary O'Sullivan. Letters, newspaper clippings, official documents.'

Daly heard the resounding thud of drawers hitting the floor.

'We're in a gypsy's house. They don't keep official documents. Most of them can't even read or write.'

'He's right. What if these documents don't exist?'

'Think about it,' said their apparent leader. 'If the documents didn't exist, why is my boss willing to pay so much money for them?'

They began ripping apart furniture downstairs. Daly could hear the shuffle and squeak of furniture being moved, the commotion shifting from room to room. The methodical sound of their destruction suggested they had done this before. He hung back in the bedroom, feeling cowardly about what might happen if he pushed the door open and confronted the men. He glanced through the crack in the door, and felt a chill travel down his spine – not fear, but a strange apprehension he could not precisely fathom, the sense that he was neither guest nor violent intruder in O'Sullivan's mansion. He was simply a mute presence, a ghost, trying to blend in with the shadows.

He tried to focus on the intruders' movements, their precise locations on the ground floor. He heard more snippets of conversation. He concentrated and tried to put them together and work out what exactly they were looking for.

'Who is this woman, anyway?' asked one of the younger voices.

'She disappeared a long time ago. If you want to know anything else I suggest you leave right now.'

'I take it her disappearance was no accident. Else your boss would be paying us to look for her body, rather than these documents.'

The youngest of the voices spoke again. 'Why should your boss give a shit about a dead gypsy?' He sounded genuinely puzzled.

'He cares enough to share his mountain of money with us. Trust me on this. Anything you've earned before is peanuts compared to what is on offer.' The older voice paused. 'Any more questions and I'll find someone else to help me. You can go back to your dirty little smuggling jobs and wonder what you missed.'

They were quiet for a while, taking things more slowly, moving carefully from room to room, standing silently for long periods. Daly was going to have to devote all his attention to not being discovered.

'The toilet downstairs isn't working.'

'Then check it out.'

'Already have. There's a tonne of cash in the drain.'

'Any documents to do with Mary O'Sullivan there?'

'No. Just money.'

'Then put it all back together again.'

The house became completely silent. Daly could hear only his breathing. He peeked out at the dark landing and the sweeping staircase with the elaborately carved roses on the banisters. It was hard to hold on to his sense of calm. A cold anticipation took over as he waited, hoping that the intruders had found what they were looking for and left.

Then a voice echoed up the stairs. 'The two of you start doing the bedrooms.'

Daly thumbed in O'Neill's number on his mobile, but it went straight to an answer message. He cursed under his breath. The men seemed to have heard something. They stopped speaking, and then a set of footsteps approached the bedroom door. Daly had a very bad feeling about how this was going to end.

A man wearing a balaclava and wielding a crowbar stepped into the room. He gave a start when he saw Daly standing by the bed. Restraining his first impulse, which was to run past him and out of the door, the detective returned his surprised gaze and nodded slowly, as though it was the most natural thing in the world for a burglary to be disturbed in this way. He also raised his empty hands slightly, just enough to let the intruder see he was unarmed.

'You're not O'Sullivan,' said the man, pointing his crowbar at Daly's face.

'Correct.'

'Then what the fuck are you doing hiding up here?'

Caught out again, thought Daly. The question reminded him of Irwin in the courthouse yesterday.

'I'm not hiding,' he said in a harmless tone.

'Get down on the ground.'

Daly stumbled back as the man swung the crowbar in the air, narrowly missing his face.

'Don't be stupid,' said Daly. The man's eyes and mouth were the only features visible through the mask. Strung-out-looking eyes with dilated pupils, and a sneering mouth with evidence of a youthful-looking moustache: the worst possible opponent for a defenceless police detective.

'Shut up,' said the intruder. He grabbed Daly and drove his head against the wall. The impact left the detective reeling, conscious only of the weight of the assailant's breath and its sharp reek, his physical nearness, and a hammering in his ears. He saw the flash of a knife's blade and felt it draw along his neck, cold and rough.

'There are police officers on their way,' Daly said. 'You won't get away with this.' He craned round to make eye contact. A pair of dark pupils locked on to his. His own pupils contracted in that pitiless gaze.

'You shouldn't be here. What the fuck are you doing here?'

Daly heard the uncertainty in the young man's voice. It was clear that he had given the assailant a nasty surprise, that being disturbed in the middle of a house raid was uncharted terrain for him, and he was now trying to work out what to do. Daly felt the knife climb higher against his windpipe. This was new ground for both of them. Meeting as strangers in this silent, desolate house, a knife-edge the primary focus of their interaction.

'What have you heard? Do you know our names?'

Daly shook his head and croaked a response.

'I don't believe you.'

Daly leaned back, trying to make some part of his body other than his neck take the strain of the intruder's uncertainty.

'You're fucking lying. You know too much.'

The intruder tightened his grip on the knife and his eyes opened deeper into a new darkness, full of youthful determination and contempt for life. Daly felt suspended from a dangerous height, about to be flung with a jerk of the intruder's wrist into a bottomless drop.

The sound of heavier footsteps in the room made them both turn round. The bigger man strolling into the room wore a balaclava also. He approached Daly's assailant and, without pause, took aim with his large boot and kicked him in the backside. There was something relaxed and deliberate in his manner as he took another aim at the assailant, low and hard, as though hammering a football into the back of a net. 'What the fuck are you doing? Get out and let me deal with this.'

Daly crouched on his hands and knees and clambered away.

The new arrival took the knife from the younger man and slipped it into his pocket, and then he slapped him with his open hand across the side of his head. 'I'm the one in charge here, not you. Go on, get out of here.'

He gave a brief, annoyed sigh and stared at Daly. He picked

the crowbar off the ground and poked the detective in the chest. 'Who the fuck are you? You're not an O'Sullivan. I can tell that right away.'

For the first time, Daly picked up a slight American accent in his voice.

'Why should it matter who I am?' Daly crawled to his feet and edged towards the other side of the bed. His sense of relief was short-lived.

'You're right. All that matters is that you're not a fucking O'Sullivan.' He followed Daly and nudged him again with the crowbar. 'What are you doing in his bedroom?'

'You don't need to know that,' said Daly quietly.

'Why not?' A look of contempt flashed in his bulging eyes.

'Because I said so.'

The masked man stared at Daly thoughtfully. He seemed to be weighing up his options. 'I don't know who you are or what you're doing here, but I can smell you. You're a fucking policeman.'

Daly decided to tell the truth. 'You're right. I'm a detective inspector.'

The intruder asked for Daly's ID and he handed it over.

'So it's you, Inspector Celcius Daly,' he said, as though they were old acquaintances.

'I'm here investigating the disappearance of a boy.'

'A boy?'

'He went missing earlier this afternoon.'

'And you think O'Sullivan's to blame?'

Daly nodded and the masked man's attitude changed. He grew interested.

'The sick old bastard,' he said.

The other two intruders stood watching them. Only their eyes seemed alive as they flicked back and forth between the two.

'Just so you know, this isn't a routine inquiry,' said Daly. 'Time is of the utmost importance. I assume you came here because you knew O'Sullivan was away. Right now, I need you to answer one important question.'

The masked man said nothing.

'Where is O'Sullivan?'

Daly also wanted to ask him about the documents he was searching for, but in the circumstances, he thought that might be pushing it. His adversary looked and sounded too smooth and hard to be a common burglar. He was collected enough to think calmly and wrest the utmost advantage from their encounter.

'If time is of the essence, Inspector, then it's bad luck you bumped into us.' Again, Daly heard the American twang in his voice.

'A child's life is at risk,' said Daly. 'Tell me what you know about O'Sullivan.'

The intruder frowned through his mask. He rested the crowbar's weight on Daly's shoulder. 'Patience, Celcius Daly. This is not the time to lose your temper.'

'You're going to have to put that down.'

'Like I said earlier, I'm the one in charge here.' He waved the crowbar in Daly's face. 'I should be the one giving the orders. Not you.' He circled Daly again. 'Agreed?'

Daly nodded. 'If that's what you want.'

The detective glanced at the other two intruders. It was demoralizing for members of a team to be standing idle and the slow escalation of tension made them agitated at their lack of involvement. Daly watched them move about in the corner of his vision. They made the room feel very crowded.

'O'Sullivan is a gypsy, and I don't like his clan,' said the leader, walking up and down in front of Daly. 'I don't like the way they look. I don't like the way they talk and I don't like the way they do business. In the old days, we would have burnt them out.'

He took a calm pride in his little speech, prancing before Daly as though he were on freer and firmer ground than anyone else in the room. It was never the nervous ones who wanted to pose and strut, thought Daly. The intruder craved to be the centre of attention and Daly tried to supply enough to keep him content.

Daly gave another slow nod. 'Where is O'Sullivan now?'

'Celebrating his daughter's wedding,' the masked man told Daly. 'The O'Sullivans are always marrying off their children – that is, when they're not murdering each other. You'll find him at Ryan's Corner, drunk and acting the big, caring, paranoid father of the bride, buying drinks for everyone and itching to shoot his new son-in-law.'

He walked over to the window and peered outside at the gates. 'We'll be going now, Inspector. If you're talking to O'Sullivan, watch the old bastard doesn't swindle you into buying a horse or a greyhound.' He circled Daly again and pointed the crowbar at his skull. 'I'm going to give you a warning before I go and a little tickle on the knee. Don't try to follow us.'

Without further ado, he swung the crowbar in the air and delivered a crushing blow to Daly's right knee that doubled him up in pain. Daly had forgotten to answer him with an unhurried nod. Perhaps he had underestimated the value of the correct body language.

'I'm a police detective,' he said through gritted teeth. 'And I'm charging you with burglary, criminal damage and assaulting a police officer.'

'Are you saying I'm under arrest?'

'That's correct.'

Another blow swung and struck him on the left knee. Daly was convinced now that the leader was a former paramilitary, one newly returned from a stint in the United States, lying low until the ceasefire took hold. It was the practised ease of his movements, his way of standing squarely, the confidence of his voice as he addressed Daly.

'I plead guilty on all counts, Inspector.'

By comparison, the other two intruders looked uncertain and nervous, barely men at all, and certainly not hardened criminals. Their white eyes followed the arc of the crowbar, miming its violence in their imaginations. The next blow left Daly almost fainting with the pain. Surely, there was a limit to the leader's violence. He would not seriously harm him, a senior detective, trying to find a missing child, but Daly was dealing with an ex-paramilitary, not an ordinary criminal, one obviously practised in the art of torture and intimidation. A ruthless man without any limits whatsoever. The detective's presence in the bedroom was a conundrum he did not have time to unravel. The search for the boy meant nothing to him.

Crouching now on the ground, the masked man began to kick Daly. There was no point shouting for help. How could anyone hear him in that desolate housing estate? He kept his mind focused on protecting his vital organs, curling his body against the man's boot, unsure if the creaking noise he heard was the floorboards shifting under the dancing weight of the intruder or the bones of his ribcage jumping from the torment. The masked intruder loomed over Daly's sprawling body, taking breath before kicking him again, this time right in the face. At once, Daly's nose bled and pinpoints of light flared in his vision. He rolled over and gagged, a drumming roar filling his ears, the blood welling in his mouth and throat. He gasped and choked for breath. He looked up at the glare of light, and saw the intruder's fiendish body writhing, swinging his boot again. He closed his eyes, the tears welling up. They were not tears of pain or even sorrow. They were tears of relief. I am gone, he said to himself. Finally gone. His mind shone with that happy thought and soared, making a mockery of his body's pummelling ordeal.

CHAPTER ELEVEN

Samuel Reid hunkered on top of the bales, cramped and unsteady, the ripe sweet smell of the hay mingling in his nostrils with the stench of the dead pig, which dangled before him, its paunchy belly poking through the badly fitting uniform.

Desperately, he tried to distinguish the figure in the darkness. He moved a couple of paces to the left and then to the right, attempting to see behind the carcass.

'Who's there?' he shouted.

He found it impossible to ignore the pig's lifeless eyes, its swinging body, its trotters tiptoeing in the empty air.

The figure of a man loomed towards Reid, the bales shifting as they took his weight.

'It's you,' said Reid, recognizing his visitor at once.

'It's been a long time, Sammy, hasn't it?'

'What are you doing here?'

The figure stared at him with hard unblinking eyes.

'Why are you watching me?' asked Reid, sounding almost embarrassed by the silent menace that filled the air, as though it somehow indicated a failure of his hospitality.

'I haven't come to watch you.'

'Then why are you here?' Reid was puzzled, annoyed even. The proximity of the gypsy camp had made him familiar with late-night intruders. He had lost his fear of human shadows in the darkness.

'I've a message from your old friends in the Strong Ulster Foundation.'

'What do they want?'

'You've upset them. They don't like this idea of you raking over the past.'

'What was I meant to do? The gypsies have been harassing me, asking difficult questions.'

The carcass swung back and forth, its little piggy eyes peeking at both of them.

'You could have chased them away with your gun at any time,' said the visitor with scorn. 'Something else has troubled you. Something else is keeping you awake at night and haunting you during the day.'

'What else would trouble me?'

'A memory. A secret from the past. You saw us take away Mary O'Sullivan, didn't you?'

This time Reid kept his silence.

'Were you afraid at the time?'

'Yes.'

'Because she had done harm to many people and was in grave danger?'

'I suspected she was an informer.'

'But that didn't stop you running after her like a lovesick puppy. You told her about our movements along the border, the times of our patrols, our weak points. And now you feel guilty because your indiscretions led to her death.'

'Yes, damn you, the guilt is always there.' Reid spoke thickly, releasing compressed breath.

'You should know that we didn't intend to kill her. Her death was an unfortunate accident. The night we took her away for questioning, we only intended to scare her off, but when we stopped the car to let her use the toilet, she ran away with the hood still over her head. She made off in the direction of an old quarry. We tried to stop her, but she slipped over the edge. We spent hours crawling around that godforsaken rat-hole, lighting our way with boxes of matches, staring into pools of deep water that had collected at the bottom, but we never found her body.'

'She had a family. If it was an accident, they deserved to hear the truth. At least her clan would have got her body back. Now they've hunted me down, demanding answers. They won't stop until they find out the truth. That's why I had to ring Alistair and ask for his help.'

'You should have been brave and ignored the gypsies. They wouldn't have dared harm you. Look at you now, a farm of land to yourself, no money worries, a healthy herd of pigs, enough distractions to happily occupy you in your old age, but that wasn't enough for you.' The voice turned ugly. 'You had to delve into the past and sort out your guilty conscience. Now you're going to choke on it.'

'That's enough of your threats,' growled Reid. 'Go back to wherever you came from, and do your threatening there.'

'Your conscience is a disaster, Reid,' the visitor hissed back. 'A disaster that will destroy us all. There is no point talking to you any more. Persuasion is useless, utterly useless, like asking a brick wall to come to its senses. You're just a thick-headed farmer, who doesn't realize his life is in great danger.'

Reid stared at the visitor's empty hands. 'What do you mean in great danger?'

The pig hung between them, its slitted eyes rolling back, its mouth gaping.

'Trust me; the foundation has spent all day plotting ways of getting rid of you.' A long-simmering hatred welled in the visitor's voice. 'We thought of stabbing you, strangling you, poisoning you in your bed, even chopping you into pieces and feeding you to your pigs. But we decided all these measures were flawed.'

Reid's expression did not falter; rather it hardened, his brows furrowing.

'The foundation has decided there should be no violence for the sake of violence. There's been enough killing in this bloody country.'

A look of relief passed across the old man's features. He waited for more words of reassurance from the visitor.

'Is there anything else you want to ask me, Sammy, before I go?' asked the figure.

The gentle sound of the pig swaying from the rope was the only noise as the two men stared at each other. Reid looked troubled, glancing at the carcass as though it might do something terrible at any moment, something that might sweep away his fragile confidence. 'Why dishonour my brother's uniform?' he asked. 'Why kill a harmless pig and lure me up here?'

The visitor advanced towards Reid, and the bales shifted, wobbling slightly, an unsteady raft in a sea of darkness. Reid stepped to one side, and immediately the bales underfoot sagged and gave way. He sank to his knees, a look of surprise etched on his face. Arms groping, he tried to stride towards safety, only to wade deeper into collapsing hay. Too late, he realized that the visitor had cut the binder twine holding the hay in place. He leaped clumsily towards the visitor, but more bales crumpled beneath him, falling to the concrete floor below.

Reid swung his arms, and grabbed on to the pig's lifeless body, pulling it with him as he slipped further. For a teetering moment, the beast seemed to lead the old man in a macabre dance, its dainty trotters guiding his shuffling feet through thin air. Reid sank deeper and the dance turned into a wrestle, the uniform slipping further from the pig, exposing more of its hairless belly and its rows of tiny teats. Reid clung on, but the dead animal seemed to lose interest in the old man, the ropes tightening and swinging it back up to the rafters. Reid gave a final agonized shout of 'murderer', his empty arms flailing in the air, before disappearing in a cascade of hay.

The visitor leaned forward in time to see Reid's hunched backward flight; his face crushed-looking even before his body slammed on to the floor. Afterwards, he clambered down and knelt by the old man's body. Wisps of hay fell all around them, grass seed and dried flower heads shaken out in their masses, lit up by the security lights in the yard, filling the air in a golden, spinning cloud. However, they were too late to cushion Reid's fall. Blood was crawling from the old man's skull in the shape of a rat's thickly coiling tail.

He checked Reid for signs of life and was relieved to find that he was dead. Relieved not for his sake but for Reid's. He did not like dealing with a botched murder, his victim writhing and begging for release. He preferred his prey to either die or escape cleanly. That way no effort was wasted on his or his victim's part. He peered down at Reid's hooded eyes. A dead farmer on his dying farm, blinded and choked by his conscience, his body sprawled upon the hay he had diligently baled last summer. The past and its guilty secrets were disappearing a piece at a time.

CHAPTER TWELVE

Daly opened his throbbing eyes to the sound of his mobile phone. He was not sure how long it had been ringing or how much time had passed since he lost consciousness. The intruders were still standing over him, but their mood had changed. They were peering down at him with gazes of cold indifference.

'Better answer that, Celcius,' said the leader with a dry chuckle. 'You're a busy man today and we don't want to detain you any further.'

Daly crawled to his feet, wincing with the pain in his ribs and face. He fumbled for the phone as the intruders backed away. It was Commander Sinclair, his voice radiating confidence and firmness of purpose.

'I've good news for you, Daly.'

'Yes?' Daly spoke thickly, his mouth hurting. He kept it short; afraid he would gag on the blood trickling down his throat. Whorls of pain tightened every muscle in his chest and made his breathing difficult. He glanced up and saw the intruders slip down the stairs and leave the house.

'I don't like leaving my detectives at the mercy of Internal Affairs,' explained Sinclair. 'The longer this inquiry lingers the greater the shadow of suspicion on you. I've told the panel I want you to lead this investigation and they've agreed. On one condition. You attend a psychologist every week.'

'Of course.' Daly's brow perspired with the effort of speaking. His cheek filled with clotted blood. He turned it over in his mouth, as though it were a fine wine, wondering which blow had inflicted the damage.

'You don't sound overly enthused.'

'Believe me, I am. I'm invigorated to have your confidence.' Daly leaned back against the wall. He stared into the emptiness of O'Sullivan's house, reluctant to move. 'What about their report? When will I see it?'

'First it has to go to the relevant authorities.'

Daly wanted to ask who they were but a stab of pain in his side silenced him.

'Listen, Daly, you don't have to prove your innocence to me, just that you can still do your bloody job. Forget that this inquiry ever happened in the first place or that a report has been written about you. Put it down to bitter experience, or whatever.'

It sounded to Daly that the panel had decided he was harmless rather than entirely innocent. He took some painful steps into the landing. 'Can we talk about this later?'

To Sinclair's ears, the constriction in Daly's throat must have sounded like suppressed emotion. 'Of course, Daly.'

He eased himself down the stairs, grimacing all the way.

His body felt like a private cargo of pain he had to nudge gingerly from step to step. He was hopeful of making it back to his car without passing out.

Before finishing the call, Sinclair gave him a final warning. 'No nasty surprises this time, Daly. I don't want you getting entangled in the private lives of your prime suspects. For my sake, if not yours.'

Too late for that, thought Daly, surveying the trashed rooms of O'Sullivan's house. He tried O'Neill's phone again. He got through this time and told her to meet him with some support officers at Ryan's Corner.

'Could you ID O'Sullivan if he's there?' asked Daly.

'Yes, of course. Has Sinclair put you back in charge?'

'He's just given me an ultimatum.'

'Which is what?'

'See a psychologist and get back to handling cases or else languish on court duty for ever. There wasn't room for negotiation.'

'There seldom is where the internal inquiry panel's concerned.'

'Anything to report about the search?'

'Not yet.'

'Fine,' he grunted. 'We'll meet at Ryan's. Bring some support.'

Seated in his car, he glanced in the overhead mirror and suffered the dreadful surprise people experience when they barely recognize themselves after an accident. His eyes, nose and mouth certainly felt swollen and tender, and his fingers had probed the sore points, but none of that prepared him for the bruised and puffy visage staring back at him with the lop-sided grimace of a bare-knuckle fighter. He tidied his hair, and wiped away some of the blood from his nose and mouth. He tried to crack a smile from his grimace, but his swollen lips hurt too much. His veneer had gone, the thin surface layer hiding the battered, ugly interior, the troubled man beneath. Tasting something hot and liquid in his mouth, he opened the door and began spitting and retching. He vomited up at least a cupful of blood. The effort left him feeling feeble but renewed. He wiped his mouth again and started the engine. He drove slowly, waves of pain rolling in quick succession through his bruised body. He changed gears awkwardly, wincing as the car bounced over speed ramps.

In spite of his injuries, he was able to drive straight to the bar. His body felt crushed but his will was not. If anything, he had grown more intense, graver, as if he had glimpsed the darkness of the boy's predicament in the empty rooms of O'Sullivan's mansion.

'What the hell happened to you?' said O'Neill, looking at him with alarm.

'We're not the only people on O'Sullivan's trail,' he told her. 'I'll explain later.'

'Hold on, you should get yourself checked over.'

'I'm fine,' he said, keen to press on.

However, she dashed back to her car and returned with some painkillers, which she made him swallow. He grimaced at the effort.

Bouncers were carrying a young man through the doors as they hurried up to Ryan's Corner, a run-down-looking hotel next to a waste site, one of the few establishments in the county that still catered for traveller functions. Worse for wear, the youth hung face down in their grip, his arms and legs dangling as though he were paddling in shallow water. Daly saw that his knuckles were bruised and bleeding.

After dealing with the drunk, the bouncers turned to Daly with a contemptuous look of familiarity.

'Been celebrating already?' one of them asked, blocking his way.

Daly had to show them his ID before they believed he was a police officer. He no longer looked like a detective, he realized: his face was a passport to a different world entirely, the dangerous world of travellers and drunken fist fights.

Rather than risk inflaming the crowd, Daly stationed a cordon of officers at the doors while he and O'Neill stepped inside. The air had force, warm and spiky, vibrating with the over-amped sound of the wedding band. O'Neill followed Daly's slightly hunched figure as he struggled to walk normally with his injuries. The crowd was not so much drunk as in the lull between successive states of intoxication. What Daly and his colleague saw differed little from a typical Irish wedding, the united families using alcohol as a form of validation, each round of drinks a rosy endorsement of the newly married couple's compatibility. The younger members of the bridal party were moving erratically on the dance floor, out of tune with the music, but full of belief for the lyrics, which were almost indecipherable above the band's deafening instruments.

Daly and O'Neill moved more deeply through the crowd, feeling a hostile mood take hold before them, the frozen stares and whispered asides from the tipsy guests, red-faced children turned away by their parents, the bubbling voices slowly quietening. They walked back towards the fringes, to accommodate the crowd's wariness. Daly's bruised face and shambling figure stamped him as a man not to be crossed, the sort of face that the guests were all too familiar with at the end of the night, drunk and vicious, beyond all reasoning. The band stopped playing and the only sound from the guests was the mutter of suspicious voices and isolated bursts of laughter.

They found O'Sullivan resting his weight against the bar, overweight, dark-haired and jovial, his tie loosened and his gold cufflinks shining amid the rows of empty drinks. In his slightly dishevelled way, he was Daly's picture of what a gypsy patriarch should look like – a father celebrating his daughter's wedding – rather than the mastermind of a daylight abduction. He gave Daly a strange dazed grin when the detective introduced himself and O'Neill, and then his face darkened when they told him the reason for the visit.

O'Sullivan looked genuinely disturbed at the accusation that he had kidnapped a child. He picked up his pint, as if to take a drink, but then returned it to the beer-stained bar. His thick fingers gripped it so tightly Daly thought the glass would break. O'Sullivan had been a bare-knuckle fighter in his youth, and legend had it he could punch the bark off trees with his unprotected fists. However, he did nothing but simply stare at O'Neill as she explained the charges.

'Let me get this straight. You're accusing me of stealing a child?'

'Yes.'

'Why would I be doing that?' The weathered bronze of his face looked rubbery with alcohol, but his voice was clear and not slurred. He waved extravagantly at the packed crowd. 'Don't you think I've enough bloody kids? Christ almighty, we're up to our elbows in them.'

Someone laughed obscenely. A young man got to his feet, seemingly to remonstrate with Daly, but swayed and fell back to his seat.

'A ten-year-old boy is missing,' said Daly. 'Eyewitnesses say he was put in the back of your van.'

'How the fuck do you know it was my van?'

'Your registration number was noted.'

'I've been in the bar all afternoon. Everyone here can vouch for me.'

'What about the van? Where has it been all afternoon?'

'I took it,' said the young man who had earlier struggled to his feet. 'I drove it to collect the McGinns from court.'

Daly showed him a photograph of Jack Hewson. 'This is the child who went missing. Recognize him?'

He looked stunned. 'I didn't kidnap anybody.'

'But was he in the van?'

'I'm saying I didn't touch him.'

'Yet you saw him in the van?'

'Yes. But no one forced him to come along.'

'Where is he now?'

He looked nervously at Daly, trying to think of an answer; it was fear the detective saw in his eyes rather than guilt.

'If he wasn't forced into the back of the van and you didn't touch him, how did he get there in the first place?'

The young man thought for a while and then shook his head. 'No idea.' His dark eyes were drenched in defiance, and something more vulnerable, too, a tiny chink of alarm, which Daly's questions had managed to place there. Daly wanted to widen the chink a fraction more, but he needed time, and that was something he did not have in abundance.

'You're suggesting he ran away by jumping into the back of your van,' said Daly.

He nodded.

'Where's the van now?'

He threw Daly the keys. 'It's parked round the back. You can check it out for yourself.'

Daly called in a dog team and more officers, but held back on arresting either O'Sullivan or his son for the time being.

'Before we check the van, we need to ask you some important questions,' said Daly. 'The boy came here in the van with you, and then what happened?'

The young man shrugged. One of the male officers lunged forward to handcuff him, but Daly grabbed the officer by the shoulder and handed him the van keys. 'Go back outside and tell the other officers everything is under control,' he said. 'Then get a team to search the van and the grounds.'

He sent O'Neill, who was also itching to arrest the son, to check the hotel's CCTV footage for any sign of the boy. Daly also felt strongly the urge to swoop in and arrest the suspects, but it was a sign of inexperience in a detective, and ran the danger of postponing a possible breakthrough. There were important questions Daly had to ask first. It was imperative that he focus the minds of O'Sullivan and his son, as they wavered between confusion and anxiety, helping them steady their nerves and recover their lucidity in spite of their intoxication. It was a game of patience and restraint, in which everything could be lost or won.

O'Sullivan turned to his son with an angry look. 'Why didn't you tell me this boy sneaked into the back of the van?'

'I thought he was a nephew or cousin of the McGinns. I didn't know the wee fucker was running away.' A viciousness twisted his thin lips. 'All day I've been tripping over nephews and nieces I never knew existed. How was I to know who the hell he was?'

A desperate look was etched on O'Sullivan's face. 'Look, Inspector. My son's been that busy bussing people back and forth that his brain is mush. He had no idea the child wasn't one of ours.'

'OK, but right now, I need to know where he is.'

A tense silence fell upon the travellers. They glanced at each other, searching for hints as to what to do next.

'What are you going to do if we can't tell you?'

'I just need to find the boy and return him to his parents, safe and sound.' Daly stared meaningfully at them. 'Right now, you're the only people who can help me do that.'

O'Sullivan took out a hanky and wiped his forehead, which was sweating profusely. 'You'd better follow me, then,' he said.

He led Daly through a side door and down a long corridor with the deliberate gait of a drunken man pretending to be sober. Walking reminded Daly of his injuries. The painkillers had failed to dampen the ache in his ribs and face. His lips felt raw, throbbing constantly. He followed O'Sullivan with his head down, clumsy as a bullock led by a nose ring. All that kept him going now was his determination to prove that he was a competent detective capable of rescuing a missing child.

125

A curious crowd followed them from the hotel, slouching men and anxious-looking women, drunk-eyed but wary, whispering among themselves, as though they might belong to a deeper part of the mystery surrounding the boy's disappearance.

'Who are the McGinns?' Daly asked.

O'Sullivan glanced back at him and pulled a face. 'They're second cousins on my father's side.'

'So they're your guests at the wedding?'

'Not at all. They're with the groom's family. They're also second cousins.'

'Is everyone here related to you?'

'Not everyone. The bar staff are from the town.'

'What ages are the McGinns?'

'You're asking the wrong man, Inspector,' said O'Sullivan, pushing open a fire door.

A group of boys smoking blocked their way. They wore the familiar stares of teenagers avoiding grown-up supervision, mute and slightly hungry-looking, dazed by whatever alcohol or drugs they had been consuming. O'Sullivan waved his hands at them with a dismissive gesture, his gold cufflinks sparkling in the evening light, but they refused to move.

'Where are the McGinns?' O'Sullivan shouted.

One of them began quietly singing a pop song and the others laughed, as though his tune hinted at an obscene joke. Their gaze rested on Daly and his bruised face. He lifted up his chin, trying desperately to maintain his dignity and authority, while feeling that somehow he had come down in the world. He had never been the focus of such insolent attention.

'I'm looking for this boy,' said Daly, showing them a picture of Jack. 'He's ten years old. He was wearing a hooded top and white trainers when he was last seen.'

'Are you a social worker?' They began bombarding him with questions.

'No, I'm a police officer.'

'Is he in trouble?'

'No.'

'Where are you going to look for him?'

'You tell me.'

'It was nothing to do with us, mister.' The other boys laughed, but the looks on their faces were entirely serious. The tension in their eyes was unconnected to joy or sadness.

'Any smokes, mister?'

They seemed more interested in needling him than helping, glancing at O'Sullivan with complicit grins. However, O'Sullivan lunged towards them, rage and confusion burning in his cheeks, veins throbbing in his forehead, his fists clenched. He grabbed two of the boys by their collars and lifted them into the air. 'Show him where the wee fucker went!' he shouted.

'He's not with us, mister. The McGinns had him.'

'What did they do with him?'

'They took him in their van. They left about an hour ago.'

Noise and movement began to follow them from the bar, bodies crowding through the fire-exit doors, stirred by the dramatic news of child abduction, alcohol fuelling the hysteria. Gypsy weddings usually imploded in a catastrophe or a brutal row, and Daly could see why: an emotional public ceremony compressed into a hotel room full of drunken people.

Keep your patience, stay calm, were the phrases he kept repeating to himself, and he hoped but seriously doubted that the wedding party was thinking the same.

'I saw him crying,' said one of the boys.

It had nagged Daly that up until now no one had reported the boy showing any signs of distress.

'Where did you see him?' asked Daly.

'We'll take you there now.'

They half led, half pushed Daly across the waste ground, as though he were a prize animal they had captured. O'Sullivan trailed behind the search party in the company of two police officers, wiping his sweating face with a hanky.

'Watch them like a hawk, Inspector,' he shouted. 'Or they'll empty your pockets.'

The boys took every opportunity to jostle against Daly as he tried to navigate the uneven terrain. A teenager manically driving a quad bike wheeled around them. Daly scanned the waste ground. In the distance, half-hidden by piles of rubble and broken tar, he spied what appeared to be an abandoned white van. The light was fading fast and the ground underfoot turned to mud glittering with broken glass and splinters of metal.

'How long ago did you say you last saw him?' shouted Daly over the din. They were far from the hotel now, on no man's land. A fire burned amid heaps of rubbish nearby. He could hear the crackle of wood and plastic igniting.

'Nearly there, mister.'

'Are you going to arrest all of us?'

'Who beat you up? Your wife or your girlfriend?'

Daly searched their expressions for signs of mockery.

What did the multitude of their eager faces conceal? They crowded him aggressively, firing more questions, tugging at his coat, disorientating him, while the adults circled in the background, watching his search slowly unravel. Question after question came at him as the rest of the wedding party hung back with knowing looks on their faces, questions that began to sting.

'What age are you?'

'Are you married?'

'How many children do you have?'

Even when he answered truthfully, they kept repeating the same question, unnerving him, picking at the crucial knot of his loneliness, the inner anxieties that had haunted him since his divorce. Part of him wanted to bellow like a bull and scatter them, but they held the key to Jack's whereabouts, if only he could persuade them to deliver it. However, their faces were unreadable, pinched with the cold and whatever intoxicants they had consumed. He spotted some of the older boys at the margins of the group picking up pieces of wood and stones. He glanced back at the faces pressing around him, trying to connect with one of the boys, but all he saw was the same insolence, the same blank looks, the same eerily empty eyes.

The questions became unanswerable and rude. Daly was less a human being and more a ball shoved into the air during a rugby scrum, an object of sport to be dragged into the mud as they pitched and swayed around him. He gritted his teeth and cursed. Perhaps taking him out here was a form of misdirection, a chance for O'Sullivan to make his exit and escape. He craned his neck, squinting anxiously for the traveller, and was relieved to see that he was still lumbering after them, several paces behind, with a look of fury and betrayal etched on his reddened face.

Afterwards, it was hard to pinpoint the exact moment Daly and his colleagues lost control of the situation. He thought he glimpsed the face of Jack Hewson breasting the flow of surging, agitated faces, his arms flailing for help. Was it really the boy or his despairing idea of what he was searching for projected spookily upon the sea of anonymous faces? Jack's features loomed before him again, and this time he reached out and grabbed him, but instantly the boy struggled to get away. He felt the panic in the child's breathing, his heart pounding in his narrow chest.

'What do you want, mister?' the boy shouted at Daly, flashing him a look of hate. The detective held on, feeling his confidence ebb; the boy's wild eyes shone with scorn. It wasn't Jack at all. The other children noticed Daly's confusion and took a cruel delight in it.

'He's too young for you, mister,' they chanted. 'He's too young for you.'

They surged around him, carrying him farther along the uneven waste ground with a momentum that made it difficult for him to stay on his feet. Ahead, the door of the white van swung and banged as the crowd enveloped it. When he was almost upon it, the door flapped open and Daly glimpsed the empty space through which Jack Hewson had vanished. A jolt threw him to the ground but he managed to scramble to his feet. He turned. O'Sullivan and O'Neill were just a few feet away, her hair disarrayed, her blouse and jacket tugged out of place. She moved her lips. She might have been shouting but her voice was lost amid the heavy breathing and cursing. O'Sullivan heaved into view, pop-eyed with anger, his arms swinging uselessly in the air, his gold cufflinks still glittering in the middle of the dark turmoil. Daly felt fists, nails and feet as his body slammed against the van. It creaked upon its axles as though it might overturn at any moment.

A male officer waded to the detective's assistance and pinned a boy against the van in an attempt to handcuff him, but another one jumped on to the policeman's back and knocked off his cap. The officer's face grew red as he clung on to his quarry, wheeling in circles in an effort to shake off his tormentor, while the crowd of youths swarmed around them, the waste ground filling with drunken delirium. More teenagers appeared, fortified by the strength of their numbers. Daly felt a sense of wider social struggle, a doomed tribe of young people targeting him and the other officers with their restlessness. Where were their parents, the adults who might call them to order? Daly saw O'Sullivan's angry face up close, hair wet with sweat, roaring for calm, before he was pushed to the ground.

Holding out her pepper spray, Detective O'Neill advanced towards the mob, but a child pushed through the crowd and grabbed the spray from her. The officer trying to arrest the youth fell to the ground and the boy wriggled free, dangling the handcuffs triumphantly from his hands. The crowd cheered him on, and Daly caught the sight of a red splash against pale skin. Someone was bleeding. The crowd lunged back towards Daly, squeezing him against the van again, their gloating faces shutting him in. He had no idea what they were shouting at him. His mind felt dull and brutish, unable to understand fully the curses and insults hurled at him, the emptiness of the teenagers' facial expressions, and the black nothings of their eyes. Perhaps it was a mark of how removed he was from their community that he did not know their terms of abuse, their words for sex acts and other bodily functions.

He reached for his phone but, in the mêlée, it had slipped from his pocket. He felt the throbbing pain of every bruise on his body. He pushed against the throng, sweat soaking his forehead. He felt an urge to vomit but held on. Hands gripped his coat, pulling him down, while more hands grabbed his collar, jerking him deeper into the crowd, twisting him round and round, like a drunk, through a trajectory of grinning faces, the vertigo adding to his nausea. He was free-floating now, as far from normal society as he could be. Sirens sounded in the distance and, in a detached way, he wondered would they arrive in time before he was seriously injured. He tried to wipe away the spit and blood from his face, but a blinding sheet of pain filled his eyes. He no longer heard the mob's taunts and shouts.

Nor did he hear the arrival of his rescuers. Half crouching on the ground, he became aware of the crowd slackening and their blows diminishing. He looked up and saw a traveller woman moving through the throng, strong and purposeful, pushing the teenagers to one side, grunting and roaring at them as though she had known them since they were babies, rows of gold bracelets jangling like armour on her plump arms. Another woman followed her with the same heavy maternal presence, grabbing one of the ringleaders by the scruff of his neck and shoving her ample bosom into his face.

The mob shifted its energy, lost its momentum, and the pair of marauding women became the point of interest.

The women redirected their efforts towards Daly, cutting a swathe through the crowd, intent on flushing out his tormentors. They slapped the bigger youths about their heads, while the younger boys danced and cheered around them, delighted to see the older members of their gang punished in such an humiliating fashion. In a moment, Daly understood the greater influence of the chastising mothers: in spite of O'Sullivan's gold cufflinks and swagger, this was a severely matriarchal society. The women made it look so simple that his jaw hung open, the urgent action of their arms, the fury of their scolding words, and the absolute authority in their eyes.

'Lucky!' the women shouted at Daly. 'Lucky they haven't torn you apart. Go now, while you have the chance.'

Daly tried to speak to their competence and authority. 'I'm searching for a missing boy.'

They threw their arms up at him. 'Well get on with it!'

CHAPTER THIRTEEN

The family suite at police headquarters was one of the lone-
liest places imaginable at this time of the night. Daly grabbed
three coffees and for a second paused at the door, surveying
the bleak room within, its blank walls and fluorescent lighting, and the huddled figures of Rebecca and Harry Hewson
sitting at a little table, looking unbearably tense and ready to
leave, if only someone would give them the word.

After he left the hotel with no further clues about Jack, the
family liaison officers briefed him with what they had gleaned
from the couple. The officers had kept them company all
evening, attentive witnesses to their anxiety, helping them talk
through and remember the odd little events of the past few
days, the suspicious signs, the ironies and innocent-seeming
omens that might have presaged their son's disappearance,
but nothing of note had emerged.

As soon as Daly entered the room, he noticed their mood
had changed. A different tension hung in the air between

them. Instinctively, he felt it was something other than parental fear, more like the moody, haphazard tension of a couple on the verge of breaking up. Rebecca looked emotionally spent, while her husband managed to give Daly a nod and a brief smile.

A dangerous light shone in her eyes when she saw him. What did Daly see there? Anger that he had not done enough to find their son or hope that Daly was their saviour? Whatever it was, it dazzled him. The opening lines he had prepared while getting the coffees slipped from his mind. He gave a little smile that felt forced, and to his surprise she returned it with an odd look of sympathy and concern, her lips mouthing a surprised 'oh' while her husband's expression turned to suspicion, his jaw sticking out in the form of an unasked question.

My face, Daly remembered. The bruised visage of a man who had been in a drunken fight. He touched his features self-consciously.

'Just a few war wounds,' he murmured. He explained that the search for their son had precipitated a near riot at the traveller wedding.

'No sign of your son, I'm afraid, but we do have some leads.'

He told them that CCTV footage at the hotel had picked up images of two older boys escorting their son into a camper van belonging to a clan of travellers called the McGinns. There had been a report that their son was crying. Immediately, Rebecca grabbed on to the edge of the table to steady herself. She was about to speak but pressed her lips together.

'Earlier you told me no one else knew you were taking Jack to the courthouse,' said Daly. 'That the camper van was already parked when you arrived, which leads me to believe that your son's disappearance must have resulted from a chance encounter. Do you follow me?'

The couple nodded.

'Unless, of course, we factor in another possibility,' added Daly.

The two of them said nothing. Daly could sense the gears of their minds spinning into motion, trying to formulate what he might be hinting at.

'What are you suggesting?' asked Harry.

'This sort of thing happens much more frequently than is reported in the press. Boys of Jack's age sometimes develop a taste for adventure.'

'You mean he might have deliberately run away with these... people?' said Rebecca.

'Something like that. Perhaps he only meant to be gone for a short while, but then he lost control of the situation.'

She shook her head emphatically. 'Why would he run away from us?'

Daly shrugged. 'The same reason why boys usually break rules. To see if they can get away with it.' He paused and continued delicately: 'And if there are problems at home, that might be another motivating factor.'

The couple were immediately on their guard. Rebecca's eyes flicked from left to right, but the journalist fixed Daly with a steely gaze. The detective stayed firm, not even blinking. He tried to convey patience, kindness even, coupled with an air of knowledge, a sense that he had already measured the depths of the difficulties in their relationship. He wanted them to be as candid as possible. A frosty smile appeared on Harry's lips, but it was Rebecca who spoke first.

'Things at home might not be satisfactory right now, but that's not enough to make our son throw himself into the arms of strangers, especially a camper van full of travellers.'

'What about at school?'

Daly could see that she had not factored in the possibility that he might be unhappy at school.

'Has he talked to you about his feelings?'

'He's more interested in reading books.'

'But does he talk to you?'

'No.' She clasped her hands on the table, her knuckles turning white.

'Then how do you know what's going on inside his head?'

'I don't.' She looked at Daly as though he were piling more cruelty on to her.

'Has this ever happened before?'

'Disappearing like this? Never.'

Harry leaned out of his seat. 'I think you're on the wrong track, Inspector. If Jack went off on purpose, why was he taken away in tears at the hotel?'

'I don't doubt that he's in danger. All I'm saying is that we might be starting off with a mistaken assumption. That he was deliberately abducted by the O'Sullivans. That implies some degree of organization from the travellers and from what I've seen I doubt that.'

'But I left him safe and sound in the car. Why would the notion to run away suddenly spring into his head? Why would he want to hurt us like this?'

'There are other things we cannot yet explain. For instance, why did Jack not try to raise the alarm or escape at the hotel?'

'You only have the travellers' word for that.'

'Of course, it's possible that none of them are telling the truth. In that case, the entire wedding party might be an accessory to kidnapping. But I don't believe that is the case. The O'Sullivans are cooperating and helping us trace his movements.'

Daly asked if Jack had any medical conditions such as asthma that they could include in their alert to the media.

'No, he's a very healthy boy.'

Daly returned to the incident involving the traveller children in their back garden. 'Tell me more about the boys. Did they threaten Jack or you, or behave suspiciously in any way?'

'Nothing happened, Inspector,' said Harry. 'If anything had, we would have told you by now.'

'What about Jack? Did he speak about it afterwards?'

'Yes, but again it was nothing important. They just asked him for old toys—'

'I remember now,' interrupted Rebecca. 'They asked me questions about Jack. They wanted to know what age he was and where he went to school.'

'Travellers always ask questions,' said Harry dismissively. 'It's in their nature.'

Daly watched the husband intently. The fact that fathers could be more rational in their emotional attachment to their children was written in the natural order of things. After all, they did not have to undergo the trials of pregnancy and childbirth; however, there was something rehearsed and focused about Harry Hewson that unsettled Daly. The way he repeated the same words, the slowness of his speech, the formal respect he showed Daly and his self-restraint. By contrast, Rebecca started involuntarily every time a phone rang or a door clicked open in the corridor.

Daly had a tendency to want to understand people who showed perfect composure in such stressful circumstances. He wanted to replay in his mind the husband's movements and everything he said more closely so that he might detect even a whisper of panic, but throughout the interview Harry's voice remained almost grotesquely calm. Daly tried to put himself in the journalist's shoes. He lingered over the relationship he might have with his son. Did he take him to football matches or help him with his homework and read him bedtime stories? Perhaps the boy was too old for that. Daly wouldn't know. He didn't have a son. He knew nothing about children of Jack's age – or any age for that matter – and the thought depressed him.

'These people were asking questions about our son,' said Rebecca to her husband. 'They were watching our house, which means they were watching you, too.'

There was a slight movement from Harry, an almost imperceptible hunching of his shoulders.

'Hold on a moment,' said Rebecca. Her expression grew darker and more solemn. 'This happened before. When we were on holiday in Donegal last summer. I almost forgot to mention it. How could I have forgotten that?' She looked at Harry with a faint shudder. 'That day we visited the monastery at Rossnowlagh. You left for a walk on the beach, while

Jack and I did the Stations of the Cross. He disappeared that day, too. One minute I was caught up in prayers with a group of nuns, the next he was nowhere to be seen. I was frantic for about an hour. I couldn't believe that he had just vanished in broad daylight.'

Harry rolled his eyes. 'Don't, Rebecca. You're twisting a story out of a couple of random events. There's no connection between what happened back then and what's happening now. You're fabricating a plot to give the detective something to go on. We should just let him get on with his job.'

'How can you be sure it's not connected?' replied Rebecca. 'You always sound as if you know everything.'

'All I'm saying is you're straying into areas that don't concern the detective.'

Daly interrupted the exchange. He could not leave her story hanging in the air. 'Let me be the judge of whether it's relevant or not. Tell me what happened at the monastery.'

'I searched the grounds, retracing my steps, and then I saw her, an old woman holding Jack's hand, leading him down a side path to the car park, as though she were making a getaway. I ran after them and grabbed Jack from her. I was shaking with anger.'

'What was she doing with your son?' asked Daly.

'I didn't stop to ask. A priest was walking nearby and I ran towards him. I could hear her calling after us but I didn't dare look back.'

'What did Jack say?'

'He said she was a traveller. He'd wandered off and met her on a path. She'd wanted to know was he lost and where were his parents.'

'Which are perfectly reasonable questions to ask,' interposed Harry.

'You seem to know a lot about travellers,' said Daly.

'I've had dealings with them. In the course of my work.'

'Your work?' A note of scorn entered Rebecca's voice. Daly had not expected her to intervene in such a manner, but Harry seemed nonplussed.

'Why did it take you so long to come to me?' she asked him. The tone of her voice made his tardiness seem like a gross betrayal.

'I came as soon as I could.' Harry looked at Daly warily, unwilling to involve him in what seemed a domestic matter. 'I already told you, I missed your messages.'

For Rebecca, however, Daly's presence seemed of less importance.

'You should have come sooner. None of your colleagues knew what you were up to. They hadn't seen you for ages.' Her voice teetered on the edge of a dangerous darkness. Harry's discomfort increased.

'I've been busy. I'll explain everything later.'

'Why are you telling me this roundabout story? Why don't you just tell me the truth?'

Harry's eyes grew small and intense. 'I already told you. I dropped everything and came as soon as I could.'

Daly watched the two of them continue their argument in curt tones, trying to keep it civilized, but everything about their strained eyes and voices suggested that their relationship was derailing. Daly had seen it countless times before: the stress of a child's disappearance or death breeding a void between its parents; the solitude of guilt and grief turning both partners into human shards, fragments that would never again constitute a functioning whole.

Eventually Rebecca fell silent. Daly and the journalist listened to her unsteady breathing. Her shoulders trembled slightly as she tried to control her emotions. She seemed to realize that it was the wrong time and place to have an argument, in the police station's atmosphere of forensic surveillance, with a detective as piggy-in-the-middle. She repeated the same reproachful sentence, but in a smaller voice. 'You should have come sooner.'

Daly decided he ought to send the couple home. The interview had reached an impasse, and he realized that the couple now craved to be on their own. They needed privacy to vent their fears and whatever marital tension was bubbling under the surface. He needed them to isolate whatever resentments they held against each other so that they would not infect the investigation.

Before they left, he showed them some still photographs from the hotel CCTV. 'These are the boys who took Jack from the hotel. Do you recognize them?'

They shook their heads.

'I want you to think carefully about these photographs. I want you to try to remember where you might have seen these teenagers before. Perhaps they have been watching you for some time and were waiting for this opportunity. Perhaps they befriended your son and encouraged him to run away. Talk about it and think it over. We need to work out what part Jack played in his disappearance.'

They stared at him blankly. They had crossed into the no man's land of conjecture and fleeting hope. Already they were forming a more troubling picture of their son, a vulnerable child tricked into joining a gang of runaway travellers in a camper van, a feral teenager stationed at the wheel, all of them outlaws on a road trip, fleeing the messed-up world of grown-ups.

'In the meantime, if you can think of any reason why these people might be interested in your son, let me know.'

Daly frowned after the couple left the station. He was still troubled by the fact that Harry Hewson's behaviour had seemed too poised and controlled. He had the nagging feeling that he had been holding something back. But why would a father desperate to find his son not tell the police the truth? He kept his suspicions to himself for the time being and organized two teams of uniformed officers to check all the traveller encampments, legal and illegal, on this side of the border for any information about the McGinns. He also made contact with the Gardai in Monaghan to launch a similar operation in the Republic. He asked Detective O'Neill to interview Jack's teachers and his friends at school first thing in the morning. He wanted her to gather as much information as possible on the boy and his state of mind.

He drove home, his thoughts teeming with the events of the day. Only when the road orientated itself towards Lough Neagh's dark mass of water did his mind begin to clear. Beyond him lay the unscathed heart of his country and one of its great wild spaces, its waves reflecting a silver mesh of moon and quivering starlight. He stopped the car and stared for a while at the expanse, mesmerized by the countless threads of reflected light rising and sinking with the ghostly slowness of the waves, which ran all the way, it seemed, to the humped silhouette of his little cottage. Even in the dark, the nearness of the lough never failed to calm his thoughts. Was it because this impassable barrier of water forced the end of all his travelling, depriving him of his restlessness?

Starting the engine again for the final stretch home, he began to think about the connections between the Hewsons and the travellers. It was a textbook procedure in criminal investigations. Explore the links, even if it meant casting suspicion on an entirely innocent party. He was struck by Harry Hewson's knowledge of traveller ways, and his admission that he had worked on news stories about their tussles with law and order. The thought struck him: what if the Hewsons' marital tensions were deeper than they seemed even to his discerning eye? What if they were in the throes of separation and custody issues had risen to the fore? The prospect of divorce changed children into powerful tools of menace and punishment. Humiliation and fear of loneliness might make a father act desperately. Desperate enough to stage a mock abduction?

Harry had seemed stubbornly calm all day. Had it been a protective response to Rebecca's panic or a symptom of his secret control over the events? Ordinarily, would a father not be frantic also, demanding more of the police, less satisfied with how the search operation was progressing?

Daly climbed out of his car and made his way towards the dimly lit front door of his cottage. It struck him that suspecting the husband in this way made him feel happier about himself. The image of Rebecca's stricken face flashed into his mind, her eyes lifting towards him, eyelashes quivering, her lips pale with worry. He remembered the soft grip of her hands in the courthouse, the way they sought out his fingers with the fervent instinct of a child. Was she the loveless victim of a plot hatched by her husband, or were his suspicions little more than the fanciful imaginings of a middle-aged man, the narcissism of a lonely detective who believed that she had singled him out to rescue her from a doomed marriage?

As he slipped his key into the latch, the black hen flapped towards him from her secret perch, as though to welcome his return home, but at the last moment, she faltered, fluttering her wings frantically and rising up on to the roof, far beyond his grasping hands. He looked up and saw that a few tiles had slipped from their places, and were now lodged precariously at the edge of the guttering. The hen hopped across the roof and nestled into one of the gaps. He called and called her, but despite his desperate coaxing, she refused to budge. Even when he pulled out a ladder and climbed on to the roof, she scrambled away from him, finding more and more inaccessible perches along the eaves. He could see that the roof was in bad shape and needed extensive repairing. He cursed to himself, thinking of the cost, and gave up on the hen. She had become his nightly trial, the antidote to his lonely narcissism.

CHAPTER FOURTEEN

'You should see a doctor,' Detective O'Neill chided Daly as he prepared to chair the first meeting of the search team at nine o'clock the next morning. 'At least get something to take the swelling down.'

Daly did not mind that his face was bruised and swollen. Somehow, it completed him. He dredged up a smile that revealed more of his cut lip and made him wince. 'Serves us right for wandering into a traveller wedding without proper back-up.'

O'Neill smiled at him in sympathy. 'Take you off court duty and within a few hours you end up with a face like a busted slipper.'

'Sinclair will think I went crazy with my new-found freedom.'

Daly began the meeting by summing up what they knew so far about the boy's disappearance. However, the face of Detective Irwin looming at the door window soon broke his train of thought. The Special Branch detective seemed to take an insolent pleasure in watching the proceedings. In spite of Daly's seniority, Irwin had invaded his investigations without qualms, asking probing questions that were just shy of being insubordinate, happier, it seemed, to do battle over the political ramifications of Daly's work rather than indulge in some proper detective work of his own. His face drifted by the window, his eyes fastening on to Daly's, vigilant and gleaming with anticipation. Daly stared back at him, wearing his bruises like badges of honour. He had sloughed off his old skin, and abandoned for good the confines of the courtroom and the pleas of shoplifting mothers. No one in Special Branch could accuse him of hiding from real police work any longer.

As the meeting went on, Irwin's lingering presence at the door and the impudence of his staring eyes made Daly's skin prickle. These days, the new police headquarters building echoed with the footsteps of numerous Special Branch officers in the mould of Irwin. So habitual and discreet were they in their wanderings through the corridors and incident rooms that they seemed like watchful ghosts when compared to their harried counterparts in CID. While other departments such as Community Liaison and the traffic branch faced drastic cuts to their workforces, there seemed to be more recruits to the Special Branch team by the day. Daly had taught himself to ignore their presence, and told his junior officers the most helpful thing to do was to pretend they were not there, to pass them by as though they belonged to a different world.

So many competing interests were juxtaposed in this gleaming new building: the policing of the past and the policing of the present, one overshadowing the other. Even the simplest run-of-the-mill investigations into a car crash or a missing boy might turn out to have sinister implications for the stability of the peace process or the career of a former paramilitary now protected within the political framework of the new Northern Ireland government. Daly had grown used over the past few years to Irwin being his tail, going wherever he went, staying where he stayed. He dreaded to think what the successes of his detective work might look like through the eyes of this cold but attentive shadow, who had forged a career out of doing little more than watching and waiting for other officers to step over invisible political lines.

Although Daly had slept poorly and was tired, the events of the previous day painfully cramming his head, the thought of Irwin prowling around the edges of the investigation had the effect of energizing him. He was determined to prove that he was fit for the job. He was the lead detective, and that meant being the driving force in the search for the boy, even though the mêlée at the hotel had blunted and sapped the collective spirit of the team. Almost twenty-four hours had passed since Rebecca had summoned his help, and so far they had secured very little in terms of tangible leads.

'Are we sure there was an element of coercion in his disappearance?' Susie Brooke, the anti-racism officer, asked him. 'For the sake of the travelling community, we need to work out as quickly as possible what actually happened to this boy. This is a closed society we're dealing with, where privacy is paramount. Unfortunately, travellers fear the consequences of talking openly to the police.'

Irwin's fish-like eyes bulged at the window in the door. Daly was all too familiar with the complacent smirk on his lips.

'Of course,' he replied, trying to concentrate on the priorities of the investigation. 'We don't want the media conjecturing the worst possible scenario and stirring up paranoia towards every traveller encampment in the country.'

'What do you mean by the worst possible scenario?' asked Brooke.

Nobody spoke. The rest of the officers, trained in the rules of political correctness, did not voice the fear that consumed their thoughts; instead, they semaphored it in a mixture of glances and throat clearances.

Daly answered for them. 'That the travellers are involved in organized child trafficking.'

'But Jack Hewson appears to have been free to play and mix with the travellers at the hotel. That doesn't suggest to me that child traffickers are at work.'

'That's true,' said Daly. 'O'Sullivan's effort at helping us in the hotel also goes some way to lessening that suspicion.'

Daly glanced up at the door and saw that the irksome shape of Irwin had passed from view. Taking advantage of the pause, Sergeant Tom McKenna began summarizing what he had gleaned from questioning O'Sullivan and his son.

'I'll make it brief,' said McKenna. 'O'Sullivan has no idea where Jack was taken to. He can't give us any leads. Nor does he know anything about the McGinns or where they might be right now. It strikes me that he's clamming up to protect his relatives.'

'Were you able to tell when he was holding something back?' asked Daly.

'How would I notice that?'

'You said you thought he was clamming up.'

'How could I tell what he doesn't want me to know?' McKenna flashed Daly a look of surprise.

Daly made an effort to suppress his annoyance. He doubted if McKenna had listened properly to O'Sullivan's answers, or probed his silences. What the junior officer saw and heard was probably based on the stereotypes he held of travellers, rather than the flesh-and-blood man before him, the rasp of his voice, the flicker of his eyes, and the movement of his hands.

'Did you ask him if he knew Rebecca or Harry Hewson?' asked Daly.

'O'Sullivan was incomprehensible for most of the interview,' said McKenna, shrugging his shoulders. 'With his thick accent and fast talking, he just kept dodging every question I asked.'

'Did he remember anything that he hadn't mentioned before?'

'I didn't see the point in asking him to go over what he had already told us.'

'What about his plans? Did you ask him what he had in mind to do after the wedding?'

McKenna looked at him in surprise. 'It was clear he intended to get as drunk as possible.'

Daly wanted to rebuke McKenna for his laziness. He wanted to tell him that a good detective should be able to build intuitions of the truth from a suspect's body language, a shift in their gaze, a break in their voice, even a change in their body odour. On the most primitive biological level, a guilty person might leak a wealth of information, but it was clear to Daly that for McKenna the thought of groping in this realm of the unspoken left him uneasy, especially when interviewing someone he felt was his social inferior. Daly sighed. He should have questioned O'Sullivan himself, instead of spending time in the family suite staring at Rebecca Hewson's devastated eyes. He was at fault, as well. The chance to console a distressed mother had seemed to offer him the promise of elevation, of somehow bettering himself, while the prospect of interrogating an evasive gypsy had done the opposite, threatening debasement.

'We'll have to interview him again.'

'I can do it,' said McKenna sourly.

'No, you won't,' said Daly, unable to keep the note of irritation from creeping into his voice. There was an awkward silence.

'What else do we have?' asked Daly. 'What about eyewitnesses at the hotel? Anything unusual there?'

'We've interviewed as many of the wedding party as possible,' said Detective O'Neill. 'None of them remember seeing the boy or noticing anything untoward happening. Oddly, not even the hotel staff said they saw any sign of a boy in distress.'

'The picture is very confusing,' said Brooke. The other officers nodded in agreement.

'You can't drag a boy across a hotel car park and into a van without making a fuss and drawing attention to yourself,' said McKenna.

'So the absence of eyewitnesses suggests he might have gone willingly with these boys,' said Daly.

'This seems to be the obvious conclusion. But his parents strongly disagree.'

Daly thought for a while. 'What do we have on the McGinns?'

'Again, hardly anything,' said O'Neill. 'They are two brothers called Patrick and Thomas, aged sixteen and seventeen, with no criminal record, except for some police warnings over anti-social behaviour. They belong to a clan who had been camping illegally at a farm near the border. The head of the family had bought a field or two and applied for planning permission to build a halting site. However, for some reason, they cleared out of the site overnight.'

Mentally, Daly reviewed the evidence they had gathered, looking for a lead or some hint of a breakthrough in understanding. He rubbed his forehead and felt a twinge of pain. Suddenly, his bruises and swollen features made him feel as though he were wearing a heavy mask, one that had grown out of his skin and flesh and could not be ripped off, no matter how hard he tried. The injuries he wore were a projection of his damaged spirit, a replica of the person he normally kept hidden from view. He stared at the rest of the team, noting how none of them maintained eye contact for longer than a second.

'We've searched O'Sullivan's mansion outside Dungannon,' he told them. 'I had the misfortune to bump into several intruders who were rummaging through his things.' At the risk of further muddying the waters, Daly recounted his encounter with the men, one of whom he suspected was a former paramilitary. 'Neither I nor the intruders found what we were looking for. O'Sullivan keeps his mansion like a show house, very neat and ordered, with nothing incriminating lying around. However, on the basis of what I saw and heard, there is no doubt that he is a man with secrets to hide.'

'Do you think their search is connected with ours?'

'They were looking for documents belonging to a traveller called Mary O'Sullivan,' said Daly. 'It seems implausible that this might be connected to Jack Hewson, but if it is then the boy's disappearance is linked to criminal elements.'

The team ruminated on Daly's words. A set of unconnected coincidences or a network of clues? To Daly's mind they resembled pieces of a troubling puzzle that were organizing themselves into a familiar pattern. Sometimes an investigation felt familiar even if at first sight it seemed completely new and challenging. Certain characteristics triggered a collective memory, as if he'd experienced and solved the case before. Daly felt that the boy's disappearance was joined to the past, to a dangerous bloodline of paramilitary violence, organized crime and fugitive rootless beings, but what were the links between this world and the Hewsons'?

Right on cue, Irwin reappeared at the window, as though he had been eavesdropping on Daly's thoughts. He rapped on the glass and beckoned to Daly, who ignored him at first.

The door opened and Irwin stuck his long face into the room. 'Commander Sinclair would like to see you, Celcius. In his room.'

'I'm chairing a meeting. Can't it wait?'

'No. He's having a conference with some senior officers. He thinks you might find it helpful.'

'A conference about what?'

'The boy's disappearance.'

'I thought I was in charge of the case,' Daly said with anger. 'Why is he discussing it without my knowledge?'

'Take it easy, Daly. All will be revealed if you come with me.'

Daly adjourned the meeting and marched out of the room. He followed Irwin up the stairs, feeling annoyance well within his chest. The Special Branch detective could have chosen a shorter route to Sinclair's office, but for some reason he took Daly along a few more corridors than he needed to. At one point, Daly miscalculated his step and bumped into a female officer coming in the opposite direction. He swayed and tottered a little before catching up with Irwin, who was bounding up more stairs. They were several storeys up now. Stretching ahead of them was a low, white corridor. The featureless walls rang with the empty echo of their footsteps.

Eventually, Irwin stopped and put his shoulder to a door. 'After you, Daly,' he said with a grin.

He pushed open the door and ushered Daly into an office that was bigger than the investigation room he had just left, with softer carpeting and more solid wood fixtures. The commander was seated at the head of a table along with Inspector Fealty from Special Branch and two stiff, statue-like men Daly did not recognize. They were both grey-haired and grim-faced, their eyes flicking over Daly as though they already knew everything about him and had their defences alerted. Behind them, the rain was hammering against a large set of windows, which produced vibrating shadows across the ceiling, bringing the features of the men at the table into sharp relief.

'Detective Brian Barclay, Superintendent Nigel Reilly, this is Detective Celcius Daly,' said Sinclair. The two men unwound from their chairs and nodded greetings to Daly. 'They're leading a special drugs team with the assistance of HM Revenue.'

'Who's in charge of this investigation?' demanded Daly, ignoring the offer of handshakes.

'You are,' said Sinclair. 'Which is why I've invited you to this meeting. In the circumstances, it's wiser you hear this in privacy.'

'Why are Special Branch involved?' said Daly, glaring at Irwin and Fealty. 'Why the need to monitor everything I do?'

'We're here to share information,' replied Irwin.

Fealty leaned forward. His thin face looked abraded by the light from the windows. 'Commander Sinclair thinks we can be of assistance in your search for Jack Hewson.'

Daly smiled bitterly. 'I can't believe this. My first case back on full duty, and I have Special Branch breathing down my neck. What connection do you have with the disappearance of this boy? What possible political trouble can my investigation stir up?'

'I've put you in charge of an important investigation, Daly,' said Sinclair. 'Hear what the team have to say before you go on the defensive.'

What unfolded, at first, was a series of grim introductions, right out of the handbook of multi-agency cooperation, a bureaucratic trap for a detective like Daly, an outsider, who felt he was floating ignorantly through the systems of policies and protocols. Daly failed to see any sense of structure to the meeting or clearly identify the competing roles of the different crime squads. He found it hard to credit that one missing boy might be the object and source of such a high-powered meeting, involving so many different departments.

Reilly began outlining for Daly's benefit how the O'Sullivans had aroused the interest of his department, as well as HM Revenue and Special Branch. A grimace flexed on his face.

'Unfortunately, within the law-abiding travelling community, there is a small, extremely violent, and well-organized gang of criminals that are members of a globally organized crime network.'

Reilly paused every now and again, checking Daly's response, as though he expected the detective to ask him questions, while his colleague Barclay seemed content to doodle on a notepad.

'The O'Sullivans have had several brushes with the law, but mostly minor stuff, until early last year, when we suspect some of Thomas O'Sullivan's nephews had become active in a drug-smuggling ring using cheap furniture imported from Eastern Europe, mostly leather sofas and armchairs to stash the drugs.'

'Why don't you just round them up and arrest them?' asked Irwin. 'You might get a prosecutor to charge them.'

Reilly grinned ruefully. 'Not unless they're going to confess. The only evidence we've been able to uncover is based on tip-offs from informers, whose testimony might be questionable. We know that the O'Sullivans have recently made a number of trips to Romania and that they've been handling large amounts of cash. Such is the flow of the money that the clan have built a number of mansions, which they hardly ever use. The source of their wealth is suspicious to say the least.'

Daly glanced at the notepad that Barclay was doodling upon. He saw a series of numbers with zeros attached. The detective was adding up sums that did not appear to have anything to do with the meeting. Probably totalling his monthly expenses, thought Daly, or working out how he was going to spend his pension. There was a semi-retired look about him already: the slightly doomed set of his mouth; the vagueness in his eyes, as though he had given up pretending to understand the ramifications of the investigation. Daly knew his type, an old RUC detective who'd spent his career resisting terrorist attacks but now felt adrift with the Troubles over and a ceasefire in place, grimly holding out against the creeping fever of political correctness and professionalism that was transforming the country's police service.

Barclay flashed Daly a good-natured grin when he saw that Daly had seen his calculations, before crumpling up the paper and tossing it in a waste-paper bin. By contrast, Reilly seemed to be intimately connected with the apparatus of Special Branch. When he wasn't speaking with his booming voice, he was flashing Irwin and Fealty secret signs with his eyes. Daly wondered what plots had been hatched between the three at a prior meeting to control the investigation from the start.

'The fundamental problem from a policing perspective is that the O'Sullivans have a brazen approach to borders,' said Reilly. 'We can't tie them down. Not to a jurisdiction or an address. Sometimes not even to a name. They're all called Thomas Patrick Joseph, or Patrick Thomas Joseph, or some such combination. Even their birth records are awry.'

Barclay stopped scrawling on his pad. 'We've obtained search warrants for their properties, but never found anything. They're like blank slates, wiped clean.'

Daly recalled his encounter with the masked intruders in O'Sullivan's mansion, and their hunt for birth certificates, but thought better of mentioning it as he had entered the property without a warrant.

'They drink hard, fight hard, and as soon as they fall under the attention of the police, they disappear. We arrest some of them but the rest of the clan break into smaller, tighter groups, travelling in convoys of two or three caravans. As such they are the most effective couriers imaginable for anyone wishing to smuggle something across the border.

'In the past month or two, we've been investigating reports of a new criminal gang using the border as a people-trafficking route into the UK with possible links to dissident paramilitary groups.'

Daly looked up and eyed Fealty, understanding the reason for his presence at the meeting.

'Which brings us to the missing boy,' interposed Sinclair.

'If this was an abduction it was a skilful piece of work,' said Reilly.

'How can you tell?' asked Daly.

Reilly raised an eyebrow at Barclay, who began to look uncomfortable.

'We've been conducting a surveillance operation on the O'Sullivans for the past week,' said Barclay.

Daly said nothing, his eyes watching each of the men at the table.

Reilly shifted in his seat and avoided Daly's gaze.

'We had two undercover teams deployed yesterday,' added Barclay. 'Our intelligence suggested that the O'Sullivans were planning to use the wedding as a cover for transporting some merchandise. We watched them at the church and then followed them to the hotel.'

'What did you notice at the hotel?' asked Daly.

'There was a much bigger gathering of the clans than we expected. We weren't able to get close enough to them.'

'Too many drunken young men strutting round like fighting cocks,' said Reilly.

'When Inspector Daly arrived we were forced to withdraw at the risk of jeopardizing the operation.'

'How did O'Sullivan behave?' asked Daly.

'He seemed restrained. Perhaps he was minding his manners. He was the father of the bride, after all.'

'Did anyone follow them to the courthouse?' asked Daly.

'Yes, but when we saw where they were going, we pulled the tail on O'Sullivan's son. We reckoned that if a drop-off was going to happen, the courthouse would be an unlikely location.'

Barclay looked sheepishly around the table. Daly now understood the reason for the tension in the air. He imagined Barclay writing the report that outlined how a suspected drug smuggler might have managed to abduct a child while under police surveillance. The press would have a field day if they got wind of this.

Reilly cleared his throat, breaking the silence. 'This was a routine surveillance operation. You can't train police officers to be on the lookout for a missing child when their minds are focused on another mission.'

Sinclair made a wry face in response. 'It's true police off-icers are trained to keep focused on their objectives, but they should always be prepared for the unexpected.'

On the defensive, Reilly turned his gaze on Daly. 'What can you tell us about the search for the boy?'

Irwin stepped in. 'Inspector Daly and his team have yet to define the boundaries of their investigation. They have a suspicion that the boy may have wandered off or run away from home. They haven't established if this is a case of some-thing more sinister such as an abduction.'

'We're examining the family background,' explained Daly. 'We're trying to judge the boy's frame of mind, weighing up the probabilities. This is the normal procedure. We don't want to start a witch hunt against the travelling community.'

Reilly stared at Daly. 'I've been briefing officers here about our operations with the travellers for the last six months. How come I haven't seen you before?'

'I've been on court duty.'

'Covering for officers who were too busy to attend the hearings,' said Irwin with a smirk.

'In the circumstances, are you sure you're qualified to lead such a sensitive investigation?' Reilly's clear blue eyes seemed to suggest that he had already appraised Daly and found him less than adequate.

'I have no doubt that Inspector Daly is more than capable of heading up the search,' said Sinclair, rushing to Daly's defence.

Reilly had kept his candid blue eyes on Daly, and now he turned to Sinclair. 'OK, I think that should conclude this meeting. Just remember that the O'Sullivans are under our watch, and we're very close to netting them. I hope that Inspector Daly solves the disappearance of this boy as quickly and efficiently as possible, and that his efforts don't derail our investigation.'

Barclay tried to mollify the sting of Reilly's last comment. 'Whatever has happened to the boy is a tragedy for his family. It is in all our interests to get to the bottom of it.' He gave Daly a reassuring smile. 'Be sure to tell us what you're doing and we'll do our best to help.'

Daly wanted to say that this was a separate criminal investigation and had nothing to do with the remit of the drugs squad, HM Revenue or Special Branch. However, he made an effort to smile cheerfully.

Fealty nodded and eyed Daly. 'A man of your seniority needs to be communicating with the other departments of this police force.'

As they left the room, Irwin came up close to Daly, who was still smiling. 'I hope you've taken all that on board.'

'Not a word of it,' said Daly. 'My investigation is none of your bloody business.'

'Then why are you looking so happy?'

'Just thinking of all the court hearings I missed today.'

Irwin's expression grew agitated. 'Consider it a few days off, Daly. Knowing your style, you'll be back skulking amid the town's petty criminals before very long, looking for your usual hiding place.'

Daly walked away, feeling Irwin's overheated gaze upon his back. A door opened and a group of young Special Branch officers crowded into the corridor, thronging both sides of his vision with their bland, watchful faces, emitting their coded signals to each other as he passed them by with his bruised face. Daly felt the hairs on the back of his neck prickle. He hoped that the surge of detective work and the urgency of his search for the missing boy would carry him safely beyond this morbid delusion that his colleagues were keeping him under constant surveillance.

CHAPTER FIFTEEN

For the next twenty-four hours, Daly and his officers interrogated and watched O'Sullivan and his son in the custody cell, but they discovered little of anything. The two slept, ate, answered the questions that were fired at them, paced up and down in their cell, and seemed not to notice the growing desperation in the officers' eyes.

'We didn't do anything to the boy,' said O'Sullivan. 'It's not our fault he sneaked into the back of the van. You can't do anything to us, so let us go.'

'I wouldn't be so sure of that,' said Daly.

'We've done nothing wrong,' O'Sullivan yelled as the door of the room slammed shut.

Daly paced up and down outside the interview room, thinking of a fresh angle of inquiry. At the very least, the father and son were key witnesses, and Daly was worried that through his own incompetence he might let them slip through his grasp.

'We're running out of time,' said O'Neill, joining him in the corridor.

'You're right. I wish we could hold them for longer.'

Back inside the room, Daly asked them for more information about the McGinns.

'We've already told you everything we know. It's time you let us go.'

O'Neill stared at Daly as if to say O'Sullivan had a point.

Eventually, the two were released and warned to stay within the police jurisdiction, but not before Daly had organized a pair of officers and an unmarked car to tail them and report on anything suspicious.

Based on his misgivings about Harry Hewson, Daly decided to launch a more low-profile and personal line of inquiry, one that he wished to keep quiet because it was based on little more than his intuition. He ordered a criminal background check on the husband and a full driving licence check. He also rang round a few of his contacts in the local newspapers, but surprisingly none of them knew of Hewson or his work as a journalist. He asked the reporters to do some digging round and see what they could come up with to shed light on Hewson's professional and personal life.

Meanwhile, Detective O'Neill had interviewed Jack's school friends and teachers. She told Daly that their stories tallied on one main detail: Jack had been having problems over bullying in the playground. On several occasions, he had come to blows with a gang of boys in an older class. His teachers had linked the bullying to a decline in his schoolwork and the fact that he kept missing classes on Wednesdays, which was the day he had disappeared.

'According to one of his friends, Jack was convinced this gang of boys had it in for him and wanted to attack him outside the school gates,' said O'Neill.

This was something the Hewsons had not seemed to know about their son, or had at least not reported it to Daly. He was sure that Rebecca would have mentioned it if she had been aware of her son's fears. Perhaps there were other things that Jack had kept hidden from them; worrying things that – magnified in the mind of a ten-year-old – might have prompted his flight.

To his annoyance, Daly saw that Inspector Fealty of Special Branch had left him a string of messages, requesting regular updates and a transcript of any interviews with suspects and eyewitnesses. Daly immediately fired back an email stating that Fealty would have to fill out an official request form for each separate transcript, clearly indicating the precise details of the information he wished to see. He sighed. The landscape of the investigation was steepening forbiddingly. Now that Special Branch were poking their nose in, Daly felt the prospect of any simple solution to the case dwindle considerably. He feared he was sliding towards another acrimonious battle with political forces within the higher command of the police service.

He left the headquarters and headed for the border. Where else could he shake off the shadows that oppressed him than amid the labyrinth of introverted roads criss-crossing Northern Ireland and the Republic? Ever since his Troubles' childhood, Daly had the sense that these neglected border roads were transient rather than fixed, capricious and unknowable, likely to disappear into a bottomless bog or end mid-air over a bomb crater rather than lead one to a desired destination. They were the secret paths of paramilitaries and smugglers: men and women who hid from the law, who sought safe passage from the police and soldiers, while the surrounding farms and divided parishes sank into decline and abandonment. The undertow of the past was strong in this part of the country, and Daly was on the alert, checking his rear-view window constantly for suspicious vehicles.

Thankfully, there was little rain, mist, or fog and he was able to find his way along the crooked roads using his instinct and vigilance, driving until he reached the site where the McGinns had been encamped before they fled with the boy. Daly had checked the police records. An elderly farmer named Samuel Reid had made several complaints about the encampment, but as the travellers had not broken any laws, the police had been unwilling to move them on. Reid, who lived in the nearby farmhouse, had accused the travellers of poking about the farm and prying into his private life. Daly was intrigued by the complaints and the similarities with Rebecca Hewson's account of the travellers in her back garden.

He pulled his car on to the muddy verge and got out. He inspected the huddle of small fields and meaningless lanes, the cramped pine forest and marshy hollow that surrounded the campsite. It was a bleak and difficult threshold to nowhere in particular. Why had the travellers chosen to pitch in this godforsaken place? Gypsies did not follow maps or GPS systems. They used older, more intuitive ways to navigate the country, but it was difficult for Daly to come up with a logical reason why the clan would have bought this particular field with plans to turn it into a permanent halting site.

He got out and walked around the abandoned field. Beyond the gate, the churned-up mud was knee-deep in places. He half expected to discover evidence of a drunken, slovenly encampment, but apart from the tyre tracks, there was barely a sign the travellers had been there. A few flecks of litter were visible in the corners of the hedges. At the sites of the campfires, someone had spread fresh sods of turf. He hung around the fringes of the field, examining the hedges for rubbish that might yield a clue to the McGinns' whereabouts, but he found nothing at all. Crows muttered at him, dropping out of sight over the windblown shapes of hawthorn and willow. Bubbles glistened in the bottom of the ditches where the marsh water had broken loose. All he saw was a fetid cauldron of rotting vegetation.

A small blue van braked suddenly on seeing Daly. The driver rolled down his window and beckoned to the detective. 'What are you doing?' he asked.

Daly did not like the look on his face, the way his eyes barely blinked, and the aggressive frown on his lips. 'I'm checking this field.'

'You the police?'

'Yes.'

'Well, when are you going to start catching the real criminals in this country?'

'Who are you talking about?' Daly wondered why he was answering his questions at all.

'It's them gypsies, always misbehaving, always making a nuisance of themselves. Turn your back for a second and they come crawling out of the night to set up camp on your doorstep, and all the time the government pays them just for

167

living. You need to round up the whole bloody lot and send them back over the border.'

'We can't arrest anyone until they've broken the law.'

The driver glowered at Daly. 'Of course they're doing something wrong. They're invading our land. This is our country, not a bloody holiday camp.'

'Did the travellers commit any crime while they were here?'

The man chuckled to himself 'Go up to the farmhouse and ask the man there. He'll tell you how they harassed the life out of his brother, the farmer who owned that hedge you were poking at.'

'Why can't the farmer speak for himself?'

'Because he died in a horrible accident. His burial is tomorrow. Go up quickly and you'll catch the brother. He's a very important person these days but he has a story to tell you.' He started up his engine. 'Must get on, now,' he shouted, as though Daly had been hindering him from his busy afternoon routine.

Daly drove up the lane towards a sky of silvery dark clouds marching along the brow of the hill. The blackthorns had blossomed and the silhouetted hedges seemed to carry their own trails of light, running up to the farmhouse like a series of simmering fuses, but the two-storey house itself was dark and dreary, reflections of the sky stifled within its small windows, and no signs of life about the place at all. Daly pulled into the back yard and parked behind a spotless black BMW. He stepped into mud curdled with straw and horse manure.

From one of the ramshackle outhouses there rose the grunting and slurping of hungry pigs, their stench fouling the air. He found it hard to pick out a safe passage to the back door. In fact, everything about the dead man's farm was depressing and low key, apart from the figure of Alistair Reid, the famous Unionist politician, who looked surprised when Daly introduced himself at the door.

Daly had been taken aback himself when the door swung back to reveal Reid's formidable features, his grey-black hair streaked back from his forehead, his eyes luminous and daunting. Daly was a simple detective based in a rural district, while Reid belonged to the most powerful political circles in the country, jetting off on regular trips to Dublin, London and Washington to bolster Northern Ireland's peace process and seek support for the region's ailing economy. Daly could not help feel a little insecure in his presence.

Adjusting quickly to the detective's arrival, Reid ushered him into the living room with an air of warmth, as if they had known each other for years. He introduced Daly to his press assistant, a woman in expensive-looking clothes sitting in a corner, and on the opposite side of the room, Reid's dead brother, who was laid out in a dark suit in a coffin, looking like a shrunken, more depressed version of the politician, his waxen features frozen in an expression of sadness, sunspots streaking his face and gnarled hands like mud-stained teardrops.

Newspapers lay spread on a low coffee table with a tray of tea, a funeral order of service pushed to one side. Socially, it felt awkward for Daly, interviewing the politician with his brother in the corner, and his unease increased. The room seemed to shrink to the size of a closet.

'It's terrible but at a time like this I can't resist checking the headlines,' Reid confided in Daly as he lifted the papers. 'I'm sure you can understand how strong an addiction it can be.'

Even slumped on a sofa, Reid managed to retain an air of condescending authority. The defects of his face – the crooked nose, the darkened bags under his eyes, and the heavy jowls – reinforced the sense of power he emanated. His was a face destined to be thrust into the public domain, to be admired and hated for his flaws.

'An addiction?' said Daly.

'Politics. Public opinion. I don't read newspapers for relaxation or their literary merit.'

Reid tidied away the papers and poured Daly some tea. In the silence, the ticking of the clock seemed muted. On the mantelpiece, a set of silver-framed pictures depicting smiling relatives had been displayed with the same loyalty and care as the bible and photograph of the Queen in the china cabinet. Someone had opened the window, but it did little to disperse the fusty smell of age that seeped from the tired-looking furniture.

Alistair Reid looked pale, the way grieving brothers were meant to look. But in his hooded eyes, Daly saw something else: the mind of a politician calculating everything, assessing the tragedy that had been dealt him, working out how to play his cards to the maximum personal benefit. He let out a sigh that was a mixture of impatience and grief, and glanced at his press officer. She was sitting stiffly by the door in a vigilant manner that left Daly thinking she might be just as attentive if Reid were dabbling in a little gardening, advising him what gloves to wear and what weeds to pull.

'I kept telling him to be more careful.' Reid shook his head.

'Believe me, Inspector, the sight of a police car calling at my house is not unusual, but when one woke me up yesterday morning, I had the sinking feeling that something had happened to Sammy.'

'Why was that?'

'My brother was feeling very troubled lately. His judgement was not what it should have been. I don't think he was sleeping that well.'

'And somehow you expected him to have an accident?'

For an instant, a wild haunted look stared out of Reid's eyes, and then it was gone.

'Why exactly have you come here, Inspector?' he asked. 'The police told me this morning that they would not be investigating Samuel's death, beyond the usual coroner's report.'

'There's another investigation I'm working upon. I believe your brother might have been of assistance had he been alive still.'

Reid's nose twitched as if he had scented something unpleasant. 'Special Branch have also been in touch with me. They wanted to go over the security ramifications of Sammy's death. They're not unduly concerned.'

'Who were you speaking to?'

'A detective called Irwin. He seemed busy. At least, busier than you, that is.'

'Special Branch are always busy,' said Daly. Whenever Irwin popped up one step ahead of him, he wondered what it was he was not meant to see or hear.

'Your brother made several phone calls to the police over the past month complaining about a nearby traveller camp. He was fearful for his life. Why would that have been?'

'I wish I knew.' Reid's eyes watched Daly, compact and still.

'He never revealed why the travellers were targeting him or what personal questions they were asking him?'

'Paranoia is not my speciality, Inspector. Don't involve me in whatever it is you're speculating.'

'But you are involved, Mr Reid. The dead man was your brother.'

The troubled look passed across Reid's features again. 'To tell you the truth, Inspector, Sammy had become a stranger to me these past few weeks.'

'Was he ill?'

'Not ill, just haunted.' He cleared his throat. 'Possessed by those travellers, I might say. Instead of just bloody ignoring the camp and waiting for the authorities to get rid of them, he grew obsessed with their presence. All these years, he was used to just his own company, you see. The travellers had camped so close to his farm. He thought their idleness was proof they were plotting against him, that something terrible was going to happen.'

'What do you mean plotting against him?'

Reid shrugged. 'He was protective of the land. It was embedded in him, a part of his blood. He feared they had come to prise him away from his fields.'

'When did you last talk?'

'A few nights ago.'

'How did he seem?'

'Confused. Full of dark fears.'

'What type of fears?'

Reid let out a pensive sigh. 'I don't know. I pretended to understand him, showed him sympathy, but his rambling got worse.' He leaned back in the sofa and stared hard at Daly. 'I want you to understand something, Inspector, something that's important to good Protestant farmers like Sammy.' He pointed to the green screen of an ancient-looking television in the corner. 'My brother lived in the past. He never changed anything in the house. Not even that TV. Now he's gone the house will be a burden to me.' He let the words hang in the air. 'Sammy will be happier if I just let the place fall apart. Like so many Protestant farms in this part of the country.'

'Why not sell up, give it to someone who'll look after it?'

Reid grimaced. He looked at Daly with an expression that combined sadness and embitterment. 'Protestants are leaving this part of the border all of the time. Not just the young and the very old, but entire families, without ever putting their homes up for sale. They'd rather they rot back into the ground than sell up.'

Daly looked confused. The property market along the border was an arcane and mysterious world, but surely there were buyers somewhere. 'House prices are on the up again,' he said. 'And land is always highly sought after. Why wouldn't they make some quick money out of their inheritance?'

'The Troubles may be over, Inspector, but what we have now is a hidden war, with farms like this one the new front line. Republicans are buying up land all the time, flush with money from fuel and cigarette smuggling.' Reid sighed. 'Soon they'll own all the farms on both sides of the border. They won't stop until they drive the Protestant people off the face of this country.'

The wind swirled under the door, making it creak on its hinges. It whispered through cracks and crevices in the farmhouse, unsettling the fine dust that covered the dark furniture and the ashes that lay in the cold hearth. Daly wondered if Sammy's ghost was planning to linger about the place, eager to oversee the slow decline of the house, rather than let it fall into the wrong hands. He stared through the window at the sombre hinterland of the border, full of shadows and bedraggled-looking trees, the darkness of the hedges and slanting fields thickening into a mist that seemed to rise into the air like a poisonous vapour, with nothing stirring in it, only the solitary shape of a crow rising and then sinking back into the thorns.

'If I put this place up for sale, my bidders will be former paramilitaries, IRA godfathers, retired gunmen,' said Reid. 'It's a matter of survival, Inspector. My people are being threatened with extinction.' He stared out of the window as though the landscape were a property balance sheet with terrifying black columns rising against him. The door rattled in its frame, incapable of holding back the wind and the ghosts of a generation of Protestants.

He glanced back at Daly, to check if he was following the story. For a persuasive politician who had held the attention of crowds, Reid seemed weak on eye contact when it came to one-to-one communication. He rose to his feet and beckoned Daly to follow him.

'You might get a better understanding of my brother's state of mind if I show you round the place.'

He took Daly on a guided tour of the farm, as though it was some sort of monument, heavy with the weight of history. Certainly, Daly found the place oppressive. The wind strengthened, unsettling the trees that bordered the outhouses, lifting their heavy branches, agitating the twigs. Reid's face looked raw and strangely elated in the cold air. A form of emptiness radiated from his watery eyes, magnified by the pride and fear he felt surveying the bleak landscape.

He guided Daly through the yard and to the burnt remnants of an outhouse.

'Another sign of poor Sammy's carelessness,' he said. 'He let this shed go up in flames earlier in the week.'

Daly surveyed the charred timbers, the blackened hay and, beyond, the backdrop of ruin. The rankness of mud and decay, and the wildness of the hedges were advancing from all sides.

'Weren't you worried about your brother? Living on his own, so far away from his neighbours?'

'My brother could defend himself, so I wasn't unduly worried. Between you and me, he still had my old army rifle and a box full of ammunition. He kept it in good condition, polished to a shine, ready to use if trouble visited him.' He grinned at Daly's look of alarm. 'In this part of the world, we're farmers at times of peace, members of a staunch militia when there's violence.'

He showed Daly the ladder that his brother had climbed before his death, and the collapsed bales of hay that had failed to cushion his fall. Daly walked back and forth, inspecting the scene. He checked the sturdiness of the ladder and began climbing it. Reid stood still and waited. When Daly returned he was carrying a loose length of binder twine, which he showed to Reid.

'I found this loosely holding one of the bales on top. Someone has sliced through it with a knife.'

A transformation overcame Reid's face as he studied the

cut twine. The wild eyes stared at Daly again and then at the twine, as he tried to work out what had happened on the night of his brother's death. His mouth gaped open and his eyes blazed in a moment of intensity. Daly realized that the politician was staring at him with an expression of mortal terror. Slowly Reid recovered his poise, his eyes flicking around the hateful circumstances of his brother's demise until they rested by default on a pair of crows attacking some rotten sacking in the nearby barn. The wind picked up, lifting the sacking into the air and unsettling the birds.

'The twine leaves an unanswered question,' said Daly. 'Who cut it?'

'I can't help you with that one.'

'But it's making you think.'

'I already told you that Sammy was growing confused and preoccupied. He might have cut it himself.'

'How can you be satisfied with that answer? Shouldn't your doubt make you more determined to find out how exactly he fell to his death?'

Reid's press officer stuck her head around the corner and flashed him a warning look. The politician walked after her. Daly put the piece of twine in his jacket pocket – a loose end in more than one sense. He doubted that Reid knew who had cut the twine, or whether or not his brother's death had been the result of sabotage. However, he had an inkling that the politician knew more than he was letting on. He would have liked to peer into Reid's mind and into that of his brother, but how do you access the secrets locked away in the heads of political heavyweights and their dead relatives?

In an effort to take control of the conversation, Reid began reminiscing about the past. The gates clanged at the bottom of the yard with a mad musical discord that made the pigs squeal in their enclosure.

'My brother and I grew up herding pigs on this land,' announced Reid. He looked on firmer ground with his press officer flanking him. 'In those days, travellers passing through were likely to steal a pig or a few hens. We used to climb a tree at the bottom of the lane and wait for them with our father's shotgun. That was when we learned to handle a weapon. Then when I was eighteen, I left and joined the army. We had to protect our people and our property against IRA gun attacks, midnight ambushes, car bombs, snipers...' A burdened look came over his face. His tired eyes blinked as though trying to rein in an inner vision. 'Later I got into politics, while Sammy stayed at home with these black hills and the herd of pigs.'

The wind hushed and the storm in the trees fell away.

'My brother believed he had enemies, but he never told me their names.'

'Did they belong to the IRA or some criminal group? Someone from the past?'

Reid shrugged. 'He said it was "them people down there". He never said who they were or where exactly "down there" was. I assumed he was talking about the travellers.' He stared at Daly with a look of impatience. 'He's being buried tomorrow. The faster you get your work cleared up the better for all of us.'

'This other investigation that I'm working upon, it's to do with the disappearance of a boy.'

Reid looked at him shrewdly. 'And you think the travellers are to blame?'

'The same ones who'd been harassing your brother. We're questioning a man called Thomas O'Sullivan.'

The mention of the name brought about another visible reaction in Reid's face. His eyes were luminous under the gloom of the sky as he stared and stared at the detective, paralysed by fear. The moments passed. Whatever Daly hoped to get out of the interview, it was not his intention to terrify the politician into this state of abject silence.

'Do you know the name?'

Eventually Reid recovered. 'No, not at all.' He pursed his lips primly. 'I suggest you keep that investigation as far away from my doorstep as possible. We don't want the press making the wrong connections and stirring up suspicions about the travelling community. Lord knows, they've suffered enough down through the years.'

'Your brother's complaints are a logical place to start. He may have met the people behind the boy's disappearance. Perhaps the camp was hiding a dangerous predator, someone trying to avoid detection.'

Reid grimaced. 'My brother never gave me a list of suspicious individuals, if that's what you're hoping to get.' He strode off. 'Be very careful how you proceed with this case, Inspector,' he said.

The politician's voice was calm and cordial, masking the threat, but the edge of menace still showed through. Daly could see that Reid was a seasoned negotiator. His mind was sharp and ranged far beyond this closet of grief, the bleak farm, and his brother's vacant life, like a falcon scouting the paths that lay ahead.

'Remember, Sammy's death was an accident,' said Reid.

'Nothing to make a fuss about. These things happen to elderly farmers all the time.'

'When a person dies after threats are made against him, then naturally there will be suspicions.'

This time Reid flashed Daly a look of irritation. 'I wish I could help you more, Inspector,' he said. 'Right now I have to bury my brother. In the meantime, I'd be obliged if you would keep me informed of your investigation.'

'It's very likely that I will need to ask you more questions at some point in the future.'

'I'll do my best to answer them,' he said stiffly, before leading Daly back to his car. A cold glint appeared in his eyes. 'The more I think about it, the more I believe Sammy's death was an abomination.' He leaned close to Daly. 'It was wrong for him to die in this way.'

'What do you mean?'

'To die out of carelessness. It seems more of a sin against God and nature.'

Daly watched Reid through his rear-view window as he drove away. The fêted politician with his press officer skulking at the back door, and his BMW waiting for him. He looked like the temporary caretaker of a doomed building, eager to flee back to his gilded world, where political success would whisk him away from the troubling burdens of the past.

Daly sought a shortcut back to the motorway, travelling through a series of border villages that were like garrison points, the derelict Protestant churches with their Union flags anchoring each stronghold amid streets of humble-looking shops and houses. He glanced at the broken silhouettes of abandoned police stations and the military fortifications that had once given these communities a sense of political prestige, but now, with the Troubles over, they looked in a much worse predicament. Their world was dying and these abandoned police stations and churches were icons of their extinction, whose ruin they were doomed to follow.

Daly drove on. He did not know if he was on the right track to get back to Lough Neagh. The landscape changed around him. The vague malaise that hung over the interlocking border parishes, the sense of a history and a people in flux, evaporated. The trees and little farmhouses seemed more rooted in place, contented and sane. The road veered south, and for miles there were no turns left or right. At first, he did not understand what the road meant. Why this melancholy feeling that it promised deliverance, a safe passage to a land without fracture or fraught history? He tried to get a grip on his surroundings but could not work out where he was.

He stopped the car, rolled down the window and listened to the hushed countryside. Which country was he in? Northern Ireland or the Republic, north or south? He drove back the way he had come. He passed a white X daubed in the middle of the road. It was a warning sign for army helicopters, marking where the United Kingdom of Great Britain and Northern Ireland ended. Inadvertently, he had slipped over the border into a different police jurisdiction, a different state, but somehow, deep down, he had known that he was leaving behind the wounded landscape of the North, where a frozen peace had covered over the troubling secrets of the past.

He found his way to the motorway and drove homewards, deep in thought. Back at his cottage, the wind had knocked his gate ajar and blown old leaves and twigs into the porch. The sound of crows settling down to roost formed a raucous backdrop to the silence of his home. There was no sign of his hen anywhere.

Entering the cottage, he heard a banging noise from the darkness within. He felt uneasy, detecting a chill in the air, a sense of trespass. He stepped around the shadowy furniture and found his torch. He flashed the light about and rested the beam at the trapdoor to the attic, watching spellbound as it shuddered with regular thuds as if a trapped and desperate intruder were jumping up and down upon it. He waited. The black hen crept in behind him, leaving muddy marks on the floor. He stared down at her and she looked straight back at him with unblinking eyes, as if to ask: What secrets have you kept hidden up there, what ghosts have you locked away from view? The trapdoor shook with even greater force, and the hen, startled into flight, stabbed itself at possible escape routes in the darkness. Daly found a sweeping brush and gingerly used the shaft to push open the trapdoor. It fell back with a bang and a strong breeze wafted on to Daly's face. He stuck his head through and found the attic was empty. However, a large hole had appeared in the roof, through which the wind was blowing fiercely.

He crept under the rafters and inspected the extent of the damage. The action of repeated storms and roosting birds had been to blame, he surmised. He could see where the rain had also got in, forming a serpentine track of damp and mould along the attic floor. The bitter stench of decay filled his nostrils. He grimaced. He had too many things on his mind to deal with organizing repairs. It would probably mean moving out and living in a caravan on site while workers replaced the roof and fixed the ceiling. The house also needed insulating and replastering in places. The idea of the disruption left him feeling tired and depressed.

Later, lying on his bed, listening to the rain falling outside and leaking through the roof, he understood why, year after year, he had put off the idea of renovating the cottage or moving out completely. How could he rid himself of the one security he had left in his life, his link with the past and his parents? And now he risked losing even that, the very roof over his head. He had sentenced himself to be a prisoner of the house's slow decay and collapse, unable to leave its cramped warren of rooms. He closed his eyes and tried to imagine a future in a brand-new house, one filled with the sound of playing children, but instead of reassuring him, his thoughts plunged him into a deeper anxiety. Whenever he willed his mind to dream up a more fulfilling life for himself, he kept returning to the same image. He saw himself trapped within the hedges of his father's farm, confused and wandering, not knowing what age he was, whether he was a man or a boy, a troubled detective running after a wayward hen or a grieving child still searching for his dead mother.

The rain stopped and the wind picked up, churning through the trees that overshadowed the cottage. Daly's mind settled eventually, listening to the branches toiling in the storm. The big oak tree in the garden sounded as though it was carrying an impossible load, its branches groaning with the force of the wind. He drifted off, thinking about his childhood, remembering lying on his little bed at night, his hands clasped behind his head, listening to the same trees lashing in the darkness. He had a sudden longing for the simplicity of those days, his boyish thoughts floating up, carefree and adventurous, with the sound of the tireless branches, all his adult worries and doubts drifting away, disappearing into another country entirely. His final thought, before he was carried off to sleep by the flights of his boyhood imagination, was what would his mother and father make of his absence when they awoke in the morning?

CHAPTER SIXTEEN

Jack Hewson woke in the cold caravan after a poor night's sleep. The traveller dogs that had been so friendly and docile during the day had barked viciously all night long, haunting his dreams with images of fanged mouths and wolf-like eyes. For a while, he lay under the heavy duvet, listening for sounds from the encampment as the dawn light crept under the curtains. A smell he had never experienced before filled his nostrils. The smell of outdoor skin and hair exposed to the sun and rain, a fugitive sense of not belonging that wafted through the cramped bedroom, and something else, darker and more thrilling: the scent of trespass. He thought about home, his bedroom packed with toys, gadgets and books, the enclosed walls, and the silent rooms below where his mother paced every evening, waiting for his father to return. Everything was different about his new abode, not least the fact that he had several sleeping companions.

He parted the curtains so he could see them more clearly. The arms of the other boys were brown and freckled, entangled together. He listened to their regular breathing, feeling envious of their easy sleep. From what he was able to understand, they were all brothers and cousins, nestled together, their bodies realigning in sleep with occasional kicks and groans. He had never before seen so many children share the one bed. This was his new family now, a ramshackle tribe hiding in a lonely corner of the border countryside. How long would he be able to stay with them? he wondered. How long before the police caught up with them?

Too unsettled to return to sleep, he slid from the bed and slipped out of the caravan. All was quiet outside. The travellers had parked along a dark winding lane that did not look as though it was going anywhere. Beyond the caravans, a mouldy-looking path disappeared into a pine forest. He walked past the slumbering dogs that now resembled perfectly behaved house pets. The only traveller awake was an old woman, who had been filling a black kettle with water from the river. When she saw him creep out of the camp, she blocked his path and grabbed him by the arm. Her dark eyebrows twisted across her wrinkled face, and a slight scent of urine wafted from her clothes. She squatted down in front of him, her lips hissing in anger, her eyes agitated.

'I know why you're here,' she whispered in a venomous voice. 'You've come to curse us all.' She cuffed him over the head. 'I'm taking you back to your own people, where you belong.'

He broke free from her grasp and ran into the forest. He hurried along a faint path, checking that she was not following, and eventually slowed to a rest. The darkness amid the pine trees was tinged with his fear over what the day might hold. However, in spite of his anxiety, the morning felt more complete than any he had experienced in the company of his mother and father. The path resonated with mystery. This was the first time he had seen dawn breaking in a forest and he was awe-struck. He breathed in with relish, wading through deep shadows dappled with light that resembled an otherworldly path hovering above the actual trail. He hauled himself over the slippery trunk of a fallen tree into a secret patch of sunbeams. No one knows I am here, he thought. No one can see me. I am safe. His third night away from home was over, and he wondered with anticipation what adventures the forest might bring him.

The path joined a stream and then parted ways, breaking up in places with large rocks and the humps of old roots. His feet stumbled into crevices draped with spiders' cobwebs. The gauze of sunlight hovering in the air fought with a deeper darkness below. In the contrast of shades, he found it difficult to make out the path. At one point, he saw a dark shadow detach itself from the columns of tree trunks, but he looked away and hurried on. The air was damp, filled with a mossy smell and the sound of hidden streams gurgling through the pine roots.

He walked on, feeling hungry. He had not had breakfast and his belly felt cold. He began to think of when he might see his mother and father again. At first light, the forest had felt like a refuge, but now, the more he thought about home, the more it began to feel like a trap, a maze to stop him from finding the way back to his parents. He stopped and, for a long while, looked behind at the route he had taken, memorizing every detail in case he got lost. He contemplated the possibility of finding his way home, thinking that somewhere beyond the forest the police would be roaming the roads along with his mother and father, searching desperately for him.

The sight of a gypsy teenager resting against a fallen-down tree startled him, even though the youth was gazing at him in an unthreatening manner. Jack looked all around, scanning the rows of tree trunks. If there were others, he could see no trace of them, but for all he knew, the forest could be hiding hundreds of invisible travellers in its gloom. The teenager smoked the butt of a cigarette, pulling a face as he took each drag, all the time gazing at the boy. The mirage of a path gleaming in the air disappeared, leaving Jack with a sense of abandonment. He approached the youth slowly, feeling the forest darken, the tentacles of its shadows reaching out towards him, a chilly spasm shooting through his body.

'This isn't the road, Jack,' said the traveller with a smile.

'I don't think I'm ready for the road,' he replied.

'Not ready for the road? Of course you are,' said the traveller patiently. 'Think of all the adventure that's ahead of us. No more school and no more rules. We're going to follow the road until our shoes fall to tatters.'

'I'm worried where it will take me. I want to go home now.'

'Don't worry, Jack. The road always takes you home, no matter how long you spend travelling it.'

There was a mysterious purposefulness about the young traveller, which eased Jack's worries about being so far from his parents. He shuddered with a thrill of dread, remembering what the youth had promised him the night before.

The youth stroked the back of his head. 'I think it's time we headed back, Jack. Cousins and uncles have travelled from all corners of the country to meet you. We've a little surprise planned for you. A ceremony will take place later today and you're our special guest.'

Jack nodded his head. He did not know what the ceremony was, but he knew that his real life was starting now, his life without his mother and father. They turned back together and kept walking until they reached the camp. The others had risen and wisps of smoke curled from a campfire. A naked toddler sat on a caravan step, crying inconsolably, his sobs shaking his plump little body. No one was paying him any attention. The child's wail rose, piercing the air, and then subsided.

Jack found himself a place at the fire. His sleeping companions from the caravan sat down beside him, wedging him in so tightly he could barely move. More children joined them. He stayed alert and quiet within the growing horde, hoping that his fear would recede. A gang of men circled the boys, sombre-faced and powerful. More men arrived, casting furtive glances at Jack. He caught their stares and glanced away. Everywhere he turned, he was blocked. What did the men know about him that he did not know himself? What was the secret that he held but did not know how to deliver to this strange race of people?

CHAPTER SEVENTEEN

The housing estate had its own eyes, dozens of them, hostile and reflective, gazing skywards as Daly drove by slowly, the windows of brand-new homes built too close for his comfort, walling him in as he searched for number 38, the residence of the Hewsons. The moment he awoke that morning, he had decided he needed to speak to the couple as soon as possible. Not that he had any good news to relay about their missing son, but the question marks over Reid's death had given him a shiver of anxiety for the couple's safety. He felt a strong need to check that they were coping with the emotional strain, and that they were generally safe and well.

It was a new estate, constructed during the boom, when builders packed houses on to cramped sites to meet the insatiable demand for property. Slender threads of front lawn were the only green spaces, unravelling into a wilderness of rubble and stagnant marsh at the bottom of the estate. Many of the houses looked unoccupied, homes with no insides, thought Daly as the reflection of his car ghosted along their windows. His experience of living in his father's run-down cottage had taught him that inherited houses were animate things, capable of cursing or blessing their occupants. The spirit of the past never faded away in an old house, rather it mustered in its nooks and crannies, ready to pour forth at unexpected moments. By comparison, these new homes were sturdy and bright and packed with mod cons, free of the ghosts of the past. However, Daly seriously doubted if he would ever settle happily in one of them.

There did not seem to be anyone at number 38. After ringing the bell and knocking on the door, Daly took out his mobile phone and tapped in their landline number, which rang and rang. He tried Rebecca's mobile and, after a few ring tones, someone answered but did not speak. Daly said hello. There was a moment of silence, followed by a sigh and then the clearing of a throat. The line went dead. Daly rang again but this time the phone went straight to an answer message. He tried Harry's mobile but all he got was the sound of static. His sense of anxiety increased.

He rang the landline again, and this time it was engaged. Convinced that at least one of the couple was at home, he rang the doorbell repeatedly and shouted their names through the letterbox.

Eventually, Rebecca came to the door, looking thinner and frailer than at their previous meeting. She had guessed from the look on his face that he had no positive news to bring. Her eyes appeared set behind glass, wary as she led Daly wordlessly through a hallway and into a comfortable living room, suffused with the light of discreetly placed lamps.

'I take it you still haven't found him, Inspector,' she said.

'Not yet,' he replied. She gestured for him to take a seat by the window.

'Then have you come with news about my husband?' Her voice hinted at bitterness and loneliness.

Her question stumped him. 'Why? What's happened?'

'He's decided to run out on me,' she said flatly. 'I've been ringing his phone all morning but there's no answer. He packed his stuff in a camper van and left as soon as we came home from the police station.'

'Why would he leave you at this time?'

She almost laughed. 'My guess is that he's hiding some-where along the border. He often takes himself off there.'

'Did he say when he'd be back?'

'No.'

'That sounds very odd, given what has happened.'

'Odd if you don't know Harry. He gets agitated from time to time and has to be on his own.'

'What about his personal documents, did he take them with him? Passport, driving licence, that sort of thing.'

'Yes.'

'His mobile phone and any other devices?'

'Gone, too.'

Rebecca sounded genuinely confused by the abruptness of her husband's departure. How well did she really know him? he wondered. What was parenthood but a man and a woman lit up by the flickering light of the children between them? Take the children away, and sometimes all that remained were two strangers staring at each other across a void.

'I've contacted his editor at the *Irish News*. He said Harry had been made redundant about a year ago, and since then he'd done some freelance work but nothing in the past six months. I rang every other newspaper I thought he worked for but none of them had heard of him, never mind employed him.'

'He'd kept this secret from you?'

'I only suspected something was wrong after Jack was taken.' There was a bitter edge to her voice. 'Whatever he's been doing all these months, it wasn't journalism. I challenged him after we came home from the station, but he just kept on packing.'

Daly nodded and struggled to think of something sympathetic to say. 'How many of us question what our partner says about their job? It's the last thing we expect to be lied to about.'

'Harry always took his profession so seriously. I thought he was committed to the truth.'

But not to his nearest and dearest, thought Daly. 'What did he do for money?'

'He always seemed to have enough. He mentioned something about an advance from a publisher for a book he was researching.' She flashed a fierce look at Daly, a woman wronged. 'I don't know what to think now – perhaps even that was a lie. What does it all mean, Inspector?'

'It means perhaps you shouldn't judge him so harshly because he couldn't tell you he'd lost his job.'

Her eyes glanced away from Daly's stare, her mind elsewhere. 'Before he left, he told me something. He thought he knew the people behind Jack's abduction.'

'How might he have known them?'

'Through work.'

'But he didn't work. His career as a journalist was over.'

'He told me that his work might have been the reason why Jack disappeared.'

'Then he must have meant that he was responsible, personally. Did he tell you how?'

'This book he was working on. It was about the history of the travellers during the Troubles.'

Daly raised an eyebrow. 'What sort of history?'

'How they suffered during the conflict. Intimidated and abused by both sides, with no one to protect their rights or ensure they had access to justice.'

Daly considered the possibility that Hewson had been unravelling a dangerous secret within the travelling community. If it was true, the abduction might make sense as a scare tactic, a warning for him to desist from his research. At the very least, it backed him into a corner.

'He told me he'd spent the last month interviewing travellers and studying library archives of the Troubles. I asked him what was so important that it made him ignore his family and his proper job, but all he said was that he was on to something important.'

'Did he give any hint as to how dangerous it was?'

'His job was about asking awkward questions, he always told me. Sometimes he offended powerful people.'

'Did you ever see this book he was working on?'

'He said he was writing a first draft, but when I asked to see it he couldn't produce a single page. He explained that he'd yet to commit it to paper. However, he'd written it in his head, and any day now he was going to type it all up. I saw files of newspaper cuttings, maps of the border, and journals, but he hadn't written a word of what they all meant.' She made his writerly failure seem like a further act of betrayal. 'When I went looking for his papers yesterday, they were gone.'

'What about his computer?'

'He used a laptop which he kept locked in his camper van. He'd been living out of it for the past month.'

'Perhaps this story he was working on was so dangerous he had to hide it.'

'Hide it? From who?' She frowned at Daly.

'From his family. From you.'

'Why would he do that?'

'To protect you and your son from the truth.'

'But why dig up something so dangerous in the first place?'

Her voice, the emotion in it, penetrated his professional defences. With her dark hair and green eyes, he realized how much she resembled his mother. Hers was a younger and more alluring face than the one he remembered from his childhood, but still the resemblance was there. Not just in her looks but in the way she carried herself and sat at the edge of her seat, her composure, her obstinate wariness, the signs of worry that appeared at the corners of her mouth. He hadn't noticed it before, or had blanked it out, but now the similarity was manifest in the intimate setting of her living room. The resemblance impeded him, distracting him from the questions he needed to ask. The sound of her anxious breathing seemed to fill the room. He could sense her inner turmoil, but the signal that drowned out everything else was the memory of another woman.

Rebecca sighed and gazed at him with a look of curiosity. There was his mother's face again, or a more intense version of it, oppressing him through the proximity of another woman's sadness. A tide of emotions flowed within him. What loss did he want to bury in this young woman's searching eyes, and in the warm darkness of her hair? He was afraid to look away from her face in case the huge gallery of his memories welled up and filled the rest of the room.

With a shudder of annoyance, he pulled himself together. Rebecca had told him that her husband was researching something dangerous, but what? A powerful truth that had activated dormant forces, old monsters from the Troubles. Her son abducted and now her husband disappears. What did that chain of events signify? The common denominator was the travellers. What was it about the past that Hewson could not discuss with his wife? Why, in the first place, had he kept up the pretence that he was still employed as a journalist?

'What about his family?' he asked. 'Have they been in touch?'

'There is no family.' She sat erect and tense in her chair.

'Everyone has a family.'

'Harry was an only child. Both his parents are dead. He never mentioned other relatives.'

'Has anyone else tried to get in touch with him? A friend or colleague?'

She shrugged her shoulders in a way that seemed to suggest every question he might ask was futile, that Harry Hewson's entire life had been an impenetrable fiction.

'Someone called Caroline rang a few times,' she said eventually.

'Did she say what she wanted?'

Rebecca hesitated. 'She mentioned something about an old

police investigation concerning a missing traveller girl, and that Harry hadn't answered her calls. I really didn't want to ask her for more details.'

'Why?'

'She sounded concerned about him. I was afraid of catching my husband in another lie.'

She had given Daly an opening for a more delicate question.

'How were things between the two of you?'

Hewson's disappearance fitted one of Daly's theories. If a separation was imminent between the couple, then the husband might have arranged the abduction and had now joined their son. When Rebecca did not speak, he probed gently: 'It's usual for a couple undergoing trauma to experience relationship difficulties.'

'It's usual', she said in a cold voice, 'for a husband to tell his wife the truth. He told me so many lies and half-truths I'm not sure where the reality begins.'

'Do you think something has happened to him?'

'I'm not sure. So much of his life was kept secret.'

'Yes.'

She seemed to realize that her husband might have been plotting something in the weeks prior to Jack's disappearance. 'Do you believe he might have been behind Jack going missing?' She tried to blink away fear.

'There is no evidence to support that theory,' said Daly. Nevertheless, he was glad she had brought up the possibility.

'But not much to discount it either?' she said.

Daly nodded. The question was what sort of plot determined that the boy should disappear first, and in such unusual circumstances?

Rebecca looked about her with an expression of eerie panic, as though the interview with Daly had displaced her from her familiar surroundings. A burst of sunlight came through the living-room window, sharpening the look of anxiety on her face. He stared at her blankly. He opened his mouth to say something but closed it again, not because he was unsure what to say, but because the ray of light had changed her face into another woman's. He must be mad, he thought. Perhaps he was suffering from some sort of premature senility. The way the memory of his mother's face seemed to resurface in bits and pieces, the flash of her eyes, the wave of her hair, but as soon as he homed in on the similarities, the image disintegrated.

It struck him how much he had tried to remember as little as possible of his mother's face, avoiding any thought or conversation that might trigger a recollection, as if that would accelerate the oblivion to which he had consigned many of the murder victims he had encountered in his career as a detective. Ever since he had unravelled the complicated circumstances of her death, he had fought to keep her free-floating face from entering his consciousness. In spite of all his precautions, Rebecca's face had sought him out on the afternoon of her son's disappearance. He should have closed his eyes and ears to her, ignored her imploring request, kept himself hooded and hidden in the depths of the courthouse.

'Are you all right?'

Rebecca's voice sounded far away.

'Yes.' Had she noticed the depth of his distraction?

'Is there something you can't tell me?'

'No. Why do you ask?'

'You look as if your mind is elsewhere. You must tell me what you know.'

He sighed. 'I know very little about your husband, but I intend to find out more. To tell you the truth, I am concerned for your safety. First your child disappears and now your husband. You are the only one left that is connected to them. Is there anyone you can stay with, family or friends?'

She moved her shoulders, gesturing resignation. 'This is my home, our home. I can't leave it now.' She expressed it without emotion, an incontrovertible fact.

Daly had one final question to ask her before he left. 'That day in the court, when your son was taken, why did you come to me?'

She looked at him in surprise, as though the answer was obvious. 'Because you were there.'

'But why pick me out of all the police officers and security staff? And the previous time, when you needed someone to look after the shoplifter's baby. Why me that day?'

'Because you have a caring face. Because your eyes looked at me, clear and straight.'

Daly got up to leave. Her answer had been too personal and she seemed to regret saying it. At the door, he said, 'If your husband returns or you manage to make contact with him, let me know immediately.'

She nodded, her eyes lingering upon his with something like reproach. He had failed to rescue her; instead, he had brought her a new terror neither of them could explain.

CHAPTER EIGHTEEN

It was a dream-like morning in a strange place full of smoke and flames. The barefooted boy beside Jack tested the hot embers of the fire with his grubby toes and then wriggled them in the ashes like worms. The other children were half-asleep, docile and resting their heads against each other, unconcerned by the increasing tension in the air. Slowly, the gypsy men gathered around the fire in a circle of makeshift seats, upturned buckets with planks across them, wooden crates, half-crippled chairs, even a rusted birdcage. So dignified were their attitudes and postures, they might have been lowering themselves on to marble plinths. Some of them had fashioned crosses from rough pieces of wood and rushes, and erected them near the fire. The effect was sinister, suggesting that the huddled throng belonged to a lost corner of a superstitious religion.

Jack had expected unusual robes, ancient symbols, or ornate statues for the ceremony, but the men had brought nothing else with them, and were dressed in their everyday clothing, their faces sullen, unshaven, and downcast. The only thing that suggested the ritual was about to begin, or had already started, was the silence, so grave that it hung in the air, heavier than the grey smoke drifting from the fire and through which their eyes glimmered and watched Jack.

A rooster crowed and the nearby roar of someone trying to start a motorbike punctuated the air. A shower of sparks rose to the pale blue sky that only a few hours ago had seemed to promise Jack a world washed clean of fear.

One of the older gypsies leaned towards his ear. 'You're a brave little bastard,' he said with a dangerous smile. Through his opened shirt cuffs, Jack could see an ugly set of tattoos roping the sinews of his muscular arms. He squeezed the boy's neck. 'You have to stay in sight. We must be ready to move camp at a moment's notice. The country folk and their police are on edge. If they find you, they'll lock us all up.'

The man had a thickset neck, and his head moved tightly, peering at Jack's face like a turtle's.

'What were you doing, skulking in the forest?'

Jack tried to squirm away.

'Next time you try to run away, we'll lock you in the boot of a car.'

A voice leaned towards his other ear. Another man with a sodden moustache, shirtless in the morning sun, his body oily and hairy. 'Why did you run away, Jack?' he asked.

He did not know there had to be a reason.

'Don't you understand why you're here?'

'No.'

'Your father has been asking some very dangerous

questions. Putting pressure on powerful people. It's better you stay with us, for your own safety.'

But he had two parents to protect him and a safe home. Why did he need more protection? The men began whispering together, their cheeks flushed and their eyes glinting.

'What are we going to do with him?'

'The boy has the key.'

'The key to what?'

'The secret that will make us all rich.'

'He's the son of country people. He hasn't been initiated.'

'But he's only a child. He's not ready for the ceremony.'

'There are things he's not allowed to know.'

'What about the father? Shouldn't he be here, too?'

'We don't need the father; all we need is the boy. And his blood.' The speaker turned to Jack with a smirking face.

'This is a dark business you're getting us into,' said one of the men, spitting. 'The boy will get in the way. He'll make us hunted men.'

'Think of him as business,' said the one who seemed to be in charge. 'A new line in smuggled goods. What he can give us is more valuable than lorryloads of cigarettes and alcohol.'

The leader began speaking softly in a language Jack did not understand. He wielded a bottle of spirits in the air and poured the contents on to the ground. The other men looked on with satisfaction as though an important part of the ritual had been conducted.

An old woman appeared through the smoke and squatted in front of the fire. Jack was sure he had never seen her before, but still she looked oddly familiar. She began scattering leaves and a fine black powder into the flames, all the time murmuring some sort of prayer or chant.

'Where are you?' shouted the old woman.

There was nothing in the air but dark trails of smoke and the light of the morning sun competing with the blazing fire.

'Where are you?'

The old woman grew more distressed. Someone should take her away, thought Jack. Stop her from burning herself in the flames.

'Where are you?' She stared about her with a blind look of grief, her eyes begging for release.

'Who are you searching for?' asked one of the men in a strangely disembodied voice.

'I'm searching for my daughter,' she shouted back, her voice cracking with emotion. Tears streamed down her soot-covered cheeks. One of the children next to Jack stared at him through the smoke. He had the disquieting feeling that he was on the brink of some great danger. The child's eyes seemed to be trying to warn him.

'Those dark shadows, it's her.' The leader was looking at the smoke in a weird way, his features hard and impersonal.

'Who?' asked one of his companions.

'Her spirit.'

'Who is she?'

A crow hovered out of the leaden air, croaked and then disappeared.

'The young woman those bastards murdered.' The gypsy's voice was hoarse, barely audible.

Jack struggled to his feet, alarmed by the conversation, the growing intensity of the fire, and the overwhelming cloud of smoke. Soot settled like thick black powder on his legs and arms. The ceremony was beyond him; beyond anything he had experienced or could understand.

'Don't go anywhere, son,' said one of the men behind him, placing his meaty hands on his shoulders and neck.

'They took her away and attacked her,' said the gypsy leader. 'When they came back they said she had ran off and disappeared. Those bastards killed her but never owned up to it.'

Jack's throat burned with the smoke. He did not want to hear any more, but the hands had him clamped in place. He huddled closer to the other boys, feeling the men's eyes boring into his back. He could not bear the fear that rose within him. The comforting nearness of the traveller children's skinny bodies was the only refuge he had left. Ashes swarmed out of the blaze like plump white grubs and his eyes began to stream with the sting of smoke.

'May God take away her killers' strength and pleasure,' said the lead gypsy in a murderous voice. 'May sterility deprive them of children.'

'May the poisonous winds strike their bellies and make them ill with deadly diseases,' said another.

'May they die in horrible agony.'

'May the earth go red with their blood.'

Jack listened to the disconcerting flow of curses, his vision breaking up under the constant veil of smoke and heat. He tried to stand on his feet but immediately felt dizzy. The face of one of the travellers reeled towards him, his lips curling to reveal dark shiny gums and the stumps of blackened teeth. The air filled with the loud flapping noise of birds' wings, or was it people clapping in a frenzy?

'I see you, daughter. I'm following you now,' shouted the old woman. In a spurt of energy, she gathered up her skirts and disappeared into the smoke-filled forest. One by one, the circle of men rose, too, and followed her path.

'Your journey has finally begun,' someone whispered in Jack's ear and hauled him behind the procession. In his confusion, he thought he smelled his mother's perfume, the distant smell of home and safety. He found it hard to believe that the world of his parents still existed, that it had not been make-believe or a dream, as he stumbled into the cold hollows of the forest. He did not know his new family at all, or what they had planned for him at the end of this dangerous path, and he feared that by the time they returned he would never be able to find the traces of the way back home.

CHAPTER NINETEEN

The interview with Rebecca left Daly hungry, eager to find out more about the travellers and their connections with Harry Hewson. He had not felt so determined to succeed in months, but the intensity of the investigation and the lack of any firm leads as to Jack's whereabouts also left him vulnerable to old weaknesses, frailties that might break him: guilt, self-blame and his growing emotional attachment to the boy's distressed mother. He worried that it was his fault the team were no closer to finding the child. He wanted to galvanize his officers, make up for any lack of confidence they might have in him as a leader, feed them with as many clues and as much evidence as possible, forgetting in his worry that a good investigative team needed to be kept hungry and encouraged to think on their own.

Daly kept cajoling his team, hauling them through a blur of false leads and misinformation. There had been sightings of the boy reported as far away as Greece and Turkey. Spirits grew low and tempers short as the searches for the McGinns and their camper van became repetitive and exhausting.

To the detriment of his deteriorating mental state, Daly missed his first appointment with the police psychologist. He had been making good time on his way to see her in Armagh but deep down he had not been looking forward to her helpful interrogation. He had visited her six months before and remembered with a shudder the gentleness and patience of her questions, and how his mind, soaked in professional anxieties, had gripped convulsively at silence. She had gently urged his confession, his confidence, encouraging him to talk about the secrets of his heart, his past, his dreams, anything at all, while the real questions bunched up behind her, filling the silence like brooding ghosts. Questions like who are you? Can you be trusted? What makes you want to be a police detective after all you have discovered in your past? What exactly are your allegiances?

When he had come up with replies to her inquiries, his voice cut off before finishing, making his answers sound broken and child-like.

Thus, when he caught a glimpse of Rebecca Hewson in the graveyard of Maghery church, something made him pull his car into the church grounds and park by the gates. He did not mean to spy but a part of him felt powerfully drawn to the sight of her quick figure, roaming along the graveyard's grid of paths like a caged creature, unable to find a way out. So preoccupied was she that she failed to notice his car, or his hunched figure at the wheel. The sight of her downcast face turned his frustration over the slowness of the investigation into despair, as if he were personally responsible for her sadness. She paused, glanced at her watch and dashed through the doors of the church, as though she might suddenly be late for an appointment. At the holy water font, Daly saw her right hand glide across her chest and shoulders, more a gesture of personal reassurance than the act of blessing, as her head drooped forward. He felt a pang of compassion in his chest, contemplating the sinking weight of her sadness.

He fiddled with his ignition keys, shifted the gearstick in its socket. He ought to make tracks to see the therapist. After all, his attendance had been one of the requirements of his return to full duties, but instead, he slipped out of the car and into the darkness of the church as if drawn on a leash.

It was Lent, and the priest had just finished the Stations of the Cross. An elderly congregation with a few young mothers drifted out of the church. Daly lingered at the back while Rebecca took a pew close to the altar and knelt down, covering her face with her hands. Daly's eyes slipped away to the sides of the church and the pictures of Christ's suffering hanging on the walls. He stared at the face of Jesus, full of arresting passion, the eyes demanding promises that he could never keep. Not so different from Rebecca's gaze, he thought. How did one console someone in her predicament? he wondered. What use were reassuring words or false promises? All he could do was keep his silence in mute adoration, as if she were an apparition of grief, rather than a real woman of flesh and blood.

Rebecca glanced round, checking the empty pews behind her. Daly shifted sideways behind a large pillar, positioning himself as though he were playing a game of hide and seek. She was going through the difficult emotions of guilt and fear, and he felt he should not interfere. Sometimes, detective work was about making oneself invisible. He sat down and waited. The silence within the church felt strange, a towering emptiness. His eyes closed over, and his hearing reached out to the sound of her breathing, which came in rapid gasps. What did he detect in her breathlessness that so intrigued him? Not anxiety, something more like anticipation, as though she were awaiting some sort of revelation.

Trying to hide was what Daly normally did in church, anyway. He sat very still behind the broad pillar, keeping his eyes closed, trying to empty his mind. Was this not the best form of therapy? To make oneself disappear, empty oneself of every thought and attachment, and pretend that one no longer existed. He covered his eyes with his hands and began rubbing them. Like a hooded man, his mind reached out with his hearing, crossing the silent space of the church. A startlingly clear image of Rebecca's face popped into his mind, her dark eyebrows framing a pair of eyes flaring with emotion, her terrible but beautiful look of loss.

He would much rather stay here, he realized, than hurry to the psychologist's office, forced to spend the best part of an hour staring at the unchanging carpet, wrestling with the armour of his silence. *At least I can do this*, he thought, *listen intently rather than talk*. He was an expert in silences, and the refuge they provided for the troubled and guilt-stricken, and the church, like the courthouse, was full of those little spaces in which people could feel safely alone, even doubting souls like Daly, trapped in the no man's land between faith and scepticism. For a moment, he thought about returning to Mass to follow this year's Lenten rites. He glanced up at the Stations of the Cross, and the images of Christ's final hours of suffering. 'Come to me,' the imploring face of Jesus seemed to say to him. 'Turn your faithful attention back to me. I've been waiting all your adult life for your return. Stop putting it off.' But Daly remained resistant. His heart did not move. He stared at his watch and counted the minutes as they ticked by.

He thought of drawing closer to Rebecca's seat, perhaps a few pews behind. He hesitated and then thought better of it. She might be disturbed by the idea that he had followed her into church. He was about to leave when the click-clack of her heels echoing in the empty church made him freeze. Still hidden from view, he listened as she walked over to a side altar, and confidently inserted some coins into the candle box. He resisted the temptation to look around the stone pillar. After a while, she returned to her pew, the rhythm of her steps slowing a little, but sounding no less decisive, as though she was determined not to feel dejected. She began praying, her voice low and even, reciting a rosary of Hail Marys.

She broke into what sounded like a stifled cough, and then the tone of her voice changed. There was wildness in it, an intensity, as though she were having a whispered argument with someone. He thought he understood her emotional shift, the despair raging below the smooth surface. She stopped and, for the length of several heartbeats, the quietness in the church deepened. She seemed to have lost the ability to string another prayer together. He felt moved. Something in him wanted to throw himself upon her hungry silence and satisfy the maternal fear and guilt he detected there. He would have allowed her, in the wildness of her thwarted love for her son, to tear at his very bones, if it helped. But then another voice whispered back, startling Daly, in lower, slightly hoarse tones.

This time he did look round the pillar. An old traveller woman dressed in a shawl had knelt beside Rebecca, and the two of them were now engaged in a hushed conversation. Rebecca's voice grew louder, shakier, and some of her words became distinct.

'I don't want to know my future; I just want to know where my son is.'

'Different places... never the same twice.' The old woman's voice came to Daly in fragments. She was talking in riddles, trying to tell Rebecca something, but not daring to say it clearly.

'I don't understand why you need him.' Rebecca's whisper penetrated the silence of the church.

'He has a special gift... no ordinary boy.'

What gift was she referring to? wondered Daly. Clairvoyance, second sight? What need would the travellers have for a ten-year-old boy? What did he have to give that was so precious they had to take him away from his parents?

'Your husband has to tell you his part... the start of the story... A debt has never been settled.'

'But Harry has left me,' said Rebecca coldly. 'Oh God, I can't go through with this. You must let me see him.'

The old woman whispered something about a plan and the vital role that Jack would play in it. They were relying on her for the plan to run smoothly.

Daly stepped out from behind the pillar. Neither of them heard him, so engrossed were they in the conversation.

The elderly woman had risen to her feet, and Rebecca was holding on to her arm with a pleading look on her face.

'We're trying to help you,' said the old woman. 'Please let go.' She seemed intent on giving nothing else away. 'You'll get a phone call every second day.' There was a finality about her voice. 'Don't try to follow me or you'll risk your son's life.'

Daly watched her hurry up the central aisle towards the doors. Immediately, he saw right through her. He heard it, the false note ringing in her voice. He would have to follow her and forget about Rebecca for the moment. He slipped out of his pew and pursued her through the church doors. Almost immediately, she sensed his presence and quickened her pace. All trace of frailty and age seemed to vanish from her figure, her steps becoming firm and quick.

When Daly emerged, there was no sign of the old woman. She seemed to have miraculously disappeared. Then he heard the crunch of gravel and the squeak of a gate as she marched into the graveyard. He shouted for her to stop and she looked back, throwing him a sharp, shrewd glance before breaking into a run, gathering up her long skirts to reveal a pair of muddy trainers.

A mourner who'd been kneeling at a grave stood up and tried to block her path, but she sidestepped him, knocking against his shoulder. A slight collision, but enough to knock off her shawl and wig to reveal a much younger woman, running hard now, weaving her way through the jumble of gravestones. Daly vaulted the low wall and tried to cut her off before she reached the road, but getting his own legs to match her pace and agility was becoming problematic for him.

A white van swung alongside the boundary wall, and

speeded up beside the traveller woman. A beckoning arm reached out of the back of the vehicle and, with a sureness of feet that would have been breathtaking in a circus horse show, the woman leaped into the accelerating van. Within moments, a yawning gap opened up between Daly and the vehicle. Soon it was disappearing out of sight, leaving him a solitary figure standing in the middle of the road. He felt more bereft when he returned, out of breath, to the church and found that Rebecca was also leaving in a hurry. He glimpsed the whisk of her dark coat pulled after her as she slammed the car door shut. Oblivious to his panting presence, she drove off at speed.

Daly was about to take off after her when his mobile phone buzzed into life. It was Commander Sinclair.

'Daly? You never showed for your appointment.' Sinclair's voice was agitated.

Daly did not reply. He was trying to catch his breath.

'I've gone to a lot of bother, getting you back on this case and organizing a psychologist. Like it or not, you have to talk to her.'

Daly felt a weight return to his shoulders.

'You have another appointment for tomorrow morning. I want you to be there, without fail, understand?'

'Can't it wait?'

'Why? Has something come up? You sound out of breath.'

'No. Nothing has come up. I've just been running.'

'Let's be clear about this, Daly. No amount of running is going to help you resolve your problems. You have things to get off your chest and it's time you started telling your story.'

CHAPTER TWENTY

Rain had fallen on the travellers as they followed the hunched figure of the old woman through the forest, a drifting veil of drizzle reducing the path to a tangled trail of mud and slime. Jack had looked up through the breaks in the cloud for a glimpse of the sun but the murky glow overhead failed to thicken to a shine. The faces of the traveller men had been indistinct, too, averted from his anxious eyes, as they passed a bottle of whiskey around and spoke in whispers.

For about an hour, they picked their way over the slippery terrain of rocks and overgrown roots, the children stepping lightly, bouncing from rock to rock, while Jack plodded behind, pushed on by the traveller men. They wandered along the side of a fern-covered valley riddled with side streams that ran into a river glittering bleakly below. They passed under a pair of vast hollies bedecked with red berries. The old woman leaned her weight against the trees, sometimes running her hand along their bark, as though she were greeting old friends.

Eventually, they reached a dim and featureless cavern in the side of the hill. When his eyes adjusted to the greater gloom, Jack saw they had reached some sort of shrine to the Virgin Mary. He doubted that anyone had prayed there for a long time. The grotto did not feel like a holy refuge. The pale and peeling statue of Mary encased in its rocky crevice resembled a larval creature that had never taken wing. Below the statue, the stunted thorn trees appeared to be in bloom, but on closer examination, he saw that the skeletal branches were adorned with pieces of string and glistening fabric, prayer tokens left behind by superstitious visitors.

The old woman crept towards a pool of water, next to which an altar had been fashioned from a piece of smooth black rock. Someone had placed a crude-looking crucifix, a bunch of whitethorn blossoms in a vase ringed by stumpy candles, and in the centre a faded photograph of a girl in a glass frame. The old woman took out a cloth and began cleaning the items. The others watched her work with her rag, wiping and polishing, engrossed, as if nothing else mattered. When she was done cleaning, she bowed her head and began murmuring a prayer.

Someone pushed Jack. He had not minded being shoved along the path because in the greyness, he had felt virtually invisible, but now, standing in the centre of the circle of watching eyes, he felt exposed and frightened. A bitter wind blew through the trees, whirling bits of old leaves and sticking them to the gypsies' pale faces.

A girl whispered in his ear: 'When she calls, you must bless yourself and walk three times around the well.'

A religious hush descended on the crowd, and then he heard the old woman say his name.

'Go to her,' said the girl.

He clambered towards the old woman. The sound of water dripping and gurgling through countless crevices in the rocks made speech unnecessary. It was hard even to hear the wind in the trees. He blessed himself and walked around the pool three times. The old woman pursed her lips and nodded her head to show her appreciation at his devoutness, and then she beckoned him closer.

She stared at him with a toothless grimace. Her face was cut with so many creases that her blue eyes seemed to stare out of the wrinkled map of all the paths she had travelled. She smiled, as though she had been waiting a long time for him, and then she dipped her hand in the murky water of the pool and scattered the drops over him.

He remembered now where he had seen her before: on the holiday in Donegal, the traveller who had blessed him at the monastery.

She leaned so close to him he could feel the weight of her sadness. The sound of someone weeping seemed to seep through the cracks in the rocks.

'I come and pray here as often as I can,' she said. 'I'm the only one who visits this shrine now. I pull away the weeds, wipe the photograph, and bring new flowers. I still mourn her. All I have is this wet lump of rock where I pray for the return of her body. Take a look at the photograph, son. Do you recognize who she is?'

He blinked and looked at the photograph and then back at the old woman. 'No.'

Above them, the statue of the Virgin watched them with her gutted eyes.

'This poor girl is what connects us. Her name was Mary O'Sullivan. My eldest daughter.'

He glanced again at the photograph. A big black beetle with a shiny back scuttled over the altar. 'I've never heard of her.'

The gurgling of the rivulets deepened like a hidden river rising beneath the rocks.

The old woman's face floated closer to him. 'Look closely. The picture was taken a year before your father was born. She was his mother.'

'What happened to her?'

'She was murdered by a gang of bad men.'

'Who?'

'Who?' she repeated back to him, her blue eyes clouding with fear. 'The same men who will kill you when they discover you have the gift.'

'What gift are you talking about?'

'The gift of bad blood.'

She rubbed her index finger and thumb together in a gesture which the boy recognized as signifying money. The men watching them began to snigger. He could hear the dregs of greed in their throats. He refused to look at her face, or the photograph of the girl. He wanted to run into the forest along the dangerous path to the river, anywhere but beside this sinister old woman, whose voluminous skirts threatened to spread out and encircle him, dragging him into the dark depths of the past.

'If my life is in danger, why can't I go home? Why can't I go back to my parents?'

'Keeping you here is not my idea. It's not the traveller way.'

216

'Then help me get home.'

'We have a path to take first.' Her voice began to grumble. 'It wasn't us who started this journey. The men who murdered your grandmother and hid her body. They're the reason why you can't leave us now.'

He forced himself to look at the photograph. His eyes wavered. He felt nervous, awed by the story the old woman began to relate. She told him he had run away too soon, but his predicament was more than just a matter of bad timing. His life was now in danger and so was his father's. A flurry of shadows fell over her face, or was it more shrivelled leaves picked up by the wind?

'We travellers count for nothing in this society. Which is why we must stick together,' she said, lowering her eyes to the altar.

Seeing that the old woman had finished, the travellers bowed their heads without a word and filed out of the grotto. A rough hand pushed Jack along the track. He began to recognize the road they were guiding him towards. It was one of the gypsy ways his father had often talked about. He had promised Jack they would travel it together some day, but now the terrain was unravelling, full of deep recesses and shadows, warped out of all recognition by greed and the desire for revenge.

CHAPTER TWENTY-ONE

On Tuesday morning, back at police headquarters, there was an email waiting for Daly about the police check he had ordered on Hewson's background. He had been due to see the police psychologist but the appointment had completely slipped his mind, such was the unusual nature of the email. For some reason, he did not have the proper authorization to access the file. He stared at the security clearance code that was required. He had no idea what it meant or who could grant it. The new computerized archive was still an alien landscape to him. He had learned to stitch a route together, navigating his way eventually to the desired information without getting too mired in the system, but in this instance, he had stumbled upon an invisible border. There were various official and unofficial ways he could respond to the obstacle, but the only one Daly was interested in involved finding out the truth as quickly as possible.

He checked the access history for Hewson's file, and saw

that it had last been opened on 22 August from Dungannon police station. He searched back through the duty rosters to see who had been in charge of calls that day. Cross-referencing the date and the name of the inspector, he came across a brief describing a road collision, which had taken place early that morning, involving a thirty-nine-year-old male, who had been subsequently arrested on suspicion of drink-driving.

A little more digging and he found the inspector's original report. The suspect had been described as a journalist, but any other reference to him had been redacted from the transcript. At the bottom of the report was a note from Special Branch recommending that the prosecution for drink-driving be dropped because it risked compromising the security of an operative.

A prickle of apprehension ran down Daly's spine. The file suggested that Hewson had been recruited as an informant of some sort. The implication of this could hardly be more serious. Hewson had been holding back a lot more than even his wife realized. He had more than one dangerous secret. Was that the reason why he had disappeared? Because he feared the police investigation into the boy's abduction might expose discrepancies within his professional life, and threaten his covert role with Special Branch, or worse, his life?

Hewson must have weighed up the dangers and somehow decided that there was no point in revealing everything to Daly, and that he had to go it alone. If so, it was a heavy price to pay. Hewson was an informer but a father, too, which was why he must have made the drastic decision to disappear with his camper van and its secrets. He had become a fugitive, following in the footsteps of his son, at the risk of destroying his family and his career as a Special Branch spy.

Since he was rooting around in the police archives, Daly decided to do a trawl for the missing traveller woman Mary O'Sullivan, who had been the target of the intruders' search at O'Sullivan's mansion. He traced the name back to a case that detectives had closed in the late 1970s. According to the records, O'Sullivan had been twenty-one years old when she was first reported missing in the spring of 1976. She was registered as the mother of a six-month-old baby, which had been found by social workers, unkempt and hungry, in her abandoned caravan.

The police investigation had thrown up an unpleasant secret within Mary's family. Since Mary was unmarried and had no partner, the neglected baby became the charge of court while social workers organized its adoption. A copy of the baby's birth certificate was located and on its examination, social workers made the appalling discovery that Mary's own father, a man called Patrick Thomas John O'Sullivan, had been registered as the baby's father.

The charge of incest had caused a stir within the travelling community, which had leaked into the press, sparking condemnation from Church authorities and politicians. Mary's father had taken off from the family's permanent halting site, disappearing over the border before he could be brought to court. Daly noted that while only one detective had investigated Mary's disappearance, a number of teams had tried to track down Patrick O'Sullivan. They had mounted surveillance operations of traveller encampments along the border, which had led to the arrests of several young traveller men for smuggling small amounts of fuel and alcohol. Anonymous callers had given the police tip-offs over Mary's disappearance, claiming she had been murdered and her body hidden after the IRA coerced her into informing on the movements of police officers and soldiers living along the border. Daly noted that whereas the tip-offs had been duly recorded, the detective in charge of her disappearance did not appear to have followed them up in any meaningful way.

Members of the travelling community had also contacted police, claiming they had seen in dreams the location of Mary's body, usually the bottom of a disused well or a bog pool, but these visions had been treated as absurd and irrelevant. Police made contact with Gardai in the South in an attempt to trace the father, but their efforts were without success, and the incest charges were eventually dropped, along with the investigation into Mary's disappearance. Daly perused the files and could find no further mention of Mary O'Sullivan, or her baby.

He leaned back in his seat and rubbed his eyes. He thought of the Hewson family and the possible connections they might have with the travellers. He did not know for sure if father and son were still alive, or hiding in some traveller caravan on the other side of the border. Perhaps they had run off to a hideaway in Spain. His thoughts kept returning to Rebecca and her downcast eyes. There had been something so alluring about the look she had flashed him in the courthouse. He tried going through all the material his team had gathered on the boy's disappearance, as if he could make the memory of her sadness disappear, but his search lacked conviction. He knew he was conning himself. He stared at the flickering computer screen for several minutes. Feeling thirsty, he got himself a glass of water, which he sipped slowly. He reached into his coat pocket and fiddled with his car keys. He went back through the archive materials he had photocopied about Mary O'Sullivan, as if he might find the origins of Rebecca's dejection in those bleak historical details. When he had finished, he pushed his chair back and grabbed his coat.

There was something much bigger and more sinister behind the disappearance of Harry Hewson and his son, and the most direct source of information he had available was Rebecca herself. A lost mother, removed from her only son. He could see now why she intrigued him so deeply. Following her was a way of probing the original wound of his childhood. Her beauty was just the bait, the erotic charge that lured him back to the loss of his mother and the confusion of his boyhood grief.

Rebecca's car was parked on the drive, yet when he rang her phone there was no answer. He watched the house from a discreet distance. After some minutes, he saw her hurry out and climb into her car. He followed her vehicle into the nearby town of Dungannon, and tracked its movements through the narrow, hilly streets. She seemed lost and wasted half an hour driving round in circles. Once parked, she moved from café to café, unable to settle, wandering through the streets, staring at shop windows, taking off in hurried little spurts.

He kept watching the surroundings, searching for any sign of a shadow, a traveller in disguise, or a white van, but there was no sign of any contact. She appeared completely alone. At one point, as he followed her through the town's central square, he thought he heard someone call her name. He was not sure where the voice came from. He steered through a crowd of shoppers, jostling his way to get closer, but she floated away from him without any sign of recognition.

He trailed her through the public park at the bottom of the town. Not once did she look back or stop for anyone. He began to suspect that she knew he was following her and that her meandering route was a ruse, a way to distract his attention. Perhaps this was all an act for the benefit of the police, and this version of her that he was pursuing was a fake, a woman pretending to be distracted by grief and fear, with no substance of her own, while the real Rebecca Hewson plotted her next move in the darkness.

He waited for her outside a shop, standing in full view as she stepped out, but either she was lost in her thoughts or ignored him on purpose. Determined now, he made his approach, walking up to her and calling out her name.

She stopped and looked at him in confusion, and then gave a half-smile in recognition, which gradually tensed into a frown. 'Have you been following me?' she asked.

'Yes.'

'Am I in danger?'

'I'm trying to work out the answer to that question myself.' He examined her face. 'How are you managing?'

'As well as can be expected.'

'Anything come to light that might be of interest to the police?'

'Nothing worth mentioning.'

'Nothing at all?'

'No. What about you? Have you anything to tell me?'

'Not at the minute. Every piece of information is important

to a police investigation like this, which is why you have to tell me all that you know.'

She studied him with a nervous glance. 'How long have you been following me?'

'Since yesterday.' He paused, watching the anxiety increase in her face. 'I was at Maghery church when you met the traveller woman.'

Immediately, she went on the defensive. 'Am I a criminal? What have I done to deserve this level of attention?'

'Perhaps you should begin by telling me what happened in the church.'

'Why are you focusing your investigation on me? Do you think I have something to do with my son's disappearance?'

'I need to know why you secretly arranged to talk to the woman.'

'I wasn't allowed to tell anyone about it. She called me on the phone. She warned me not to talk to the police. It was stupid and impulsive of me, but I wanted to go and confront them. I wanted to know why they had taken Jack.'

'We could have organized covert surveillance, advised you what questions to ask and recorded everything.'

'They told me they had a contact in the police force who would let them know if I told you about the meeting.'

'Most likely a scare tactic.'

'I wasn't willing to take that risk.'

In the circumstances, a desperate mother would do anything her child's kidnappers wanted. It was pointless to add to her stress by making her feel at fault. She stared at him with a calm, resolute gaze. A thought occurred to him.

'You've been very composed in spite of everything that

has happened,' he said. 'How did you know the traveller was genuine? What proof did she give that she was holding Jack?'

'They sent me an email though his own account. Jack and I were the only ones who knew the password.'

'You believe that only Jack could have given them access to it?'

'I think so. Someone could have hacked his account, but our home computer has all the latest protection.'

Daly nodded. It seemed unlikely that the travellers had penetrated the family's computer. They had connections everywhere in the real world, but he doubted that they extended to the internet.

'What about your husband? Any word from him?'

'Nothing. Not even a text message.' Her voice grew more earnest. 'You have to understand, Inspector, this was the first time I felt I could do something since Jack disappeared. It gave me strength. I wanted them to see how determined I was to get him back.'

Daly noticed how quickly she had changed the subject away from her husband.

'I need you to tell me more about Harry. Anything unusual about his behaviour. Any sudden show of anxiety or annoyance over a topic of conversation.'

She shrugged and fidgeted with her handbag.

'I need to know the real Harry Hewson. What is there about him that you haven't told me?'

'What makes you think there's another side?'

Daly wondered if he should tell her about his discovery of Harry's possible links to Special Branch, but thought better of it. The revelation might plunge her into a darker territory of worry.

'I have a right to know if you suspect my husband is behind Jack's disappearance.'

'Why did he leave immediately after coming back from the police station?'

'I've already told you. I don't know.'

'Did he ever mention the names Samuel or Alistair Reid?'

She pulled a face. 'Are the names important?'

'They might be.'

'Tell me more about them.'

'Samuel Reid was an elderly pig farmer who lived along the border. He died in mysterious circumstances a few days ago. He is survived by his brother Alistair, the politician.'

She nodded. 'I remember now.' She paused for a moment. 'I think he found their names on a list of directors for a property company.'

'What sort of property company?'

'You should talk to his work colleagues.'

'Why?'

'I heard him talking about it on the phone.'

'I'm finding it hard to trace anybody who worked with your husband,' said Daly, wondering if Hewson's phone calls had been to his handlers in Special Branch. 'What did you hear?'

She vacillated for a moment. 'The organization was called the Strong Ulster Foundation. Harry was obsessed with it. He discovered that it relied on funding from people's wills and political parties. Since the property crash, it went on a spending spree, buying hundreds of empty farms along the border, but it had no office or contact number. The only details registered with Companies House were the names of its directors.'

Daly made a mental note of the details. 'Any more phone calls for your husband? What about the woman called Caroline?'

'She rang again this morning. I didn't answer so she left a message. She still didn't say why she wanted Harry.'

'And the traveller woman? Has she called again?'

'No.'

'We're going to place a tap on your phone to help us trace any calls that come through. It's important that you cooperate with us and let us advise you if either of the women ring again.'

'Of course. All the traveller would tell me was that Jack's alive and being looked after, and that they had taken him because of something that happened in the past. They said my husband would explain it.'

He considered carefully what they had told her. 'They're keeping you in a state of suspense by acting in this mysterious way. It's their way of manipulating you into becoming more compliant.'

'But what they could possibly want from me?'

'Only your husband can tell us, I'm afraid.'

She caught a glint in Daly's eyes. 'I don't know what he has been keeping secret. But what about you? Do you know more than you're letting on?'

Rather than answer, Daly stared at Rebecca, throwing the question back at her.

'I've been telling you the truth,' she said. 'I have no idea what is going on with my husband and the travellers.'

'If the travellers try to get in touch in any way, you must contact me immediately. Understood?'

'Yes.'

'At some point they are going to start making demands, for money or for whatever else it is they believe they can use Jack as a bargaining tool.'

'What should I do in the meantime?'

'Sit back and wait. Trust us on this, Rebecca; we will get your son back, but you have to cooperate with us and be patient.'

She nodded resolutely. However, her determined expression began to dissipate when she saw the shadows of worry on his face. 'Do you really think my husband could be behind all that's happened?'

He stared at her unblinking eyes. 'It's a strong possibility,' he said.

CHAPTER TWENTY-TWO

As soon as Daly returned to his car, he rang Inspector Fealty. However, the Special Branch inspector was in an important meeting and would not be free until lunchtime. Daly sighed. He felt uneasy about what lay ahead. He asked the secretary to pass on an urgent message requesting a meeting with Fealty as soon as possible, and then drove back to headquarters. When he returned to his desk, he was surprised to see Fealty standing there, waiting for him.

'What are you doing here?' asked Daly. 'I thought you had a meeting.'

'I got your message and decided to pop down.'

Daly briefed him on what he had discovered about Hewson's background, and the news that he had disappeared from his family home. He handed Fealty the printout of the redacted police file.

Fealty glanced at the pages, pulled a face, and slipped them back into the cover.

'I understand that the full report on Hewson is confidential,' said Daly, 'and that ordinarily its details can't be shared with other police teams. However, given that the man is the father of a missing son, and can't be traced at the current time, I thought you might be able to share the details informally.'

'Oh,' said Fealty. The coldness of his stare reminded Daly of a bird of prey. 'Everything relevant in terms of Hewson's background is already available to you.'

'But that's not the full story, is it? The boy's disappearance has turned a spotlight on Hewson, on all that he knows and did, whether Special Branch like it or not. I need to know if he was on your payroll.'

Fealty stared at Daly's face with a look of annoyance that transformed itself into a glare of hungry fascination. 'Listen, Daly, you're currently under internal investigation, suspected of helping a dangerous spy escape the clutches of the police. You've also been accused of potentially destabilizing the political settlement and bringing Special Branch into disrepute, and now you want to access secret intelligence reports to satisfy your curiosity about a person who happens to be the father of a missing child?'

'That's correct.'

'I can't show you them.'

'Why not?'

'That would be breaking the rules.'

'I'll swear I never saw them.'

However, it was clear from Fealty's attitude that he was not going to volunteer Daly any further information on Hewson's secret life.

'Let me educate you a little on the territory you're threatening to tramp all over,' warned Fealty. 'While you've been
stumbling around your farm and hiding in the local court-
houses, Special Branch have been waging a secret war with
dissident paramilitaries linked to smuggling and organized
crime. For the first time in Northern Ireland's history, we
have national crime agency officers on the ground unravelling their networks, following the cash trails, unpicking their
secret bank accounts. This file on Hewson you're requesting
is sensitive to the highest degree.'

'I have been out of touch,' said Daly. 'But you should have
informed me of Hewson's role with Special Branch. I believe
he has forged some links with dangerous individuals. I had
been working on the theory that he might have been complicit in the boy's disappearance, but this revelation raises
the possibility that the kidnapping was a warning or a form
of retaliation.'

'What makes you believe that Hewson's links with Special
Branch had anything to do with the disappearance? I've
already checked with your colleagues, and they say there are
no grounds for this line of inquiry. In fact, they tell me you've
yet to make any significant progress in the investigation.'

'That's not entirely true. I'm investigating the suspicious
death of Samuel Reid, which may or may not be connected
to the same travellers behind Jack's disappearance. There
are also links with a missing person case from the 1970s.
A traveller girl called Mary O'Sullivan, who her family
believe was murdered.'

'What sort of links?'

Daly thought of explaining one of the theories he had

formulated, but decided against it. 'Links we have yet to understand fully.'

'You're not making much sense.' The increasing proximity of Fealty's body intensified the criticism in the words. 'Let's start with what you do understand.' Fealty's face broke into a sneer. It was almost an involuntary reflex. Daly thought of walking away, but stood firm. He would not lose his sense of calm. He was determined because he believed Fealty was counting on him losing his temper.

'I don't know how you manage it, Daly. You take a clear-cut abduction case and with a bit of clumsy detective work you turn it into some sort of political conspiracy. I've already had a phone call from Alistair Reid, objecting in the strongest possible terms to your line of questioning.'

'Has he lodged a formal complaint?'

'If he had, we wouldn't be having this chat. You'd be at the sharp end of an internal inquiry.'

'His brother was fearful for his life. He made several complaints to police officers that the travellers were menacing him, prying into his private life.'

'Close the Reid investigation.' Fealty gave Daly a cold look with his controlling grey eyes. 'If the travellers drove the poor old bastard to a fatal accident, they succeeded. There's no way we can prove it in a court of law. Work on the missing boy. His life is at stake. Not to mention your reputation as a detective.'

'Driving someone to kill themselves is not accidental death.'

'Let's try to keep the politicians happy, Daly, and work on this one together. In the past, you've shown an unpleasant talent for embarrassing and compromising your Special

Branch colleagues. You should think of us as a valuable asset to have at your side, rather than dreaming up links to the past and itching to get your name in the newspapers.'

Daly flinched at the last remark. Getting his name in the news was the last thing he desired. He found himself doing exactly what he had intended not to do, getting angry with the Special Branch inspector, and that made him angry with himself.

'Trust me on this, Daly. If Hewson's involvement with the security services was relevant to your investigation we would let you know.'

'His involvement is relevant if it turns out he was out of control, a rogue agent. What role did he play and what influence did you have over him?'

'He provided information on an ad hoc basis. Sometimes it was useful; sometimes it wasn't. In return, we fed him stories that were of use in firming up the peace process. However, the details of that information are too sensitive to divulge at this current time.'

'If you won't let me know informally, then I'll have to make an official request to see Hewson's full file.'

Fealty stood so close that Daly could feel the hot breath of his nostrils. 'You'll need to be given special security clearance to see it. This will have to go to the highest levels of the police service.'

'Tell them it's urgent.'

'It will take several days at least to get the relevant clearances.'

'And while you're at it, tell them I want a copy of the file you're keeping on me.'

'You?'

'Yes. I'm sure you don't need me to spell out my name.'

Fealty's expression was a blank, and then a makeshift grin formed on his lips. 'I have to warn you that it might be uncomfortable reading.'

'What do you mean?'

'I believe the last entry was an observation about you following Rebecca Hewson into church yesterday.'

Daly's face froze.

'What were you doing there, by the way?' asked Fealty.

'Observing my Lenten obligations.'

'Whatever that means.'

'It means none of your business.'

'Has she caught your eye?'

Fealty's line of attack was getting too personal, and Daly felt his temper bristle. He had been keeping their voices low but the intensity of the conversation drew looks from a group of officers passing by the door. Detective O'Neill appeared amid them, waving a sheaf of papers in her hand. Fealty backed away a little and some of the harshness in the air dissolved. The Special Branch inspector's face relaxed, grew less ravenous.

'Very well, Daly, I have to go now,' said Fealty. He nodded at O'Neill, and then turned back before leaving the room. 'Remember, this missing boy is your chance to rehabilitate yourself and get back into the force's good books. Don't muck it up.'

After Fealty left, O'Neill handed Daly the sheets, which were printouts of the calls that had been made to Rebecca Hewson's house over the past week.

Some of the numbers belonged to friends and relatives of Rebecca. Other calls were from her firm of solicitors and Jack's school.

'There are two numbers that are of interest,' said O'Neill. 'One of which was from a pay-as-you-go mobile which can't be traced. The other is a Belfast number, which rang the Hewsons' home several times over the past month, including twice since Jack's disappearance. It belongs to a government office. Unfortunately, we can't find out the extension number that rang or the staff member who made the call.'

Daly's eyebrows rose when he recognized the number.

CHAPTER TWENTY-THREE

From under the camouflage of shadows, the black hen's eyes glinted at Daly when he arrived home that evening. He did not glance in her direction as he inserted his key in the door. He knew that she was waiting for him to turn his head, rustling her wings slightly, begging for his attention. She gave a little cluck and challenged him to approach. However, he was reluctant to spend another evening cursing and chasing after her, afflicted by the worry that she might come to harm flapping over the muddled fields and ruined hedges. Resolutely, he refused even to look at her when the key shifted, and he slipped into the house.

He switched on the lights and lit the fire. He listened to the silence of the rooms, waiting for the ghosts of the past – his dead mother and father – to join him from the cottage's nooks and crannies, but there was no trace of either, and the place felt empty and cold. A lingering sense of guilt and loneliness made him check through the window for the hen's huddled form, but she had vanished from the porch. He felt bereft, like an old woman unable to accept that her children had finally left home.

Eventually, he went back outside and scanned the unruly garden for the bird. He stood waiting to hear a cluck or scratch or catch a glimpse of her beady eyes. Where was she? Was she behaving in this way because he did not give her enough attention? In the chill of the early spring evening, with dogs howling on the neighbouring farms, his guilt over the hen's welfare intensified. He checked the roof to see if she had returned to her roost there and to his annoyance saw that several more tiles had slipped from their places, hanging over the edge and ready to fall on an unsuspecting head. The moon came out from behind a floating cloud, and lit up the broken tiles, giving Daly the impression that the roof was tilting and about to collapse on top of him. He forgot about the hen and hurried back into the cottage.

He opened the phone book and contacted the first building contractor he came across. This was the house he had been born in, and it was time he started taking care of it, even if it meant moving out for a while. He gave the builder the details and asked him to come out as soon as possible and organize a complete renovation of the cottage. Afterwards, Daly realized he had forgotten to ask him for a quote.

In the bathroom, he was able to shave fully for the first time since the attack in O'Sullivan's mansion. His eyes peered back at him from a shifting landscape of plum-coloured bruises. The swelling around his cheeks and jaw had gone, and he was able to close his lips without smarting with the pain. He would miss his suffering visage, he thought. Its pattern of injuries had been a mask to hide his vulnerabilities.

He went to bed and lay awake for a while, waiting for the rain to come, listening for it dripping through the holes in the roof, but it was a still, frosty night, and all he heard was the flapping of birds' wings and the cluck of his hen merging with the sounds of other creatures settling down for the night.

He felt a pang of jealousy at the freewheeling existence of the travellers, playing musical chairs with their lives and wandering from place to place in their caravans. Here he was, desperately trying to maintain his dignity and place in the world, the trapped custodian of a crumbling cottage, struggling to fall asleep beneath a roof that let in the wind and the rain. Perhaps he should embrace the house's ruin, and glory in it, rather than empty his bank account to prevent it from melting back into the earth. He had always been at odds with the idea of being its owner. Better to hand the place over to the snails and mice, the bats and birds, the ivy and nettles, which were always trying to poke and burrow their way through the damp walls and mouldy window frames. A brand-new caravan might prove to be a less squalid and cosier abode. He could even pitch it up in a field with a better view of the lough, or move it from corner to corner of the farm, as his whim dictated. The rest of the world might judge that he had come down in his fortunes, but what difference would abandoning the property really make to his self-esteem?

He drifted off to sleep with a smile of contentment, imagining that he lay huddled in the bunk of a caravan parked in the darkest, most secluded corner of an impenetrable forest.

*

Jack Hewson and his companions spent the day hiding in the back of a fleet of caravans towed by vans, criss-crossing the border, separating into smaller and smaller groups, as though trying to shake off an invisible pursuer. A teenage traveller showed him the crossing points in the landscape. Not so long ago, during the Troubles, long stretches of the border had been impassable. Rolls of rusting barbed wire still lay at the sides of the road, ensnaring blocks of concrete and iron fenders. In other places, Jack could see where craters had been blown in the middle of the road, and later filled in with gravel and rubble. The land all around had been emptied of people.

'I'm frightened,' he told the youth.

'What are you frightened of?'

'The road. I'm frightened of losing my way.'

The more they travelled, the more the road unravelled, as though they were trapped on an endless circuit. He had the suspicion that time itself was unravelling. He no longer had any idea what day of the week it was. The wind blew and the caravan rattled on open stretches of the road. He could feel the side panels shifting in the turbulence.

'I miss my family.'

'Don't think about them.'

'I want to go back.'

'Back where?'

'My father will be looking for me. He won't stop until he finds me.'

'We have a story to piece together. Remember?'

'Keep your stupid story.'

At one point in the journey, the teenager shifted his focus

to the back window of the caravan. A car was gaining on them. They stared through the net curtains as the strange vehicle drew closer, the face of the driver seeming to bulge against the windscreen, so intent was he on narrowing the distance. Jack recognized the car from the filling station they had stopped at for supplies.

'We've company.' The youth spoke into a mobile phone to the driver towing the caravan. 'Might be the police.'

The sound of the tyres deepened, the road turning smooth as it swept into the northern end of a long valley lined with pine trees. They pulled sharply on to a gravel track that climbed into the forest. The car came rocketing behind them, gaining all the time, but the traveller did not seem unduly worried by the threat it posed.

'In another minute, we'll be over the border,' said the teenager. 'If he's the police, he'll have to turn back.'

The youth drew a calm satisfaction from the chase, watching with interest and approval the manoeuvres of the stranger's car over the potholed track. They crossed a small river, and then the jolting shadow of the car disappeared.

'The police are everywhere,' said the traveller. 'That's why we have to keep moving.'

When they turned back on to the road, he leaned over to reassure Jack. 'Look,' he said. 'The road is empty again. It's just a road, nothing to fear.'

That night, their encampment felt wilder and more dangerous. The constant moving left the boy unsettled. He could not believe how much time had passed since he had last seen his mother, and wished he could at least whisper goodnight to her. The incessant travelling made the road seem a vacant and lonely place, the journey in the back of the caravan so tedious that it might have easily been a journey of stillness, the only thing moving the thoughts in his head and the blood pumping anxiously in his veins.

Out of the darkness, more vans and caravans joined the camp. He heard a lot of whispering. The new arrivals were twitchy and jabbering in voices so fast he barely understood the words. A teenage girl undressed him in the caravan and made him wash in a basin of hot water with some soap. She seemed to take a sulky pleasure in watching him.

'What's your name?' he asked.

'Call me whatever you like.'

The metal bangles on her wrists jangled as she poured more water into the basin.

Later, around the campfire, the conversation of the travellers grew rough and aggressive. Jack listened to their monotonous stories about past grievances and mad schemes for the future. They talked about the great wealth that awaited them at the end of the road and bickered over how they would spend it. All they had to do was draw their enemies out of their hiding places.

One of the men sidled up to Jack in the darkness, his breath reeking of alcohol. He ruffled the boy's hair and whispered in a voice deformed with drunken affection, 'We're your new family now, Jack. Make sure you stay close.'

'Who are you?'

'My name is of no importance.'

'But I need to know who you are.'

'I'm your protector. That's all you need to know. I will watch over you tonight. In the morning, you will have to disappear again. You might not see me for days, but I will be there in the background, watching over you.'

'What if I run away? I'm not your prisoner.'

'I'm meeting your father very soon. He has an important message for you. Don't you want to know what it is?'

He felt a stab of relief that the travellers had mentioned his dad. 'Why can't I wait here for him? Why must I keep travelling?'

'There are things none of us know at this stage. Knowledge comes at an expense. The way of the road is to find out step by step, a little at a time.' The traveller grew pensive. 'A long time ago, my sister was killed by some bad men. Ever since, I've been travelling this road constantly. I've had to make myself invisible in my own country, all the time waiting for her killers to reveal themselves.'

'But you can't make me invisible, too. I don't want to go back on the road.'

He sighed. 'We travellers know that what divides us is bad. The border, hedges, walls, property boundaries. They are all bad. But the road is good. The road flows and joins people. Life should flow like the road. This is why you must keep travelling with us.'

CHAPTER TWENTY-FOUR

A ringing sound mounted in Daly's ears. He awoke in the early-morning darkness, waiting for the thud of a hangover headache, but none came. I haven't been drinking, he thought, it's the phone. He groped his way to the hall.

'We've found Hewson, Inspector,' said the caller.

'The father or the son?' He knocked over a half-filled cup of cold tea and cursed quietly.

'The father.'

'Alive or dead?'

'Quite definitely dead.'

Daly felt dread curdle his stomach and wished it were whiskey. He listened to the scant details of the discovery and took down the directions.

The road to the border lay cloaked in mist. Shapes loomed ahead of him, barely visible in the headlights of his car, trees and desolate farmhouses swimming by and disappearing in the darkness. Eventually, he pulled up on to an unpaved road that was not marked on the map; his car rocked and swayed as though the ground beneath were battling the churn of a hidden sea. He found a solid-looking patch of earth next to the other police vehicles and eased the car to a halt.

Clambering out in the early-morning light, he found himself tramping upon bogland. Peat and water sloshed beneath his feet under a thin skin of grass and heather. He looked up, hearing disembodied voices chatting ahead. A silvery plume rose from the eastern rim of the bog. Not another swathe of fog but the breaking of day. The sun forced its way through, dispelling the freezing mist, pulling its white shroud back from the crime scene, unfolding the black shapes of trees and the still figures of the police officers, ushering them closer to Daly as he orientated himself towards the single tragic note in the landscape, the murdered body of Harry Hewson.

The reporter and his camper van had turned up along a lane that looked to be on the point of disappearance, ribboning into the vast tract of bogland straddling Tyrone's border with the Republic. *The authorities, north and south, will never make these crooked ways straight, nor bridge the bog's yawning trenches*, thought Daly. This was the wilderness that shaped the theatre of border life, the decades of smuggling, the illegal dumping of rubbish and the secret burial of informers during the Troubles. A dangerous habitat for an outsider like Hewson, whose body now lay floating in a bog pool, his opened eyes looking oddly alert yet exhausted.

Blood from the wound in his forehead had seeped thick as oil through the black water, which had sucked up the lower half of his pyjama-clad body and left his bare feet, creased with grime along the soles, bobbing up like flotsam. The face looked rough and stubborn, the eyes squinting balefully at the clearing sky. The jaw needed a shave, the stubble bristling in the frost. As the rising sun warmed the skin, rivulets of water streamed down from his frozen eyelashes and collected in the corners of his mouth.

The last remnants of frost clung to his dark hair. Now that the thaw was taking hold, his death seemed less complete, his body softer and more relaxed-looking. The features of his face grew slack as though he was returning to the sleep his killer had disturbed. Daly prised open his hands and checked for evidence but they were both empty. His fingertips met the corpse's, their coldness greedy for his warmth.

'A passing farmer noticed the van hadn't moved in a few days,' one of the officers told Daly. 'He went to investigate and found the body. It had been lying here for a while.'

He watched Daly. 'Looks like he was dragged from his bed and executed. What do you think?'

Daly did not know what to think. His eyes lingered over the body, but his mind was consumed with worry for Jack Hewson. Were the same people who had done this now in charge of the boy? For a while, he paced restlessly around the police cordon. *Someone should inform Rebecca*, he thought, *before the press gets wind of the killing*. He lifted out his mobile phone and noticed his hand was shaking. He rang O'Neill and relayed the barest details of the murder scene. He asked her to send a family liaison officer to the wife's house to break the bad news and reassure her that as yet there was no evidence her son had been harmed.

The scene-of-crime officers walked past him, men and women who had the scientific equipment and ability to read the landscape of a murder, but who would never detect the dark shadows that disturbed Daly. A camera began flashing, over-exposing Hewson's grizzled face, blasting the scene with light, simplifying everything, laying bare the final indignity of Hewson's death and his loneliness.

Daly tried to assemble the sequence of events. Had the reporter been killed as a direct result of the boy's disappearance, or could it be the other way round? Perhaps they were both the consequence of another set of events entirely. Sometimes a detective had to work back to front. Moreover, where did Samuel Reid's death fit into the pattern? If that was murder, too, then the killer had accomplished it with cruel perfection, but why the need to make it look like an accident and not the reporter's?

In an attempt to preserve the crime scene, officers set up a winch, and hoisted Hewson's body out of the water. A squelching sound filled the air. Daly wandered off to check the camper van for clues. The track leading to where the reporter had driven his vehicle resembled the wake of a boat amid the sea of heather. It stretched south to the border, reminding Daly that there were hidden ways running through this landscape, connecting secrets and people, ways that petered out into wilderness, into danger and death.

His attention sharpened as soon as he entered the van. Surveying the ransacked interior, he felt he was at last on the trail of Hewson, if not the murderer. He let his gaze wander over the creased map stuck to the wall. He searched the cluttered bedroom and cupboards for Hewson's briefcase of research papers but found no trace of it. Nor was there any evidence that his son had been living with him in the camper van. He picked up a heavy photo album from the dining table and began leafing through it. It was a collection of traveller encampments, photographs from different decades of cleared spaces within forests or bogland. The old black-and-white pictures were filled with caravans, while the more recently taken photographs were empty of human traces. He flicked through pictures of men and women standing huddled together with sullen faces that looked as though they had been repeatedly rebuffed, abused and threatened. At their feet sat half-naked children. There was an air of oppression about the scenes. Beyond the caravans lay the dark siege of the ever-present forest. What had connected Hewson to these wild halting sites?

What intrigued Daly the most was not the photographs, or the map on the wall, which was a standard Ordnance Survey publication of the border counties of Ireland, but the lines that Hewson had drawn upon it in red ink, zigzagging the border, traversing bogland, forest and rivers, sometimes following the routes of roads, sometimes abandoning them. Now and again, the red lines were crossed out or corrected, and in places, there were gaps marked out in dotted lines. He had a sense that these lines could tell a story if only he could decipher their meaning. Given that they crossed the border in the most remote of places, perhaps they had something to do with concealment and escape.

At regular points along the route, Hewson had placed a series of pins. Daly noticed that some had ripped the map and were slightly discoloured, suggesting that they had been stuck there a long time ago. He noticed the distance between the pins was about thirty miles. There was a handwritten key at the bottom of the map linking the pins to a series of numbers. Daly went back to the album and noticed that the pictures were numbered and appeared to correspond to the locations of the pins on the map. Had Hewson been tracking old halting sites or secret border crossings? What connection did the reporter have with these wild places?

The travellers had meandered along these roads for centuries, seeking out their ancient resting places miles from human settlement. What had prompted Hewson, a journalist from England, to follow in their footsteps? His work as a reporter had expanded into helping Special Branch, but what else had he been involved in? A journalist, an informer and a father. A middle-class life full of connections and commitments, which had been uprooted so violently on this road into the unknown.

At least that was how it looked to the casual observer. Daly suspected that Hewson's marriage had been at the point of collapse, but had that been enough to propel him into this dangerous terrain, driving a camper van with a map full of traveller secrets? He wanted to spend some time alone with Hewson, not the water-soaked corpse but the inanimate map and photographs, in the hope that he might be able to chart Hewson's inner terrain, the secrets he had carried in his heart.

A breeze wafted through the van and rustled the map. It was as if the dead man were whispering at him, drawing him closer to a hidden landscape. These roads that were not roads. Riddles on a map. A sequence of pins joined by zigzagging lines. A death trap.

He stepped outside and shifted his attention to the terrain surrounding the body, moving in ever-widening circles.

Behind a hump of rotting turf, he retrieved a briefcase half-submerged in a pool of peaty water. It was soaked through, filled with what looked to be the blackened dregs of the bog. He dipped his hand in and examined them with his fingers. Wet ashes. Someone, probably the murderer, had burnt the contents of the briefcase. These ashes sticking to his fingers were all that was left of the documents that had probably cost Hewson his life.

He climbed into his car. The ashes still streaked his fingers. He tried to wipe them with a hanky, but he only succeeded in blackening the rest of his hands. He drove to headquarters, a detective with his hands smeared in ashes, the only material proof he had of the treachery that had ended the journalist's life.

CHAPTER TWENTY-FIVE

The Police Ombudsman's Office was a shiny new construction with a glass front tipped by the architects at a slightly oblique angle to the rest of the offices in the row, reflecting a sky full of clouds slipping off the building's edge. It gave the impression of an office aslant from the rest of Belfast city's huddled skyline, as if only it were new and clean and worthy of this early spring weather, and the envy of the passing pedestrians hunched up against the cold.

Daly had not been mistaken when he thought he recognized the number of the female caller so keen to speak to Harry Hewson. He had rung the ombudsman's phone line himself several times over the past year, not out of professional need, but on a more personal basis. After discovering that his former colleagues were implicated in his mother's killing, Daly had contacted the office and lodged the details of the murder triangle out of a desire for justice and the truth.

Now he wondered if Harry Hewson had gone to the office

with a similar purpose? Perhaps the journalist had asked the ombudsman to launch an historical investigation into an unsolved crime against the travellers, one that his research had uncovered. As Daly stepped through the building's glass doors, he felt his heartbeat quicken. If his suspicions were correct, the answers he needed were simple and straight-forward. What were the precise details of the unsolved crime, and how might it be linked to Hewson's murder and his son's disappearance? He suspected more than ever that the whole business of Jack's abduction was connected to something much bigger than his mother could ever imagine, and now he hoped to find the information that would make everything clear.

The receptionist was not sure what to do when Daly intro-duced himself and got the office manager, who recognized Daly without having to check his identification. She ushered him through to the ombudsman's office immediately. Daly got the impression that the front desk rarely had to deal with a police inspector turning up for an appointment.

The ombudsman, Caroline Black, a retired judge, was seated at her desk, surrounded by towering files of unsolved murders, complaints against the police and historical inquir-ies dating back to the start of the Troubles, files that might never see the light of day, but which loomed more oppres-sively than the clouds against the window. Daly had read that the office dealt with more than six hundred complaints a week. Some related to the recent conduct of officers, but most belonged to investigations that ran between 1968 and 1998. He wondered grimly how deep the file on his mother was buried within the stacks of unsolved crimes.

She rose from her seat when Daly entered and shook his hand warmly. 'Good to see you again, Inspector Daly. I had a meeting scheduled for this morning, but when I heard you were coming, I immediately postponed it. Take a seat.'

The lively wrinkles around her eyes gave the impression of an energetic but serene mind.

'The story of your mother's murder is really a shocking one,' she said before he could speak. Her eyes shone brightly, as though he were bringing her a gift rather than a contentious investigation and a burden for the resources of her office. The mention of his mother's case unsettled Daly. He frowned and interrupted her.

'That's not the reason I need to speak to you.'

She faltered. Like a doctor who had misdiagnosed the patient.

'Your office has been ringing a home number belonging to a journalist called Harry Hewson.'

She was silent. She shifted in her chair. She looked as if she now wished she had not cancelled the scheduled meeting.

'I suspect that Mr Hewson was working undercover for Special Branch,' said Daly. 'But that he was also carrying out his own investigation into secrets from the past.'

'Was?'

'He was found murdered yesterday morning. I need to find out if he had talked to you about an historical crime or a justice campaign.'

'I'm afraid I can't give you any details about what he might or might not have said to me. Everyone who comes here is entitled to confidentiality. You of all people should know that.'

'Of course I do,' said Daly, trying to keep the annoyance

out of his voice. 'But I'm a detective in a murder investigation. If it's necessary I will get a warrant and go through every file you have connected to Harry Hewson.'

She sighed. 'What secrets do you believe he was trying to uncover?'

Daly thought of the unsolved crime he had in mind, the scant details of Mary O'Sullivan's disappearance. 'It's not a line of investigation at this stage. Mostly a leap in the dark.'

'If, as you suggest, Mr Hewson had been working for Special Branch, why didn't he go to the police with his suspicions, rather than wait for my office to process them?'

'That's the missing piece in the puzzle. Either he had already spoken to someone or he was too nervous to bring it to police attention.'

'Why would he have been afraid?' The nets of wrinkles around her eyes tightened.

'Perhaps he suspected the police of a cover-up, which is why you should tell me about your meetings with him.'

She leaned back in her seat, disconcerted by the intensity of Daly's demands. A few moments passed, and then she coolly began telling him what he needed to find out.

'Very well, Inspector, here's what I know, or at least what I think I know. Harry visited me a few times with a file about a missing traveller girl called Mary O'Sullivan. He claimed that she was at the centre of a crime that had never been properly investigated.'

Daly felt a surge of confidence; he was on the right track, after all.

'Right from the start, he struck me as different from the usual complainants.'

'How?'

'Brisker. More arrogant. There was a professional air about him. He carried his research in a briefcase but only opened it long enough to show me a few pages. At first, I thought he was demented because they were blank. But then, on the other sides, I got a glimpse of some photographs and a birth certificate. He was afraid of the documents getting stolen or damaged. I asked him to leave copies with us, but he was paranoid that they might fall into the wrong hands.'

'What information did he have?'

In spite of her smile, she reminded him of a headmistress. The nets of wrinkles at the corners of her eyes gave her an astute, scrutinizing look.

'He had no suspects, no witnesses, and no motive. He kept turning up in the foyer with his bundle of files, which amounted to little more than newspaper speculation and the claims of uneducated travellers. He was obsessed with the story.'

Daly nodded. He knew the type very well. Hewson had been one of Northern Ireland's tribe of answer-seekers, individuals who lived in a form of limbo, spending their days in the waiting rooms of their solicitors' offices or the archives of libraries, going through old newspapers. They formed queues as grim as those lining up to see a back-street faith healer, clutching their files, their assortment of photographs, their half-pieced-together accounts of murder plots. They wanted the truth, but the political establishment cared little about their quests. In his darkest moments, Daly suspected that it was the justice department and the ombudsman's job to keep stringing them along, keep promising them the truth, all the time inventing more excuses for the delays, sidestepping them with legal jargon and excuses about budget pressures, in the hope that one by one they would give up their campaigns or die.

'But you must have thought there was something to his claims. Otherwise why try to contact him?'

'I wanted to encourage him to do more research. With more work, he might have had a case worth pursuing.'

'What made you think that?'

'Call it instinct.'

'Still, I don't understand why you went to the lengths of ringing him on several occasions in the past week. Do you follow up every complainant's case with such urgency? There is something here you are not sharing with me.'

'What do you know about Harry's history?' she asked him, her eyes shining, it seemed to Daly, with the superior knowledge of a secret.

'It's been difficult discovering anything,' he replied. 'He had an income, but apparently he had not worked as a journalist for some time. He may or may not have been an informant for Special Branch, but any police files relating to him have been classified as top secret. Nor had he any relatives who might have shed light on his behaviour or his past.'

'It's not surprising you find him such a mystery. In Harry's case the simplest fact of his identity, the seed of who he was, had been kept hidden from him all his life.'

'How?'

'Tragically, his birth was recorded as a terrible crime, one hushed up by the authorities.' She paused as Daly waited expectantly. 'Harry was the son of travellers. The O'Sullivan clan to be precise.'

She moved to a filing cabinet and, after some searching, removed a document that turned out to be a birth certificate.

'This belongs to Mr Hewson,' she said, handing it to him. 'His mother is recorded as Mary O'Sullivan and his father as Patrick Thomas John O'Sullivan. A traveller, who was also Mary's father. This was one of the crimes he wanted me to investigate. The crime of incest.'

Daly looked at her in surprise. 'I read that there was some sort of investigation by the police and social workers but it never led to charges.'

'Precisely,' she replied. 'At first I was reluctant to look again at the investigation and the conclusion of the social workers. It was a deeply unpleasant family matter. But Harry persuaded me that it might have some bearing on what happened to his mother.'

Daly thought about the photographs in O'Sullivan's mansion: the dirty-faced children standing in the doors of caravans, the bundled-up possessions, the straggling line of their convoys; a race of strangers in society's midst. He tried to place Harry Hewson among them, and immediately his image of the journalist underwent a transformation. Hewson's lustreless dark hair, his tendency to disappear for days on end, his restlessness, his reluctance to blame the travellers for the boy's abduction: it all made sense now. Of course he was a traveller. Daly took a deep breath. He felt as though he had been crawling through forest undergrowth for days and had finally reached a clearing, a place where he could stand up and take his bearings. The mystery of Harry Hewson was beginning to clear. He was no longer a shadowy journalist, operating at the boundaries of his profession.

He was the son of a missing woman who might possibly have been murdered, obstinately and courageously trying to bring his mother's killers into the light, in spite of hostile forces. As the son of a murdered woman himself, Daly understood the journalist's reckless behaviour. Sometimes the shadows of the past were more important than living people, even loved ones.

Caroline Black explained to Daly why the social workers had dropped their investigation. After many interviews, and taking into account social and cultural differences within the traveller society, they had concluded that Mary's family, confronted by the bureaucratic challenge of filling in the birth certificate of a child whose father was unknown, had decided to enter the name of Mary's father as the baby's dad. Not because it was the truth, but because they feared Mary would be viewed as a delinquent and her illegitimate child taken into care by the authorities. In fact, within the travelling community, it was not unusual for the children of unmarried women to have their grandmother or grandfather recorded as one of the parents. The cover-ups were partially an attempt to protect the mothers and the children, and partially a means to outwit the authorities of the state, making lies of their written records.

The case of Mary O'Sullivan was one instance when the practice had terrible consequences. Caroline suspected that the charge of incest brought by the police was used as a means to dissuade the travellers from demanding further investigations into Mary's disappearance. With parts of the family having to disappear over the border to evade police questions, the official search for her whereabouts soon collapsed. The baby, without a mother, was handed over by social workers to adoption services in England, where the authorities thought it stood a better chance of growing up and succeeding in life without the disadvantages of its past at its doorstep.

Caroline told Daly other things. Among the most important facts was that Mary's brother was none other than Thomas O'Sullivan. It seemed likely that the traveller had been aware all along of the link with Harry Hewson, and that he might have an idea about what happened to the journalist. Daly also accumulated a general sense of the O'Sullivan family. It was a poignant impression, a family who had botched Harry's birth certificate in an act of protection and love for their daughter and her infant.

'Harry's wife, his deceased parents, his employers and even his police contacts knew nothing of his origins,' she said. 'They were his secret. But many people carry secrets like his. Northern Ireland is a country full of secrets, its clandestine paramilitaries, its covert agents and informers, not to mention its carefully concealed network of business interests. The more I stay in this post, the more I realize there is no end to the secrets of this country.'

'Do you have any idea who Hewson planned to meet in the past week or so?'

'No idea at all.'

Daly thought for a moment. 'How do you think I might go about retracing his steps?'

'That is beyond me, too.' There was something approaching exasperation in her voice. She glanced at her watch.

'What about now that he has been murdered? Will you

be launching an official inquiry into Mary O'Sullivan's disappearance?'

'Quite possibly.'

Daly nodded. Getting himself killed meant that Harry Hewson now had an audience. He was no longer an insignificant protagonist, but a murder victim, one who had successfully moved beyond the waiting rooms full of shadowy complainants. Now he understood the essence of Hewson's restlessness, how reconstructing the secrets of his mother's disappearance and his birth had sidelined everything else: his family, his work, even his awareness of approaching danger. He imagined the journalist hunched over the steering wheel of his camper van, traversing the old killing ground of the border roads. Last winter, Daly had been in a similar demented frame of mind, unpicking the clues of his mother's murder through the labyrinth of the border parishes. He frowned. For several moments, his mind felt overwhelmed by her memory, the lilt of her soft Tyrone accent, her blue nurse's shoes lying on her bedroom floor.

Caroline watched him closely.

'This is a difficult subject for me to investigate,' he said. 'I thought that when I found out why my mother was murdered that I would be released from...' He struggled to find the right word. 'That it would ease my guilt, this... torment inside.'

'Torment?'

Was that really the right word? he wondered. He had not planned on opening up in this way, and he regretted the emotional intensity of his phrasing.

'Not torment. I mean this preoccupation. This fixation on something that happened almost forty years ago. I keep circling the day of her death, trying to see it from a different vantage point, to find out if anything else has been kept hidden from me. Now I'm worried that what I remember from that dark portion of my childhood is just a dream. There are so many twists to the story, so many reverses that it no longer feels real.'

'It seems to me that your memory is perfectly clear,' said Caroline. 'The truth is a terrible murder disrupted your childhood. You will always be the carrier of unresolved questions. That is why you have come here seeking my help.'

She smiled with her calm blue eyes. Her intelligent poise resembled a form of legal authority, but it was sympathy and kindness she was displaying towards him, he realized. What was she offering? Dangling before him the possibility that she might be able to answer those irresolvable questions, that with the powerful legality of her office, she might be able to administer a satisfactory ending to the story of his mother's murder?

'Be careful of ignoring your own grief and anger in your quest to solve this case, Celcius,' she warned. 'There is a dangerous emotional component at work here. Until you find a clear connection between the disappearance of Mary O'Sullivan and Harry's murder, your reason for digging up the past is based on little more than conjecture.'

'There has to be a connection,' replied Daly. 'There must be a link between the two. And Jack's abduction, as well.'

She pushed back her seat, smiling as she led him out of the office. 'All you have to do is work out how.'

'I believe I already have,' said Daly. 'Or at least Jack Hewson's part of the story.'

She paused at the door and looked at him expectantly.

'I have to assume that there is a logical reason for the boy's disappearance,' he said. 'Even travellers and smugglers do things for a reason. These are not irrational, impulsive people we are dealing with. However, the normal motives of greed and exploitation don't seem to be operating here. This isn't a traveller crime we're dealing with.' He glanced at her. 'It's a crime hidden in the past. A crime committed by settled people with a lot more to lose.'

Her brow creased with furrows as she tried to follow Daly's reasoning.

'And if greed is operating at its heart, then it's not the greed of travellers, but another group of people entirely. A group that intimidated Samuel Reid and orchestrated his death. A group whose carefully laid plans for the future are threatened by Jack Hewson's very existence.'

As Daly left the building, he took a final glance at the sleek glass exterior. The blankness of the reflected sky felt like a subtle architectural point he had missed earlier. The front of the building symbolized nothing and everything. Perhaps the emptiness of an ever-changing sky was the only symbol his divided country could take in the aftermath of the Troubles, he thought. It had accumulated too many competing symbols over the war-torn centuries to be at peace with itself for many years to come.

As he climbed into his car, the weariness that had weighed so heavily on him all winter began to lift. Someone had pushed Samuel Reid to his death and executed Harry Hewson with a bullet in his head, but there was something incomplete about the pattern of deaths. The killer had not finished and would strike again, Daly was convinced of that. He felt the tension inside him swell, dispelling all traces of his melancholy as he drove back to police headquarters.

CHAPTER TWENTY-SIX

Dogs roamed the fringes of the gypsy camp, nosing through the overflowing rubbish bags, sniffing in sombre fashion at the new vans that had arrived, and skulking away from the drunken men who came to relieve themselves in the darkness. They jumped up with their filthy paws to greet Jack, but he whispered at them to be quiet as he scanned the circle of caravans and the fire still burning at the centre. The men had run out of beer and sent a couple of the teenage boys to drive to the nearest off-licence. Knowing that they would not be back for at least an hour, Jack had decided to make his escape.

When he was sure no one was watching him, he slipped into the surrounding trees. Immediately, the branches stirred with birds flapping and squawking from their roosting positions. The entire forest shivered with eerie life. Startled, he glanced back at the encampment. In spite of the disturbance, none of the travellers seemed to have noticed that he had taken flight. He ran into the forest, the noise of the birds swelling all around him like a hurrying wind, the movement of their wings meshing the forest floor with moonlit shadows. A blackbird clattered into the higher branches, scolding him at full throttle.

He dipped his head and ran harder. The sky opened above him, and he found himself on a track leading down to the main road. Traces of the crescent moon guided him along the rutted path. When he made it on to the road, the first thing he saw was a car parked at a lay-by. He recognized it as the same vehicle that had been following them. The one the travellers said belonged to the police.

Excited and fearful, anticipating his rescue and the welcoming embrace of his mother, he drew closer. The headlights flicked on, dazzling him with their light. He raised his hands to shield his eyes and the light dimmed. They flashed on and off, beckoning him closer. He took a few more steps.

'Come here,' said a voice from the driver's window. 'I won't harm you. I'm a policeman.'

'My name is Jack Hewson,' he shouted. 'The police are looking for me.'

He walked closer to the driver's window and saw a look, puzzled yet knowing, flash across the driver's squinting features. His eyes were bloodshot, and he seemed very old to be a police officer.

'What makes you believe the police are looking for you?'

'I ran away with the travellers. My mum and dad are searching for me.'

'Your face is dirty. You look like a gypsy to me.'

Jack did not know what to say. The encounter was not going as he had expected.

'Why did you run away?'

He held back from answering the question. Instead, he asked, 'When is my mum coming to get me?'

'That depends. Where's your daddy?'

'He was meant to be here. But he hasn't shown. Are you really a policeman?'

'Yes.' The driver's eyes narrowed. 'I've been a policeman a very long time. Before you or your father were born, as a matter of fact.'

'So what are you going to do?'

'What do you want me to do?' Not a muscle moved on his face. In the moonlight, he resembled a tired old owl staring at its prey.

'I want you to take me home.'

Dogs from the camp began yelping in the moonlight.

'I will, very soon. But first you must be patient.'

'Why?'

He grimaced, and craned his neck out of the window. He looked up and down the road. 'Do you know where you are, Jack?'

The boy stared into the bottomless darkness of the pine trees, their needles shivering with drops of rain. Deep within the forest, he could see lights from the caravan camp, swaying through the trees.

'No.'

'You're on the wrong side of the border, son. Which means I can't do a damn thing for you right now. I'll have to make contact with the Gardai station in the next town and get their permission before I can rescue you. Do you understand?'

'Yes.'

265

The driver glanced at his watch, leaned forward and sniffed the air. 'In a little while, I'll come back with a team of officers. We'll rescue you from the gypsies and take you back home. But first I need you to tell me some things. OK?'

Jack nodded.

'How many travellers are in the camp?'

He made a rough guess, and then the driver fired more questions at him. He wanted to know about the travellers' vehicles. He mentioned some names but Jack did not recognize them.

'Are there any other children like you? Children who are missing?' His eyes bored into Jack's.

'I'm the only one.' He hesitated, unsure whether to mention what was on his mind. 'But I've heard them talk about a woman who is missing, too. Someone called Mary O'Sullivan.'

A shadow crossed the driver's face, darkening his eyes. 'What do you know about her?'

'Nothing.'

'You're lying. You're keeping a secret. I can see it in your eyes.'

Watching the driver's empty staring face, he no longer felt elation at the thought of being rescued. Instead, he felt fear, the same fear that had been plaguing him for days. Why was the policeman asking him so many questions? The lights from the forest played across the man's face. Their movement gave Jack the feeling he was staring at a dangerous border, a point of intersection, where different stories and identities criss-crossed each other.

'Your gypsy friends picked the wrong place to run with

their secrets,' said the driver. In spite of his age and tiredness, he looked capable of swooping down with his claws and carrying off his prey. 'Their backs are to the mountain, and there's only one road in and out. In an hour or so, my men will arrive and tear the camp apart. Then you and I can continue our little conversation.'

Jack said nothing as the driver leaned back in his seat.

'Are you going to run back and tell everything to the gypsies?'

He shook his head.

'Good.'

For the first time, the driver smiled. He gave Jack the thumbs up and drove slowly away. For some reason, the gesture did nothing to alleviate Jack's worries as he lurched back through the trees.

Daly's conversation with Caroline Black had given him a new edge. When he returned to the incident room at police headquarters, he got himself some coffee straight away and read the latest updates on the search for Jack Hewson. He was completely absorbed in his concentration. It had been at least a year since he felt so like a proper police detective. The leads were beginning to come to him, the urgency and complexity of the investigation growing like a balloon, slowly taking him up and away from his dispiriting personal life.

His eye caught a name in the duty inspector's summary of the previous night's crime reports. He was at pains not to show his surprise as Irwin was lurking somewhere behind.

He did not want to draw the Special Branch detective's attention to what had snagged his interest, but now that he had spotted the name, it was unignorable, hovering above all the tawdry details of car accidents, petty vandalism, assaults and attempted burglaries. As soon as Irwin slipped away, he scrutinized the bare details of the crime report, and then he tracked down the duty inspector, who was about to go home.

'What happened last night in Culdaff graveyard?' Daly asked him.

'Some vandals attacked a grave.'

'Can't you tell me more than that?'

The officer wore a tired expression. 'A passing motorist spotted two men with a mini-digger just after midnight. The vandals scarpered when the police patrol arrived and left the digger behind.'

'What damage did they do?'

'They'd dug right down to the coffin.'

'Any fingerprints on the digger or other evidence left behind?'

'No, thank goodness.'

'What do you mean, thank goodness?'

'They were a couple of mindless vandals. Most probably drunk. What's the point pursuing them and causing more work for us?'

Daly was silent for a while, thinking through the details he had gleaned from the duty inspector, who was so clearly keen to get home to his bed.

'Anyone inform the next of kin?'

'Yes.'

'Good. Get some rest and say no more about this.'

He tracked down Detective O'Neill in the incident room.

'How's Rebecca bearing up?' he asked.

'Not very good at all.'

'Did you tell her about the map in Hewson's camper van?'

'Yes. She doesn't understand what the pins mean.'

'Do you think she's telling the truth?'

'I can't believe she had no idea what her husband was doing or thinking. It makes me suspicious of her.'

'It's not unusual for husbands and wives to keep secrets from each other. What else did she say?'

'She remembered more about the telephone conversation with the traveller woman. They asked her for copies of Harry and Jack's birth certificates.'

Daly said nothing. He was thinking of his conversation with the police ombudsman.

'What does it all mean, Celcius?'

'It means that everything is connected. Samuel Reid's death, Jack's disappearance, the intruders raiding O'Sullivan's mansion, and now Hewson's murder. Our only problem is finding the evidence that will lead us to the murderer before he strikes again.'

Daly grabbed his coat and made for the door. 'Let me know when the forensics team come back with their report on Hewson's camper van. I want a full analysis of all finger-prints and DNA traces. See if they match any paramilitaries or former members of the army or the police. Check with the records of anyone who was even held in custody during the Troubles.'

'Where are you going? You just got here.'

'To talk to someone I should have brought in for questioning last week.' Then, before leaving, he shouted back: 'I almost forgot. Get some officers down to Culdaff graveyard immediately, and tell them not to take their eyes off Samuel Reid's grave. Someone very dangerous is desperate to remove his remains.'

CHAPTER TWENTY-SEVEN

Jack waited for the sound of the policeman's car trundling along the track. He listened above the crackling of the fire, the drunken murmuring of the travellers' voices and the pounding of the blood in his head. He shivered. His back was wet with sweat and cold, while his chest and face almost hurt in the blaze of heat. He slipped into a restless doze and woke to the sound of a hoarse cough. In the darkness beyond the camp, he sensed the presence of strangers gathering silently.

'Who's there?' shouted one of the travellers, scrambling to his feet. Sparks erupted from the fire, illuminating the shadows with a flickering light. Jack heard a series of small metallic noises that might have been the sound of weapons being prepared. The darkest of the shadows drew closer.

'I can see you,' shouted the traveller. 'Who are you?'

A figure materialized out of the gloom. A man with a red face and a grey handlebar moustache tinged yellow with cigarette smoke. There were others with him, but they ignored the fire and began rummaging through the caravans, searching for something.

'Take it easy,' said the visitor to the travellers, who were all standing now. 'I haven't come to do you harm.' There was a slight American accent in his voice.

'Black Paddy, is that you?' asked the traveller.

'Yes.'

Although the men sat down and resumed their drinking, they did not look relaxed. Jack felt a deathly prickling shiver pass through the children assembled around the fire.

The head traveller tipped his bottle of beer at the new arrival. 'Good to see you, Paddy.' However, the tone of his voice suggested it was anything but.

The other men joined the circle by the fire, followed by a teenage girl with a single black plait, who kept looking at Jack as though she had a secret to communicate. One of the children explained to Jack that Black Paddy was a cousin and the girl his daughter. They had recently returned from the US after getting into trouble with the law there.

'Why creep up on us in the dark like thieves?' asked the head traveller.

'I like creeping around in the dark,' replied Black Paddy. 'Besides, we're all thieves, we O'Sullivans, aren't we? We thrive on opportunity and risk.' He lifted a stick, seared it in the fire, and used it to light a cigarette.

'We're not thieves.'

'Are you sure?' He threw a glance at Jack, his eyes glinting with a sinister light. 'If you're not a thief, why did you steal the boy?'

Edginess uncoiled in the travellers' bodies, bringing some

of them to their feet, empty bottles in hand. None of them took their eyes off Black Paddy.

'Nobody stole him. He's here under our protection,' said the leader. 'You've spent that long in the States you've no idea what's going on.'

Black Paddy rubbed his forehead and moustache. 'Relax. I haven't come to steal anything. Or cause trouble.'

The group calmed a little. 'It's our way to always welcome visitors,' said the leader. 'Why don't you have a beer?'

'That's decent of you.' He pushed his way through the circle until he was sitting next to Jack. There was a long silence as they drank their beers.

'Where's the boy's father?' asked Black Paddy after the final slug of his drink. His voice was cold and knowing.

'What do you mean?'

He turned Jack's head round so there was no escaping the interrogation. 'Missing your dad, son?' He spoke in a voice intended to hurt.

Jack shrugged. 'He was meant to be coming here. Now I don't know where he is.'

'Your dad's gone,' said Black Paddy, sniggering.

'If he's gone, he'll come back.'

'Believe me, son, he's not coming back.' Black Paddy turned to the travellers. 'Really, folks, I'm sorry, but like I said I haven't come to cause trouble. It's not worth my while.'

'We appreciate that.'

Bitterness crept into his voice. 'I've only come to take what is owed. I might have been away for a long time, but I know what my due is.'

'We owe you nothing.'

Black Paddy leaned over and peered too closely into Jack's eyes. The firelight made his face look yellow and waxy, like a grotesque dummy of a gypsy. He poked Jack in the ribs with a stubby finger lined with grease and dirt. 'You think I don't know how valuable he is?'

One of his accomplices, a man with wild black sideburns and baggy eyes, forced his way to the other side of the boy.

'I want my share of the money.' Black Paddy placed his heavy hand on Jack's neck and squeezed it. 'I've come to do business. Tell me what compensation you're prepared to give me and I'll let you keep the boy.' From the waistband beneath his exposed belly, he removed a gun.

'This is private business, Paddy. Nothing to do with you.'

'We're the same family. You and I. Nothing is private between us.' He squeezed Jack's neck so tightly hot wires of pain shot down his shoulders. The boy wished that the travellers would just pay the visitor and make him go away. However, none of them moved or said anything as the two visitors lifted him into the air. They backed away from the fire, pointing their guns at the travellers, some of whom broke from the circle and sprinted into the darkness.

When he understood the travellers could do little to save him and that he was in great danger, Jack kicked at Black Paddy's knee. It buckled satisfyingly and he grunted in pain. However, more of his accomplices pressed in towards Jack. He struggled in their grip, and bit at their hands. He saw flushed cheeks, grabbing arms, bodies twisting and turning in the mêlée. He felt their hot breath on his neck.

'He's like a wild animal.'

'Not so rough.'

'Easy. You're hurting him.'

He had never been hit before, and the first blow to his head left him dazed. He looked back at the fire and saw the figures of the other travellers moving about like moths fluttering in the light. A gun went off, and the figures stirred frenziedly, roars and shouts filling the darkness.

He fell to the ground with a heavy thump. The last thing he heard was the cursing and shouting of his kidnappers. The coldness of the ground was dense and palpable. He felt the darkness rise up and devour him. Very soon, there was no ground or starlit sky, no fire, no road, no travellers, no space or time, no story left to tell, just darkness and the cold ground.

CHAPTER TWENTY-EIGHT

Daly made eye contact with several burly-looking men hovering in the shadows of the hallway, before a young woman led him upstairs and ushered him into a lowly lit room, where a faded individual greeted him from behind a mahogany desk. Alistair Reid seemed to have lost weight. The veins stood out on his greying temples and his shirt collar looked too big for his neck. His thick eyebrows resembled ragged slashes in a hood through which his frightened eyes peered. He looked as though he had just returned to this dark sanctuary after weeks of wandering lost and hungry along the border.

'It took me a while to track you down, Mr Reid. Your office said they didn't know where you were. I'm glad they passed on my message.'

'I needed the privacy.'

Daly's eyes adjusted to the light and took in the emblems and flags blazoning the walls and the shelves of leather-bound books. A dark tapestry depicting a bloody battle with men on horses masked the wall behind Reid along with banners marked with vaguely Masonic symbols. If Reid had ever derived a sense of comfort or pleasure from the surroundings, he did not show it this evening. He looked agitated, with dark smudges of worry beneath his eyes, and the smooth charm he had displayed towards Daly at their prior meeting was now transformed into churlishness.

'Your privacy is well protected,' said Daly. 'Do all politicians have so many security staff?'

Reid glared at Daly. He flexed his thumbs and folded his hands at the desk. Another physical barrier to be penetrated. 'Is that what you're here to talk about, my desire for privacy at this difficult time?'

'What I've come to talk about is the attempt to remove your brother's body from his grave.'

The rings beneath Reid's large eyes seemed to grow darker. 'That was a senseless act of desecration by mindless vandals. What else do you want to know about it?'

'I suspect it was something a lot more sinister. I believe they were trying to steal your brother's body.'

Reid continued to stare at Daly, his face taut with reserve. 'Who would be crazy enough to steal the body of my dead brother, an elderly farmer who led a solitary life?'

'That is precisely the question I have been asking myself.'

'And what have you concluded?' The politician's tense face seemed to grow heavier, as if his apprehension had a weight, burdening his eyebrows and flaccid features.

'They wanted to remove his remains because they are an important piece of evidence. One that is linked to other crimes.'

'How?'

'At first, I suspected that your brother's death was directly connected to Jack Hewson's disappearance. Now I see that the links are more indirect. The two crimes run parallel to each other.'

'What proof do you have?'

'I have one or two leads.'

Reid's mouth twisted into a grim smile. 'For Christ's sake, Daly, don't play the plodding detective with me.'

'I *am* a detective. I'm not playing the role. I believe your brother was murdered, possibly by an individual you and he knew.'

'Believe me, if it turns out Sammy was murdered I wouldn't be able to live with the thought of it. We didn't get on that well in recent years, but he still meant everything to me. He wasn't just my brother; he was the last connection I had with my roots, my land, my people.'

Daly sat quietly, waiting as the politician grew more tense, his folded hands turning into claws, his shoulders hunched and ready to spring forward.

'Listen, Inspector, I don't think you understand how serious this is.' Reid's throat grew rough. 'If, as you believe, Sammy was murdered by someone, then it won't be long before they strike again.'

'Who's next on their list?'

'Me, you bastard.' Another part of the mask slipped from Reid's face, revealing the frightened man beneath. 'You need to talk to Thomas O'Sullivan. If his people hadn't stuck their noses in Sammy's business, none of this would have happened.'

'You've taken a while to express your suspicions about the travellers.'

'I've been distracted.'

'What were the distractions?'

A flush rose through his features. 'I will have no more discussions about this matter,' he said, rising to his feet.

'Sit where you are, Mr Reid,' ordered Daly. 'I have more questions to ask you.'

The politician lowered himself into the seat with a glowering expression. All his faculties were engaged now, his eyes fully alert and focused on Daly.

'Tell me about the Strong Ulster Foundation.'

'Is this something the police need to know?'

'I'm not sure until you tell me the details. Harry Hewson had been digging around the organization before he was murdered. My understanding is that he found out you are one of its directors.'

'Was, Inspector. I resigned my position a few years ago, when the property boom collapsed. In those days, everyone was throwing money at houses.' He bared his teeth in the form of a painful smile. 'I was exposed personally to some bad investments and was forced to hand over everything to do with the foundation.'

'Who took over for you?'

'The people who stumped up the cash in the first place. The foundation was really an investment vehicle for a group of retired security force personnel. It bought up properties and then rented them out while waiting for the market to pick up.'

'Give me the names of the investors.'

He grimaced and stirred in his seat. 'That's confidential business information. All you need to know is that there are a lot of highly trained military operatives in this country surviving on very small pensions, who were keen to build up a property portfolio.' He gestured to the tapestry and banners hanging on the walls as though they were a battlefield from which he had just emerged. 'I don't think you understand anything of my people's culture, Inspector Daly, what we went through during the Troubles. Seeing our family members murdered one after the other, watching our communities falling apart. Some of us had to make a stand and form organizations to protect and support our people.'

'And did these organizations ever cross the line?'

'What do you mean?'

'Were they engaged in violence against their enemies?'

Reid sighed and rose from his seat. He stood with his back to Daly, contemplating the tapestry on the wall, and then he turned back to the detective.

'Let me tell you something about border country, Daly. It's a bottomless labyrinth. I'm not talking about its landscape of winding roads, or its interlocking sectarian parishes. I'm talking about border people themselves, both Protestant and Catholic, their unfathomable minds, the dark turmoil of their history. They are the true labyrinth.

'Even if there was a united Ireland, the Republicans living there will always belong to border country,' he added. 'Their fight is with authority of any kind, not just the British Army or a civilian police force.' He stared meaningfully at Daly. 'And that is why some of us will always have to take matters into our own hands to protect our community, no matter the political outcome. The Strong Ulster Foundation was set up, as the name suggests, to lead my community through times of weakness and confusion.'

Reid turned his back on Daly again. He opened a drawer and removed a file of documents. He faced Daly and carefully handed him one of the sheets, as though he were transferring a wafer of ice. Daly read a long list of farming properties, agricultural land and abandoned building sites, entire terraces of houses alongside contentious parade routes, as well as disused churches and police stations from border villages clinging on to existence. He could not imagine a bleaker property portfolio.

'But this isn't the complete story of the foundation's history,' said Daly. 'You're holding something back. Hewson was on the trail of something sinister linked to the foundation's past. Something so sinister he was prepared to risk his own life in bringing it to the light.'

'Then finish his work.' Reid glared at him. 'Bring it into the light, if you feel that's what this country needs at this present time.'

Daly chose his words carefully. 'We have a twisted view of our leaders in this country. We know that some of our politicians once operated at the margins of society, doing violent things with guns and paramilitary gangs, but still we keep voting them into power. We put them into positions of responsibility where they feel so threatened that they have to hunt down every shadow from their past, every secret that threatens to be revealed.'

The politician stared at Daly, wide-eyed. 'I've done nothing violent. I've broken no laws.'

'But for years you lived on a vision of violence. And now because of that vision, you are a hunted man. That's the reason for all the security here, isn't it? You're in fear of your life.' Reid might never have pulled a trigger, thought Daly, but the clamour of conflict had always been at his back. He had much more to lose than his reclusive brother, a border hermit, eking out his final days on a lonely farm.

A knock came from the door and Reid's PA stuck her head into the room and gave the politician a look as if to ask whether the meeting was going as planned. Reid shook his head slightly, and she hesitated, unsure of what to do next.

She exited when Daly cleared his throat. The detective posed another question. 'What if the travellers thought that your brother was connected to an unsolved crime in the past?'

'You'd have to ask Sammy that.'

'Unfortunately, we can't find out what fears were preying on your brother's mind. His words will never be heard. We have to go back to what you know about your brother's connections with the travellers. What earlier involvement did he have with them? Did he ever meet a woman called Mary O'Sullivan?'

Reid did not react to the name. Instead, he appeared to be expecting it. 'I don't remember.'

Daly could see that Reid clearly did remember. The politician stiffened to attention, and the mood in the room seemed to darken and contract to a point. Even the horseback figures on the tapestry appeared to rouse themselves from the wall and lean into the room, their swords glinting.

CHAPTER TWENTY-NINE

Jack's kidnappers hauled him from the car the next morning and bundled him through the door of a dingy caravan. Inside stood the girl with the black plait, studiously paying no attention to the three rough men as they undid the ropes that bound his body. She barely flinched, a calm, composed figure putting on make-up before a mirror perched on a filthy stove, as though this world of violence and disorder could not touch her. She leaned forward a little and stared at Jack through the mirror, her eyes bright and curious as if she were peering into a very dark well. Before he could say or communicate anything to the girl, the men steered him into a small bedroom and locked the door.

He was alone again. All he had to set against the gnawing fear that his life was in great danger was the conspiracy of the mute exchange with the girl, the nagging sensation that she was transmitting something coded and important through her eyes. He waited, listening for the sound of the men transmitted through the caravan, but all was silent. Overcome with the feeling that he was on an excursion into someone else's nightmare, he banged on the walls of the caravan with his fists and shouted until his hands and throat ached. After a while, he gave in and lay down on the cramped bed. He slept fitfully through a gloomy afternoon; rain glistening on the caravan window; black leaves clinging to the wetness and then whirling away in the wind. Dark clouds poured across the sky. The caravan rocked to the movements of men coming and going, disturbing his sleep, but no one entered his room.

He awoke to the sound of a radio blaring from the front of the caravan, and the movement of his captors. Then a noise from outside his window made him look up. From the radio, he heard the roar of a horse-racing crowd, and the rising tones of the commentator. Someone turned the volume higher. Closer to the window, he heard his name whispered, followed by a set of fingernails rapping on the glass.

'Shit, he's going to win it,' yelled one of the men in the front of the caravan as the commentator's voice grew more excited.

The noise from the window came again, harder, more urgent. Someone was using the sound of the radio as cover to contact him. For a second, the commentator's voice died to silence, and when he spoke again, the men roared in unison and the caravan rocked to their movement. Jack pulled back the curtain. On the other side of the window was the girl, beckoning him to open it. Her face was deathly pale, and her knuckles raw and red-looking in the subdued light.

The window had been screwed shut, and would not budge

more than a centimetre or two, but it was enough to hear her urgent breathing. She stared at him with her dark eyes, her plait drenched in the rain. So deep was her imploring look that he thought she might be deaf or mute.

When she spoke, her words jammed together in a stammer. 'You... have to escape, Jack,' she said. 'Something... bad is going to happen.' She shivered with more than the cold. He saw in her white-faced fear the dreadful things her uncle was capable of doing.

'What do you have, Jack? What is so... important to them?' She did not move or speak, waiting for his reply.

'I don't know.'

'Then why did the travellers steal you from your... parents?'

'The McGinns didn't steal me. They took me on their journey.'

'But they took you to a place no one would find you.'

'They were meant to take me to my dad.'

'There's a... man here I've never seen before.'

'What does he look like?' For a moment, he hoped it might be his father.

'I only saw him from behind. They say he is an important... policeman. He was carrying a gun and shouting. I thought he was going to cause trouble and arrest someone, but then I saw him paying money to my uncle. He was doing business. He kept asking questions about you.'

'Did he mention my name? Jack Hewson?'

'Yes. And I heard them talking about your dad.'

'Your uncle shouldn't have taken me. He should have waited until my dad showed up.'

'Do you want to go home now?'

'Yes.'

'Then tell me what it is you have.' She looked him straight in the eye, challenging him.

'I keep telling you, I don't know. Why are you speaking to me at all? Aren't you afraid of your uncle?'

'I don't fear him. I... hate him.' She stared at him in defiance.

He still had no idea why her uncle had kidnapped him. What had started as a harmless adventure with some friendly traveller children had turned into a rootless journey from one camp to another with disaster looming ever closer like the constant threat of rain and wind.

'I want to go home, now. Help me get out.'

'You'd better listen or I won't help you at all. If we leave now, they will find us very quickly. Wait until it's dark, and in the meantime, do everything my... uncle asks you. Eat what he gives you; answer his questions; pretend to go to sleep when he tells you. You must not raise their suspicions in any way.'

When he did not reply, she asked, 'Do you want my uncle to catch the two of us together?'

'No.'

'Right then. I'm going to wait until night-time and then I'll come back.' She instructed him to have a bundle ready to place under the duvet so that it would look as though he was fast asleep in bed.

In the front of the caravan, someone lowered the radio, and then the caravan shifted as the men began moving. He glanced at the door, cringing at the thought of them entering the room. He looked back through the window, but the girl had disappeared. He stared through the glass at a campsite strewn with ugly rubbish. His childhood was over. He knew that now. All that confronted him were intimidating shadows and the thick cursing voices of the men outside his door.

CHAPTER THIRTY

The afternoon light flashed along the windows of the police building like a blind gun fired in random directions. Daly hurried from his car, catching glimpses of the sun's burning reflection. Amid the usual careful figures standing and chatting behind the glass, Daly spotted Special Branch Inspector Fealty, leaning against a railing on the third floor and staring down at the car park, as if waiting in ambush. Was it his imagination or did Daly see a smile form on his lips?

The blazing sun followed Daly, filling the glass pane behind which Fealty was standing. The Special Branch inspector looked imprisoned in the light, a tall thin insect in amber. When Daly looked back up again, another figure moved casually into view behind Fealty. It was Commander Sinclair, hanging back a little in the other man's shadow. Before Daly slipped through the entrance doors he glanced up again at the third-floor window, but the figures were now invisible, the glass filled with a radiant darkness.

Detective O'Neill was waiting for him in his office. Her expression was grim, yet an excited light shone in her eyes. 'O'Sullivan called to say he's found out who is holding Jack Hewson,' she told him. 'He claims that a traveller gang led by a man called Black Paddy McDonagh kidnapped him from the McGinns last night.'

Daly took off his jacket and digested the news.

'But there are complications. He doesn't know where they've taken the boy or what they plan to do with him.'

'How did he sound on the phone?'

'Tired and worried. I think he was telling the truth.'

'Do we have any record on this McDonagh character?'

'He's just returned from America, where he'd been jailed for low-level criminality, mostly assault and intimidation. The intelligence understanding is that since his return to Northern Ireland, he's been muscling in on Thomas O'Sullivan's territory, breaking the travellers' normal code of conduct. O'Sullivan is now offering to intervene on our behalf and negotiate the boy's release. He's promised to get back to us as soon as he has more details.'

'Sounds like a long process. Meanwhile, the boy is in the hands of this dangerous gang. Why should we trust him in the first place?'

'If we bring him in for more questioning we run the risk of losing his help in finding Jack.'

Daly and O'Neill lapsed into silence, going through the possibilities in their heads. The tension in the room increased as they considered the new and sinister directions the search for Jack, which had been dragging for days, might now take.

'If what he is saying is true,' said Daly, 'then the boy is

in the middle of a war between rival traveller gangs. The danger level could not be any higher.'

He came to a conclusion. 'O'Sullivan's claims might look dubious, but this is the closest thing we've had to a break-through. For the time being, we have to behave as though we believe him.'

He asked O'Neill to go over the details of the police sur-veillance on O'Sullivan's camp that day. However, nothing of interest had emerged.

'Has he made any demands or placed any conditions upon helping us?'

'There was just one. He wants to deal only with you.'

'Where is he now?'

'We assume he's still at the camp. There have been no reports of him leaving.'

Daly asked O'Neill to send out an alert to all police patrols to search the local halting sites, and then he grabbed his jacket and strode along the sunlit corridor towards the nearest exit. However, a burly-looking silhouette stepped out to block his way. He stopped in his tracks, surprised to see the figure was Detective Brian Barclay.

'I've something confidential and urgent to discuss with you,' said Barclay. His face looked sharper in the afternoon sunlight. Even his eyes had a cutting attitude that Daly had not noticed before. He was smiling but there was an unpleas-ant edge to his grin.

'Do you want to speak somewhere private?'

'No. Here is fine. As long as Special Branch aren't listening in.' He glanced around, and then he faced Daly squarely, as though trying to shield him from the light streaming through the windows. 'I haven't seen you around for the past few days, Celcius.'

'I've been busy.'

'Irwin is spreading stories about your mother,' he said in a low voice.

'What stories?' Daly had been keen to push on, but now he lingered, suddenly on the defensive.

'I'm just alerting you,' Barclay replied flatly. 'He's telling his colleagues that she was involved with the IRA, and that's why she was murdered.'

'My mother had no links with any political or paramilitary group,' said Daly in a thick voice.

'It's clear to me that—' Barclay cut himself short. He manoeuvred himself so that he was completely silhouetted against the tall windows, the sun shining directly into Daly's eyes, making him squint.

'What's clear to you?'

'That Irwin has a personal vendetta against you.'

Daly stared at Barclay's impassive profile. Why was he disclosing this? Out of professional courtesy or something else? Barclay turned and looked at him sympathetically. Daly felt furious but also disorientated. In the past year, he had never felt so ill at ease with his fellow police officers and superiors, and it was an even longer time since he had felt able to make a personal friendship with another officer. He retreated from Barclay's friendly smile.

'What other stories has he been saying? Who else has he told these lies to?' He felt stirred into launching an all-out fight for justice, to clear his mother's name finally, but he also felt a wave of revulsion at the underhand manner in which the Special Branch detective was undermining his reputation.

Barclay averted his gaze. 'I'm just letting you know what I've heard.'

Daly wondered if this was the reason why so many of the Special Branch team had been eyeing him suspiciously. He wanted to vigorously defend his mother's name, tell Barclay about the woman she really was, a hard-working nurse devoted to her family, that she had been targeted because they had been a Catholic family planning to build a new house, that their dreams for the future had stirred mean little jealousies in their neighbours, but that was something he had wanted to forget. He remembered how his father had told him that his mother's death was over and in the past. That had been on the day he joined the police force, long before he discovered the carefully concealed truth about her murder. If only it were that simple to forget. Now he had a sour taste in his mouth.

Barclay watched Daly closely. 'Irwin is a police officer and has to observe the rules of conduct. He's not free to say anything he likes about a colleague.'

Daly nodded. He did not know whether to despise Irwin or to pity him.

'You should ignore him,' continued Barclay. 'He's just one police officer who can't control his tongue.' He rubbed his neck. 'Right now, both of our reputations are under more serious threat.'

Barclay was right, thought Daly. He had been stirred with anger and ready to tackle Irwin, but he had more pressing problems to deal with.

'I hear that Thomas O'Sullivan has changed his approach,' said Barclay. 'All of a sudden he's turned into a perfectly reasonable negotiator.'

'What have you heard?'

'That the travellers are so keen on kidnapping that they abducted the same boy twice.' Barclay laughed cynically. 'A rival family member took the child by force with the intention of ransoming him back to the original kidnappers.'

'Whatever the truth, time is the most important factor now. We need to track down McDonagh using all available resources.'

'But in spite of our surveillance on the travellers we've got very little to work on. The investigation is mired in confusion. You're annoyed over your colleague's bad behaviour and I'm scratching my stupid head over how we allowed Jack Hewson to disappear right under our noses in the first place. None of this is helping the investigation.' He stared meaningfully at Daly.

'What are you suggesting?'

Barclay hunched his shoulders. He stared at Daly as though he badly wanted to share a secret with him. 'Jack's disappearance was not a random incident,' he said. 'It's part of a deeper pattern of criminality within the travelling clans. It's time someone was brave enough to crack their wall of silence.'

'How do we do that?'

'First we need some leverage.'

Daly reverted to his usual silence. He had no idea what Barclay was hinting at, but he was intrigued.

'O'Sullivan isn't going to volunteer the whereabouts of McDonagh, Celcius. He'll divert blame from his own people,

but he'll never willingly help the police arrest another traveller. Whether you're investigating drug smuggling or searching
for a missing boy, you have to apply pressure to the correct
people. Disgruntled business associates, angry spouses, nosy
neighbours, to name but a few.'

'And how do you apply pressure?'

'Look, I never had the temperament of detectives like you,
Celcius. Patiently questioning one suspect after another, teas-
ing out the leads. But in my own way, I can be very persuasive.'
Barclay gave Daly more eye contact, level and sustained.

'You're still not making yourself clear. What are you pro-
posing we do to the O'Sullivans?'

Barclay flashed Daly a delayed grin. 'When it comes to
the border you're an outsider, Celcius. You don't know what
policing the place is like. Don't make the mistake of thinking that it's easy to reason with people like the O'Sullivans.
If you're not prepared to take measures into your own
hands and use some force, you'll never find that boy. What
I propose is we should invent some charges to do with drug
dealing and use that as leverage.'

Daly felt a measure of disappointment in Barclay and also
distrust. Why was he brazenly suggesting they should break
police rules? 'I prefer to make my own judgement as to how
the investigation should proceed.'

Barclay was distracted by a column of fresh-faced police
officers moving down the corridor. He turned sideways into
the sunlight and shadows scooped at his bony face. He looked
back at Daly and tipped his head closer with a confidential
air. 'I like how you operate. I've seen how you deal with the
top brass. You don't talk the bureaucratic crap of all these

new officers eager for promotion. What do they know about policing? Their heads are filled with all these fantasies of a new Northern Ireland. They can't see the truth, even though it's staring them in their faces.'

'And what is that?'

'That political power and justice come from physical force. Look at all those politicians and their advisers in our government. How many of them have blood on their hands?'

Barclay's eyes widened, as if he were remembering the grisly past. Daly knew that Barclay had started in the police reserve, and had moved around a lot between stations along the border. He would have had to tough it out before rising to the rank of detective. Daly sighed. How had they got on to the contentious subject of the past when they had more pressing problems to deal with?

'I'm heading to O'Sullivan's camp right now,' said Daly. 'I'll let you know how I get on.'

'I'll follow you. We'll take him by surprise. That's halfway to winning the battle.'

'No. I'd rather go alone.'

'You don't know O'Sullivan.'

'I've known dozens of men like O'Sullivan, sitting on secrets all their lives. If he hasn't told the police anything up to now, the two of us barging in and trumping up charges is not going to make any difference.'

'Is this about territory? You don't like me muscling in on your investigation, is that it?' Barclay grinned. Almost everything Daly said seemed to make him grin. Not because he somehow saw the funny side of their conversation, thought Daly. More that Barclay was trying to lighten the mood, and convince him they were immersed in a light-hearted caper instead of a serious investigation veering towards disaster.

'Look, let me talk to him,' said Barclay.

'No. This is my investigation.'

'He'll tell me everything. Who knows, maybe he's been waiting for someone like me to appear. Someone who knows how to bargain and haggle over the truth. Maybe you've never raised the stakes with him. I know how to do that. I know how to get the answers.'

'What if the truth cannot be told? At least not to you or me?'

'What do you mean? Of course the truth should be told to us. We're police officers. We uphold the law. We are beyond reproach.'

'What if O'Sullivan is keeping silent not because he's afraid of incriminating himself but because he's protecting a family secret, one that has been hidden for decades?'

Barclay took a few steps backwards. His voice went flat again. 'OK, Celcius. Have it your way, but you're at serious risk of getting yourself into a tangle again. I heard about the near riot you caused the last time you went looking for O'Sullivan.' He took out his mobile phone and began punching in a number. 'I'm going to inform Special Branch and have them monitor your progress with O'Sullivan, whether you like it or not. The stakes are too high to let you risk doing this on your own. Detective Irwin will give you back-up on the ground, should anything go wrong.'

Daly sighed. 'Fine with me,' he replied, forcing aside his earlier antipathy for Irwin. 'But make sure he keeps at a discreet distance. I don't want anyone spooking O'Sullivan while he's this close to helping us.'

CHAPTER THIRTY-ONE

Jack awoke from a half-slumber to the sound of metal scratching against the window. He pulled back the curtains and saw that the girl had returned. Her nose and cheek were pressed against the glass, her skinny arms wielding a crowbar, which she had wedged into the tiny gap between the pane and the window frame. She was strange and feral-looking, forcing the window open in the moonlight, but somehow alluring with her black plait and large eyes, which immediately cautioned him to be silent. She strained and pushed, using the weight of her body, and eventually one of the window locks snapped, creating a gap large enough for him to clamber through by twisting his body sideways. He dropped to the ground with a grunt. Immediately, she slipped her cold hand into his and held it there as they crouched in the darkness beneath the caravan.

They hunkered lower as a group of men carrying heavy cans lumbered towards them. Fearing capture, they crawled to the other side of the caravan. They listened to the men whispering, a period of silence, the hoot of an owl, and the sound of a liquid sloshing against the sides of the caravan. The acrid smell of petrol coiled up their nostrils. They rubbed their eyes, which wept in the fumes. He felt his throat choke and he tried to stifle the noise, but it came out as a broken cough.

The men stopped moving. There was a tense hush. The pair lay still and closed their eyes in the cramped space, barely breathing, and then the sound of someone flicking a cigarette lighter made them desperately drag themselves from beneath the caravan and run for cover. He heard what sounded like grim laughter, mirth incorporating a murderous delight, and then the licking roar of flames taking hold, engulfing the caravan in a ball of yellow and orange hues.

Jack's father had told him there were different types of travellers, and not all of them belonged to the same road: some had settled in houses and stayed put for generations. But in most cases they were a proud and insecure people, their loyalty centring on their extended family. The men who had doused the caravan with petrol were different, however. Their hair and moustaches were matted and greasy, and they seemed to spend most of their time arguing drunkenly among themselves. They had shown contempt for family bonds. They were not travellers; they were thieves and criminals.

Black fumes of smoke and a trapped violence burst forth from the caravan's shell, as though it had been harbouring weeks of pent-up rage. The windowpanes splintered and their frames melted in the heat.

They kept moving, glancing behind every now and again. The burning caravan grew brighter, their only landmark in the darkness. Then an explosion filled the air. They ducked for cover and for several moments they stared back, entranced by the blaze, the wind and flames opening the guts of the caravan to a howling roar. Even from this distance, they felt a heavy blanket of heat roll over them. What had prompted such murderous violence? wondered the boy. Was it his fault or his father's?

Then they were running again. He allowed her to keep possession of his hand. In the circumstances, it was all he had to give. Beyond the glowing encampment, the forest was filled with mist and faint blue starlight. They scurried into the trees. The sense of a new adventure, private to just the two of them, filled him with a sense of relief and excitement. However, as the pine branches swept over them, she slowed, tugging him back.

'Am I going too fast?' he asked.

'No.' She withdrew her hand and pulled away from him. 'It's time you told me what you're keeping... secret.'

A pale light seemed to emanate from her face, a light without any warmth, her eyes like ice.

He grew exasperated. 'Don't you think if I knew, I would tell you?' He felt anger rise in his throat. 'You know something I don't,' he shouted. 'What makes you so certain I have a secret?'

'All I know is you've gotten me into a lot of trouble.'

'I didn't ask you to help me.'

The shouts of men began to draw near with the searching beams of torches.

'Jesus and Mary look after us,' she said, gripping him by the hand, and then they were off again, running with one mind, fending off the branches and briars with their free arms. They paused for breath and heard the voices grow louder, torch-lights wavering in the darkness. One of the beams glanced across her face, lighting up the tiny cuts on her cheeks from the briars. Her eyes gleamed with the sheen of a wild animal. She made a sign of the cross, and dragged him after her.

The trees grew thicker, the terrain more uneven. Branches seemed to spread and solidify all around them, their gorged roots rising up from the slimy ground. Sweat poured from him and the muscles of his legs burned with exhaustion. Eventually, they broke from the forest on to a grassy bank that ended abruptly in a deeper darkness. Are we free? he wondered, staring back at the trees. Where were their pursu-ers and which direction should they take now? What about the girl, was she his ally or his captor, leading him on to a darker trap?

They stood apart, contemplating their next move. A cold wind buffeted their bodies. Was it a river or a silent road that stretched before them? It was so black, he could not tell. She turned to him with a smile, and then she climbed to the edge of the bank and leaped into the well of darkness. Without hesitating a moment, he ran after her and jumped.

CHAPTER THIRTY-TWO

The traveller camp was a fairground of discordant noises, doors banging on the caravans, brakes squealing as children rode round on rusted bikes, babies wailing from battered prams pushed by girls laughing and talking in high-pitched voices. Daly could feel the adults watching him surreptitiously through the caravan windows as he made his way along the muddy paths. He spied a drunk-looking man sprawled on a set of steps, bent over and gulping. He was unsure if the man was laughing to himself or vomiting. A magpie flapped away, sharing the detective's look of unease.

Daly tried not to attract too much attention. He wanted to wander and poke around a bit. However, the children began to follow him around, drawing closer to satisfy their curiosity. He turned upon them and asked for Thomas O'Sullivan's whereabouts.

'What do you want him for, mister?' they asked.

'I'm here to do business.'

A horse and rider emerged from between the trees. A large piebald mare with a touch of Irish draught, and seated on top was O'Sullivan, bare-headed and grinning, taking a leisurely tour around the margins of the camp. He urged the animal towards Daly and circled the detective, his bearing radiating authority.

'I hope you haven't come to arrest us, Inspector. Or chase us away.' His eyes were challenging, and in the wet dusk, his drooping moustache looked even more impressive. His darkly haired hands, covered in gold rings, held the reins loosely.

'I've come to warn you that everything has changed.'

'Has it?' replied O'Sullivan. He seemed more focused on his horse and the fading light. 'How has it changed?'

The children swarmed around them, and the horse shivered, taking several steps backwards. The light thickened into darkness.

'Whatever reason you had to take the boy, it no longer holds.'

'Why do you think that?'

'His father was murdered. Another man has died in mysterious circumstances. Who is there left to apply pressure on?'

'You're missing the point, Inspector. The motive for taking the boy still stands.'

'Then tell me what it is.'

O'Sullivan reined the agitated animal to a stop and stared towards the entrance of the camp, distracted. Had he seen Irwin's back-up car or was he just checking if Daly had come alone or not? He turned his attention back to Daly.

'He was taken to apply pressure on you, Inspector.'

Daly stood in the deepening gloom as children on bikes

302

and pushing prams ran and played around them as though they were both invisible. What did the traveller mean? O'Sullivan slid from his horse and plonked his considerable frame beside Daly. What the detective saw etched in his face was worse than animosity. It was triumph.

'We took Jack to see how you and your colleagues reacted.'

'Which colleagues?'

'Senior detectives in Special Branch.'

'Who are you talking about? Irwin or Fealty?'

'That's still the problem; we don't have a fucking clue who they are.'

'But they know you. You've been a person of interest for a long time. For the past six months, an extensive surveillance operation has been focused on you.' Daly considered O'Sullivan's grinning face. 'Is that why you took Jack? To divert police attention away from your criminal activities?'

'The people most anxious to find Jack are the ones with the biggest secrets to hide,' said O'Sullivan.

What sort of conspiracy was he hinting at? What links and secret associations lay at the heart of the case? Daly thought of Special Branch's interest in the case right from the start and their recruitment of Harry Hewson. To the foreground loomed the figures of Irwin and Fealty, police officers whose main skill and rigour lay in concealment. The journalist had been sitting on a very large story involving travelling families but also secret smuggling routes, politicians, business companies with a special interest in property, and a woman who had disappeared a long time ago at the heart of it all. Did the story also include police officers working in a conscious effort to hide a crime?

A look of concentration settled on O'Sullivan's face, as though he had finally made up his mind about something important. 'I've nothing else to tell you, Inspector. Other than it's time you met the boy.'

'Is this a confession?'

'No,' said O'Sullivan. He led Daly to a van, and opened the passenger door. He waited for the detective to climb in. 'I'm providing you with some secret information. I want to see what you think about it. But first, you have to trade a secret with me. It's the traveller way.'

'I have no secrets,' said Daly cautiously. Nevertheless, he wanted to keep the line of communication open. 'What secret are you talking about?'

'The one involving police officers and the Strong Ulster Foundation.'

Daly stared at him with growing interest.

O'Sullivan grinned. 'To help you make up your mind, I'm going to trade you another secret. I'm going to double the stakes by telling you who blew Harry Hewson's cover.'

The only good thing about O'Sullivan's face was that his thoughts and emotions played so clearly on it. He seemed to be taking pleasure in administering the truth in neat little portions like pieces of bait.

'It was his son,' said O'Sullivan. 'Hewson should have kept the boy completely in the dark, like he did his wife. Jack was old enough to ask questions but not old enough to understand the great danger his father was in. That morning in the courthouse, he climbed willingly into the van and blew apart all his father's carefully laid plans.'

O'Sullivan gestured at Daly to climb into the vehicle.

'I can tell from the expression on your face that you know all about the Strong Ulster Foundation. You can take your time and share your secrets with me. We have a long journey ahead of us.'

Daly had little choice but to clamber into the seat and buckle in. The engine of the van sounded suspiciously souped up as O'Sullivan revved it into life. As Daly took in the view from the windscreen, the rain-glistening path of the road winding through the trees, the wing flashes of birds diving for cover, he felt completely in the dark. However, he decided that not being in the know was fine for now, that a new perspective awaited him at the end of this journey. Besides, he had Irwin following behind. He could see the headlights of the detective's car swing out on to the road behind them. The car hung back and followed at a discreet distance. Things were set in motion and O'Sullivan seemed ready to explain or confess his role in the kidnapping.

CHAPTER THIRTY-THREE

In the darkness of the passenger seat, Daly concentrated on arranging what he knew about the travellers, the Reid brothers and the Strong Ulster Foundation, and why O'Sullivan was taking him on this road trip. He tried to bring order to the unanswered questions, the coincidences that linked the different protagonists in this complicated tale. He tried to project O'Sullivan's intentions on to the circle of darkness that lay ahead of the headlights' beams. The traveller was a lot more intelligent than he seemed. He was the head of the clan, one of the richest travellers in the country. He could have vanished over the border but he had remained at the campsite in full view of the police. There was still something he was overlooking.

'Where's Jack?' he demanded.

'Travelling.'

'Where?'

'In the old country.'

'Where's that?'

'Just wait and see, Inspector.'

Daly reached into his pocket and took out his phone, but O'Sullivan reached across and deftly removed it. 'I'm dealing with you and no one else,' he warned.

'These travellers who took Jack, I need to know what they want,' said Daly.

O'Sullivan took a tricky corner in fourth gear, the force propelling Daly against the passenger door, the front tyres whining with the strain.

'Don't you get it, Inspector? There are no fucking demands.' O'Sullivan expertly changed gears.

'Then why kidnap him in the first place?'

'Because there's a price on his head.'

'I don't understand.'

O'Sullivan flashed him a grin broader than his usual one. Travellers were professional spinners of riddles, and he seemed pleased with Daly's confusion. He took the next corner at even greater speed.

'That was a bad bend,' said Daly.

'Don't worry, I'll go easier on the next.'

Daly worried that there might not be a next time. He glanced in the wing mirror for a sign of Irwin's car, wondering if O'Sullivan had spotted the tail. The traveller braked sharply and swung on to a side road. He ignored Daly's questions and began talking about the secret roads and border crossings the travellers had been using for generations, the old cart tracks, the green ways, the hare paths and the high-sided lanes so deep and dark they felt like tunnels into another world. He told the detective stories about the charmed lives of smugglers and vagabonds, who spent their lives criss-crossing the border and camping in the wild. Then, during the Troubles, how the criminal enterprises of paramilitaries began to intertwine with the wilful wandering of the travellers, murderers and fugitives mingling with his people along the ghost roads of the border. A brigade of broken men had found a temporary home along the old traveller halting sites, he told Daly, but they did not really belong to the road. Living rough was not in their blood and they could never be trusted.

Daly suspected at first that O'Sullivan was trying to trick him with his openness. He was used to sullen hostility from travellers, not this earnest gabbling from behind the wheel as they sped towards the border.

'Tell me this, why did you build such a grand mansion and then abandon it?' asked Daly.

'I haven't abandoned it.'

'But my officers were able to enter it without setting off any alarms. It's no secret that you choose to live in a caravan instead.'

O'Sullivan's eyes glittered. 'For all the money I've poured into that place, I could never love it like the open road. It is a grand and sturdy house, but it always felt strange to me. Houses are dead places and the people who live in them are stuffed dolls. There's nothing natural about a man and a woman trapped by the same four walls year in year out.'

'Don't caravans have four walls, too?'

'But caravans are more like living things. They have their own personalities and quirks.'

Houses, rather than caravans, were where the heart of the

mystery lay, thought Daly. Houses and the people rooted to them, pottering about their possession-filled rooms, nurturing evil thoughts of revenge and betrayal, rather than the border roads winding before them and the traveller's primitive way of life. A more sophisticated mind had been at work, plotting the murders of Samuel Reid and Harry Hewson. A mind locked down and deepened by greed and the fear of a decades-old secret being exposed to the light.

The van rolled and bounced over the potholed road, splashing and rocking from side to side. The lights on the shaking dashboard caught the gold jewellery on O'Sullivan's hands. His eyes were hooded and evasive as he glanced at Daly.

'If you settled people really knew the dark thoughts in my head, you'd lock me up without question,' he told the detective. 'You'd lock all the travelling people up, if you could only read our minds. That's why we keep moving on.'

Daly frowned. O'Sullivan was revealing something true and personal from deep within, and he believed he understood something of the traveller's inner torment. Thoughts welled up and prodded at his conscience: his mother's murder, his divorce, his father's silence and all the things that had been left unsaid between them. What would it be like to leave behind everything that reminded him of who he was? To join the travellers on the open road, to lead a life uncluttered by the baggage of the past, to stop stumbling in the darkened interior of his cottage and step into a simpler, clearer story, one made up of roads, forests, the moon, and a winding border?

'We're not that different from you,' murmured Daly. 'We lock ourselves up for the thoughts in our own heads.

We hide ourselves away in brand-new houses we can't afford, or old cottages falling down around us. We even trap ourselves in relationships and jobs that we hate because of the dark thoughts inside our heads.'

They lapsed into silence, as though too much had been said. After a few miles, O'Sullivan swung the van back on to a main road. Daly glanced in the mirror and saw what he hoped were the headlights of Irwin's car following them.

'This price on Jack's head, was it set by a criminal gang?' asked Daly.

'Correct. The same gang who murdered Mary O'Sullivan.'

The car swerved through a puddle, smearing the windows with a suspension of mud. O'Sullivan did not bother to use the wipers. They were travelling blind now. Daly could feel the exhaust pipe thumping upon the uneven terrain as the vehicle clattered along the lane.

'By holding on to Jack, we wanted to send the murderers a message. Come after him if you think the price is worth gambling everything for.'

He swung the car violently into the overgrown mouth of a hidden lane. They were on a muddier, more slippery surface. The pale trunks of pine trees flashed by.

'Turns out, the price was even greater than we suspected. The camp is close by.' He gave Daly a cold glance. 'Everything will be made clear when we get there.'

He switched off the headlights. The lane ahead was barely visible, wriggling into the darkness, but O'Sullivan increased his speed. 'Are you Special Branch?' He glanced at Daly again.

'No. Did Hewson say I was?' Daly wished O'Sullivan would stop looking at him and concentrate on the road.

'He swore you weren't Special Branch. But if you aren't, how do you know about the Strong Ulster Foundation?'

Another thread to clutch at. They were ransacking each other for hidden information, peeling away the shadows. Their eyes met again, challenging the other for some secret that could not be disclosed.

'What I find more interesting is *how* you know about the foundation,' replied Daly. 'It's a secret organization, known only to a chosen few.'

'Hewson gave me the whole story in exchange for permission to travel with us. He said he did not want any payment, just our company on the road. I thought he wanted to leave behind his settled life, but that wasn't the case at all. He made it sound as though all he wanted was a nostalgic holiday, spending time in the camp, he and his son in their camper van, enjoying the traveller way of life.'

'What did he tell you?'

O'Sullivan leaned very close to the windscreen, cradling the steering wheel in his hands as he concentrated on the dim track ahead. 'Nearly there,' he said, his drooping moustache almost brushing the windscreen. He wound his window down and drove so slowly they could hear the chittering sounds of birds disturbed from their roosts in the overarching branches. He leaned out of the window and shouted something incomprehensible. From the depths of the forest, a light blinked, once, twice, and then vanished. O'Sullivan braked and stopped the van with a jolt. He stared attentively at Daly, as though he was trying to read his thoughts. Daly looked back at him, unsure of what to do or say.

'I'll make this easier for you, Inspector,' said the traveller.

There was a slight change of tone to his voice. A hint of urgency, perhaps even fear, as though time was running out for them. In the corner of his eye, Daly could see a set of headlights appear in the wing mirror.

O'Sullivan told Daly everything that Harry Hewson had discovered about the Strong Ulster Foundation. It was a complicated story to do with control and money and sectarianism that revealed a world of invisible political forces operating at the heart of society. According to O'Sullivan, the reporter had heard rumours from other journalists, and picked up information from disgruntled estate agents and his police contacts. He found out that the foundation had been collecting donations from wealthy Protestants as well as illegally diverting political and church funds to build up a vast war chest of cash. The money was used to buy up abandoned farms along the border in order to keep them out of Catholic hands. It was all done very discreetly, through different holding companies with separate boards of directors. The foundation began to accrue large amounts of land in the run-up to the property crash in 2008. To the casual observer there had been no signs to suggest that the organization was acting through this host of property companies. The business of bidding on properties was done stealthily, and the buyers were at pains not to attract attention. Once bought, the properties were kept vacant. The foundation had large reserves and did not need to rent them out.

One of Hewson's contacts had gone so far as to reveal the foundation's secret list of directors. One of the names on the list was Alistair Reid.

'When the property crash came along, Reid was bankrupted

by some bad investments,' explained O'Sullivan. 'His creditors began to sniff out his involvement in the foundation. The whole house of cards threatened to fall down. Reid had to resign his directorship.'

'What did that mean?' asked Daly.

'It meant the story didn't end there. His stake in the foundation was signed over to someone else.'

'Who?'

'There was a shadowy group controlling the foundation from behind the scenes. Reid had been running the show, but he was acting on behalf of someone who wanted to remain invisible. To keep up the secrecy, Reid's directorship had to be transferred to someone trustworthy, someone who had not been personally exposed to the property market collapse. The circle of silence was closed again, and the foundation continued its secret business.'

When O'Sullivan had finished he stared at Daly with glinting eyes. 'Have you worked out who that person was?'

'No.'

'Think about it.'

The pieces of the puzzle finally fell into place. 'Samuel Reid.'

O'Sullivan grinned. 'You can draw one more conclusion.'

'His death was not an accident.'

'And the individual who pulled the strings in the background, who is he?'

O'Sullivan stared hard at Daly. 'He's the reason we kept Jack. He's the reason you and me are taking this journey.' He pulled a rifle from the back of the van and, pointing it at Daly, ordered him out of the vehicle.

'What about Jack Hewson?' asked Daly. 'You told me you knew where he was.'

O'Sullivan pointed with the gun towards a dim set of lights flickering through the trees.

'The rescue party are waiting in the forest for you. Go to them and they'll give you the boy.'

Daly clambered out. He glanced along the forest road. He did not see anything that might have signalled Irwin's presence, nothing that resembled another vehicle. He peered in at the traveller.

'You're not coming?'

'For what? The case is almost solved. Harry Hewson was Samuel Reid's son and Jack is his grandson.' He waved the rifle at Daly. 'Go up to the lights and you will find the boy. Don't be expecting me to hold your hand the entire fucking way.'

A set of headlights flickered further down the road. Daly hoped that it was Irwin coming with reinforcements. Strangely, the approach of the vehicle seemed to settle O'Sullivan, almost reassure him. He levelled the rifle at Daly and told him to hurry.

'I can see now how good a detective you are,' he said.

Daly took the flattery to be a sign of deep mockery. The investigation had been a catalogue of failures and delays, with not even a sighting of the missing boy, only a landscape of empty farms and roads, and dead bodies.

'You've helped me crack a forty-year conspiracy of silence,' added O'Sullivan. At this, he raised his rifle through his window and fired it, as if in celebration. Daly had the strong sense of a deal going sour and that he was expendable.

The worst sign was the look of manic satisfaction on O'Sullivan's face. Earlier he had been uncertain around Daly, veering between suspicion and trust. This elation was a more dangerous state altogether, one in which the faculties of reason were suspended. Men quickly turned to violence when high emotion took over.

'Don't fail Jack Hewson now, Inspector,' shouted O'Sullivan. 'You've worked hard to find the right track, now go and get the boy.' He fired the gun again.

Daly made a break for it. He plunged into the forest towards the light of the camp, his arms raised before him. At first, he stumbled through the darkness, and then as his eyes adjusted to the lack of light, he broke into a bent-over run. When he looked up, he was relieved to see that O'Sullivan had not moved from the van. However, the lights of the camp had drifted to the side. He adjusted his direction, panting heavily as he negotiated the almost invisible terrain of fallen tree trunks, upended roots and trenches of water. Soon traveller voices began to waft through the trees. A child's voice called 'Daddy, Daddy' from the somewhere close by, adding urgency to his run.

'All is ready,' he heard O'Sullivan shout. 'The bait has been set.'

Silence fell. Daly made long zigzagging sweeps, trying to keep the camp in sight. He had no guide left, or tracks to follow, but he was sure he was nearing the end of his journey.

CHAPTER THIRTY-FOUR

The scene that Daly stumbled into was empty of life apart from two grey horses standing statue still in the light of the roaring campfire. The only other sound as Daly approached was the rippling of the wind through the pine trees. However, the air felt charged with the static of danger. He scanned the shadows cast by the flickering firelight, wondering where were the traveller youths waiting to pounce and harry him. He stepped into the undulating light of the flames, feeling a sense of suspended animation. The horses bolted at his presence, taking off with the minimum of effort in a long flowing movement, a wave of pale shadows silently dipping and rising into the darkness. Their synchronized flight intensified the air of unreality.

When the horses had gone, Daly saw him, hunkering by the fire on his own. A skinny pale-faced boy shuffling his hands over his ears. He walked up to him and touched his head.

'Jack Hewson?'

'Yes.'

Daly noticed he was wearing the same clothes as on the day of his disappearance. His hair was matted and curly, and his trainers filthy wet.

'You're safe now, son.'

'Are you taking me to the police?' His eyes were dark with fear and hope. Rebecca's eyes had looked at him like that.

'No, I'm taking you to your mother.'

'What about my daddy?' In spite of the proximity of the fire, the boy shivered.

'I'm sorry he won't be there for you, but your mummy will.'

He took off his coat and wrapped it around the boy. He was about to lead him back through the forest to the road when a branch cracked underfoot and a figure appeared from the trees. The person waved a hand in greeting at Daly. It was Detective Barclay, looking composed and wary as he wandered along the edges of the fire's ring of light.

'Where's Irwin?' asked Daly.

'He couldn't come, so I decided to tail you instead.' Barclay spoke in a low voice, scanning the shadows around Daly. 'Surprised?'

'No.'

Daly thought it strange that Barclay had decided to follow him, but he had no time to question the detective's judgement. 'O'Sullivan has made off through the trees, along with the rest of his gang,' he said. 'If you get some reinforcements we'll stand a chance of apprehending them.'

Barclay appeared slow to respond. 'First let the boy come with me, Daly. I've already phoned his mum and she's keen to get him home.'

Jack stared at Barclay, his eyes full of suspicion. He seemed frozen to the spot and was breathing heavily.

'Is something wrong?' Daly asked the boy. He steered him by the shoulders towards Barclay, but the boy's body had stiffened and he refused to budge. 'Come on, Jack.'

Barclay waited just beyond the ring of light, watching them both but saying nothing. Somehow, the burden of negotiating with the boy had fallen to Daly.

'We haven't got all day,' said Daly. 'This is Detective Barclay, a colleague of mine. He has a car that will take you back to your mother.'

However, the boy kept glowering at Barclay, refusing to leave Daly's side.

'You have to trust me, Jack,' said Barclay. 'This time I'll make sure you get home.'

'What do you mean, this time?' asked Daly.

Neither Barclay nor the boy responded. They stared at each other, the silence intensifying between them.

'What's wrong?' Daly asked Jack. Clutching him closer, he felt something fluttering against the boy's chest, like a tiny bird trying to escape. He realized that it was the boy's heart beating wildly.

'What do you think, son?' said Barclay, his tone changing. 'Do you want the story to end here in this filthy fucking camp? That would be a very sad story, wouldn't it?' His eyes caught Daly's and glinted.

The silence grew so dense that Daly's ears began to ring. He stared at Barclay in alarm as he produced a gun from his jacket.

'It's a pity Sammy Reid never got to meet you, Jack,' said

Barclay. 'He would have been curious to meet his grandson. To see the same stubborn streak repeated in his heir. But, unfortunately, your father led you into this no man's land.' He pointed the gun at the detective. 'The game's up, Daly. You and the boy have reached the end of your journey.'

Daly hunkered a little further into the shadows.

'What do you intend doing with the gun?' he asked. The blood pounded in his temples as he tried to keep a measure of composure in his voice. The realization that Barclay had double-crossed him left him sickened, darkening further his vision of justice and order. It was a vision soiled already by the murder of his mother and the years of police cover-up. He did not need to hear a confession from Barclay. He knew already. The detective had murdered Samuel Reid and Harry Hewson, and was now intent on killing the boy and eradicating the final bloodline link to Mary O'Sullivan and Samuel Reid. As he had suspected, this was also the reason an attempt had been made to remove the farmer's body from his grave, to destroy the DNA evidence of paternity.

'It depends on who you've been talking to,' said Barclay.

Daly tried to buy himself more time. 'You've kept your role in this scheme secret from me. I applaud you on that. The day of Jack's disappearance, you were watching the travellers and organized the search of O'Sullivan's mansion. You were carefully erasing all traces of Mary O'Sullivan and her story. The last thing you expected was the appearance of her grandson on the scene. All of a sudden, her story threatened to engulf all the carefully laid plans of the Strong Ulster Foundation.'

'What do you know about the foundation?' Barclay

lowered his gun slightly, his voice sounding slightly agitated. Daly hoped that he might distract the detective long enough to grab the boy and dive into the shadows beyond the fire's circle of light.

'What sort of question is that?'

'You're killing me, Daly.'

'Killing you?'

'You and your stupid questions.' Barclay raised the gun again.

'What about Alistair Reid? What does this mean for him, knowing that you murdered his brother?'

Barclay shrugged his shoulders. 'It means that his reputation remains intact and you've turned out to be little more than a foolish amateur. While your friend O'Sullivan is either a complete coward or a scatterbrain.'

'Does Reid know what you did to Hewson?' Daly took another step to the side. All he needed was a little more time, and a few feet further from the light of the fire. Then he and the boy might find an escape route through the trees.

'Hewson was dangerous. Asking too many questions of his Special Branch handlers. He had to be stopped. He manipulated the gypsies, too, feeding them snippets of information, while all the time he was busy digging up the past. He even used his own son in his attempt to blackmail his way to the truth.'

Barclay aimed the gun at Daly and stepped closer. Daly tensed and waited, holding his breath. Barclay was still too far away for him to throw himself upon the weapon.

'What are you going to do now?'

'Kill you first, and then the boy.'

'You'll never get away with this.'

'Of course I will. No one knows where we are. Not even you. For all you know we could be on the other side of the border. I'll arrange this to look like you botched the boy's rescue and got shot by the travellers. Then I'll round up a suitable number of O'Sullivans and charge them with murdering the boy. No one will think to question my word over theirs.'

Daly heard the faintest of noises from the forest. He shifted a little, and saw a rifle glinting in the moonlight behind Barclay. A figure stepped out of the trees as stealthily as a shadow. Daly ignored the person and concentrated all his attention on Barclay.

'You still have time to surrender,' he shouted. 'Give me the weapon now before it's too late.'

Barclay stared at Daly with a look of annoyance. 'Why are you shouting?' He took aim with his gun, but before he could squeeze the trigger, Daly saw a flash from the rifle, the face of the gunman lighting up in the glare like a stage demon's, and then a shot rang out. Barclay's face turned to a sheet of ice.

Daly launched himself towards the detective, who stumbled forwards with the impact of the bullet. Barclay pointed his gun at Daly's lumbering frame and fired. Daly closed his eyes and tumbled to the ground, thinking that he was about to die. When he realized the bullet had not struck him, he looked up and saw Barclay still staggering, as though battling a shift in his centre of gravity. Another shot sounded and this time a rose of blood erupted on Barclay's forehead. He collapsed against a tree trunk, his eyes bulging in surprise, his lips moving slightly as if he were a murmuring a final prayer to himself, the hand holding the weapon trembling to the ground.

The broad-shouldered figure holding the rifle drew closer to Barclay's dying body. He lowered the weapon. It was O'Sullivan, grim-faced, his eyes scorching the shadows, until a big grin broke across his face at the sight of Daly and the boy. He wore the look of a conjurer that had pulled off something quite special.

'How long were you watching us?' asked Daly.

'From the start. I didn't step in until I heard enough to confirm my suspicions. Your colleague was the man I've been hunting for forty years.'

'I'm glad you acted when you did.'

'This beast was one of the men who killed my sister.'

'And I and the boy were the bait set to trap him?'

O'Sullivan nodded. 'I've made my living along the border, Inspector. You can't do that without meeting killers. Men who murdered for politics and men who murdered for money. But I'd never been able to trace the men responsible for Mary's death. All I ever found was a wall of silence.

'Then Harry came along, the nephew I thought I had lost. I realized I had a means to draw them out from their hiding places. This fear that they would lose their property empire to an illegitimate son. I wanted to take them out of circulation once and for all.'

Daly could see how the disappearance of Jack Hewson had appealed to a special traveller tradition – the business of going on the run to draw evil from its source.

'I didn't realize he would murder again so ruthlessly.' The

anger in O'Sullivan's voice was replaced with sorrow. 'Poor Harry paid for the truth with his life.' He spat at Barclay's body. 'His mistake was to think we were motivated by greed. That we were holding on to Jack to get his rightful inheritance. We had no interest in the foundation's empty buildings, its contested fields. What use had we for the money?'

Daly felt his impression of O'Sullivan changing. He had thought his openness, his child-like appetite for life rested on his desire to accrue as much wealth as possible. He'd been wrong. It rested on something deeper: revenge and the desire to hold together the fragmented pieces of his family.

O'Sullivan spoke again. 'In a few minutes this place will be crawling with police, and then the journalists will come, sniffing over the story, falling on top of each other, asking questions, but by then I'll be long gone.' He took another spit at Barclay's body. 'My family has wandered the road for hundreds of years, Inspector. Our freedom is limitless, and so are our resources. What would we be doing with a string of abandoned farmhouses and their muddy fields?'

The dead man's eyes stared up in O'Sullivan's direction, but looked right through him. As though the traveller, the living, calculating survivor of their contest were now the unreal one in the light of the dwindling fire, as though O'Sullivan were little more than a ghost, fading into the cold atmosphere of the night. The traveller grunted a goodbye to Daly and then he turned to the boy.

'I have to go now, Jack.'

'I don't want to travel any more. I want to stay with the detective.'

'You can stay for the rest of your life.'

CHAPTER THIRTY-FIVE

Daly sat in his car and watched the fleet of mechanical diggers tearing with military precision at the stony terrain of the quarry. The site had become a dangerous frontier in the landscape, cordoned off by police tape, and patrolled by officers and excavation experts, with a few journalists and photographers watching the unfolding drama. In the passenger seat beside Daly was a plane ticket to a foreign country and the holiday he had been long overdue. However, his mind was elsewhere.

Alistair Reid had revealed the location of the quarry after Daly arrested him over the disappearance of Mary O'Sullivan. Investigators were busy unravelling the complex financial documents relating to the Strong Ulster Foundation, and interviewing the other members of the organization. The media were all over the story, hoping to get live footage of the missing woman's remains being lifted into the air by one of the digger's claws. It was part of the modern obsession, thought Daly. If it was not filmed or photographed, it did not happen. History was no longer what existed in books or the human memory but what flashed up on a computer or mobile phone screen.

One of the reporters spotted him and walked towards his car, his press credentials and a mobile phone in his hand. Daly started the engine. A photographer aimed her camera at him and took a few shots. Then she lowered her camera and watched him drive off.

He travelled a few miles and then pulled on to the side of the road. He was tired and thought of catching up on some sleep. After that night in the forest with O'Sullivan, he had handed over the investigation to a team of officers flown over from London. He still had more interviews to do with the Metropolitan detectives, outlining what he knew of O'Sullivan's possible whereabouts, but he doubted if they would find the traveller any time soon. The investigation into Barclay's death would continue for weeks, if not months, but it would not deter the charges brought against Alistair Reid.

In the meantime, his domestic circumstances had grown more precarious. The builders had forced him out of his dilapidated cottage and into a small caravan, which he had parked up at different locations on the farm, trying to find a berth that suited him. They told him it would take several weeks to do the necessary repairs to the roof, which was why he had booked the holiday in the sun.

He stared through the windscreen at the border landscape. The round hills loomed black and foreboding. The remnants of a British Army watchtower were still visible, a shard on the horizon. Daly wondered if he would ever lose the prickle of anticipation that signalled he was about to enter disputed territory. He rolled down the window and listened to the sound of birdcalls and flowing water, trees and boggy fields suffused with a sense of peace. He would have got out for a walk, but a sudden rainstorm kept him confined to the car. The horizon darkened as the rain drummed on the roof, the windscreen wriggling with the distorted shapes of trees. The horizon changed again as the sun broke through.

A strange feeling preoccupied Daly. He sat in silence. He did not know what had overcome him, but he felt as though the landscape still held secrets. What was it about the little road, dwindling through bogland and forest, now brightly shimmering in the aftermath of the downpour, that felt so alien? As though when the rain had stopped he had somehow crossed an invisible border, and was already in the country he had booked a flight for? He felt far away from everything. This was the true foreign country, he realized. Not the country on the other side of the border, nor the one he was due to fly to, but this landscape that was his own, so familiar from his childhood, but made strange by the hundreds of reconciliations, the countless little acts of truth-telling, the search for disappeared bodies like Mary O'Sullivan's, the unravelling of cover-ups and secret betrayals.

This was the foreign country that he and his fellow citizens were coming to after a long journey, to rebuild lives darkened by the Troubles. The notion gave him a strange lift. That he and his neighbours might finally find refuge here, like asylum-seekers in the landscape they had always carried inside themselves.

He switched on the engine and drove back the way he

had come. The border was not just a powerful physical presence. It stretched like their own lives, zigzagging through an interweave of darkness and light, birth and death, grief and happiness. He was glad that he was no longer an internal exile, a prisoner of his country's painful history, that he could physically reach the landscape that nurtured him, and to which he had a profound and lasting attachment. This was his final consolation.

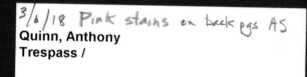